Apocalypse 666

Rory Johnston

AmErica House
Baltimore

First printing

ISBN: 1-58851-434-X
PUBLISHED BY AMERICA HOUSE BOOK PUBLISHERS
www.publishamerica.com
Baltimore

Printed in the United States of America

To my wife, Catherine, the first person I cared enough about to listen to her thoughts on God.

To my children, Jeremy and Chase, for being such incredible, terrific people.

To my mother, Daphne S. Reed, for her loving contributions to my work and my life.

To all those out there who don't just talk the talk, but also walk the walk.

And, of course, to The One.

Chapter 1

This is a true story.

It hasn't happened yet. Not yet.

But millions upon millions of people believe that the following events, or similar ones, will take place.

Soon.

Maybe tomorrow.

Maybe...

"Today!"

"I'm coming! I'm coming!"

Stan Washington turned to his wife, Brenda, and grinned. "About time. You want burgers or briquettes?" He took the plate she handed him and turned his attention to the three hamburgers sizzling on the barbecue grill, scooping them off onto the waiting buns.

She gave a little curtsy. "Well, excuse me, your majesty. May this lowly scullery maid return to the kitchen now?"

Stan frowned. He didn't like the inference, even in jest. His mama had been forced to spend most of her life cooking and cleaning for rich white people. She'd died, an old woman at age forty-eight, only fifteen years older than he was now. "Don't even say that."

"Yassuh, Mazza," she said, in an old slave accent.

He felt himself begin to burn. How could she joke about hundreds of years of suppression and worse? He was just about to voice his opinion about that when the back screen door opened with a creak and slammed with a bang.

"I got the tata salad!" came a small voice. Hobbling out the door, her legs wrapped by metal braces and crutches wedged into her armpits, his five-year old daughter, Katie, was struggling valiantly with a huge pink bowl that looked like it would topple her over at any moment. Brenda rushed to her side and swept the container from her small hands.

"Thank you, baby! You're such a big help!" She carried the bowl over to the faded wood picnic table and added it to the feast.

Stan looked at his little girl and his irritation disappeared as a wave of love washed over him. She was still in her church outfit, a frilly yellow dress with matching hair bow. If there was a more precious child on the planet, Stan wouldn't have believed it. "Do these burgers look scrumptious, or what?" he asked, heading toward her with the plate.

"Scumptious!" she said with a big smile, revealing a missing tooth. She set the crutches against the arm of a small wheelchair and slid onto the bench of the picnic table.

"Yeah, 'scumptious,'" laughed Brenda.

"Okay," said Stan, folding his huge frame into the small space between bench and table, "Let's eat!"

Katie and her mother automatically held hands and reached out toward him. Reluctantly, he enclosed them in his large paws, completing the prayer circle. The ladies bowed their heads and shut their eyes.

"Thank you, God," said Katie, "For our many blessings..."

Stan stared past his daughter at the tiny wheelchair and crutches and felt resentment well up. *Blessings? How could she speak of blessings?*

"... for this fine food and for our wonderful life."

Wonderful life? Born with dark skin in this country was curse enough, but to be doubly struck with a crippling disease? What kind of God would allow such an innocent, sweet child to suffer like this? No, there was no God, that was clear. *And if there was some sort of twisted entity, why thank Him? Why go to church and sing his praises?* Stan refused to support such a hypocritical institution. He saw it as nothing more than a warped way to give false hope and collect money from deluded suckers.

"Please watch over us."

Yeah, right! Look down on us and laugh yourself sick.

"Amen."

Brenda looked up and her peaceful countenance turned to a frown as she caught his angry look. He forced himself to smile before Katie noticed and lifted his glass. "Cheers. I love you." He did love them; with an intensity so powerful it was almost a physical hurt.

His wife gave him a reproachful look, then smiled and lifted her glass in response. "Cheers. I love you."

Katie held up her cup of red Kool-aid. "Cheers! I love you!"

Stan felt his anger melting away as all three touched glasses. A low rumble shook the air, growing in strength by the moment. Katie grinned and pointed. They'd lived in this low-rent neighborhood only one mile from the airport since before she was born but she still got excited when the large 747 aircrafts flew close overhead. Personally, he hated them. With his luck, he figured, one day one of them would drop out of the sky, exploding in a firestorm of flaming jet fuel.

He figured right.

Twenty minutes into the flight, First Class Attendant Lisa Keeler offered a selection of magazines to a conservatively dressed man in the second row. He scanned the titles quickly then made a selection. "I'll take that one."

Lisa smiled. *People* magazine was always the first to go. The headline read: JORDAN MASTERS - WORLD'S SEXIEST MAN, with a picture of Hollywood's latest heartthrob. She started to hand it over when it was snatched out of her hand.

"I'll take that one," said a low, gravelly voice.

She turned, with a frown. The man in 3A was studying the cover of the magazine, intently.

The first passenger turned around in his seat. "Excuse me," he started.

"What?" came the brusque, challenging answer. The man behind had jet black hair cut into a stiff, military flattop, a thin, clipped Errol Flynn mustache, and a serious, don't-get-in-my-face attitude.

"Never mind." The first man turned quickly away. "I have a lot of work to finish, anyway." He focused his attention on a laptop computer.

Lisa was tempted to snatch the magazine back, roll it into a tube and swat the second guy on the nose for being so rude, but experience told her to let it go. If both passengers were okay with the outcome, so was she. She had seen worse behavior in her thirteen years on the job. Much worse, especially here in First Class where people often seemed to feel it was their duty to behave like jerks. She checked out the man, now intently studying the magazine's table of contents. He wore what was clearly an expensive charcoal gray suit with a high-cut collar. For some reason it reminded her of a military uniform. The first finger of his right hand sported a large onyx ring bearing an unusual design, something like the lens of a camera. She recalled that he'd stored an expensive metal Haliburton case in the overhead compartment, so perhaps he was a photographer. Without taking his eyes off the magazine he reached into his jacket pocket and produced a silver cigar holder and a gold Dunhill lighter.

"I'm sorry, sir," she said, putting on her friendly-but- firm face, "this is a non-smoking flight."

The look he shot her made her feel like something slimy was crawling in her esophagus. He inserted a cigar between his teeth defiantly, but put the lighter away.

She smiled, acknowledging the sacrifice, and moved on, grateful that it hadn't become an issue. She worked her way down the aisles, graciously helping other passengers, until she arrived at the small food prep alcove between first class and economy. Shutting the curtain, she leaned back against the counter and rolled her eyes at Jenny Cole, her associate and best friend. "Full flight," she sighed.

Jenny nodded. "Like sardines." She was, as they said in the deep south where Lisa had been raised, 'a big ol' girl.' Six foot tall and nearly one hundred seventy-five pounds, her heart was as large as her body and Lisa loved her like a sister. "Any trouble from 3A?"

"Cigar man? Naw. I thought there might be, but no. Not yet, anyway." She shifted gears. "Okay, Jen, I've waited long enough! What is this little surprise you've been hinting about all day?" Ever since the preflight check her friend had been practically oozing with mysterious excitement.

"Nothing little about it, girl friend!" She presented her left hand and waggled her fingers. A gold band with a huge, tear-drop diamond was perched on her ring finger.

Lisa let out an excited squeal. "Oh, Jenny! When?"

"Last night!"

"Finally! How long have you been waiting for this?"

"Since I was five years old, when 'Stewardess Barbie' met 'Pilot Ken!'"

Lisa laughed, thrilled for her and her new fiancee, Gerald, who happened to be the navigator on this flight. She'd known them both for two years and they seemed to be the perfect couple. She studied the massive stone, which refracted the light into a million sparkles. "My goodness! How do you change the batteries in that thing?"

They laughed. Lisa threw her arms around her oldest, closest friend and hugged her. This was surely a day to end all days.

A scream echoed down the nearly deserted hallways of Vandenberg Military Hospital. Lucretia "Lucy" Burton had never been to a Lamaze class–her husband clearly hadn't had the time and neither had she, therefore she didn't know contractions from dilations from dish water. But she did know pain, and this was it. She screamed and stiffened again as another stab of agony shot through her. When the pain ebbed, she glared up at the irritatingly calm young woman standing in the corner. Although she couldn't see the woman's eyes behind the dark glasses, she was certain they were glittering with secret satisfaction. The spooks all hated her. "Where the hell is he?" she snapped.

The Secret Service agent touched the earpiece she was wearing and spoke into her sleeve. Her voice was low, but Lucretia heard. "Bobbit wants to know where he is."

Bobbit. Lucy was well aware of her nickname. She didn't mind it. She took it as more of a reflection on her husband's "short comings" than on herself. The truth was, she agreed with the assessment, he was lacking in the manhood department.

"He's on his way, ma'am."

"Well, the little cretin had better be here when this happens or the press'll eat his reputation alive with some fava beans and a nice Chianti, and this whole damn thing will be for no–thi–ing!" Another wave of pain started to swell, coming on fast. This baby wasn't going to wait much longer. "Get him here. Now! And get this baby outta me!" She screamed as the pain peaked once again. "Haaaa!"

"–llelujah!" cried the fat woman.

"Hallelujah!" answered the twenty-person choir, then broke into a rousing gospel tune accompanied by Brother Michael on the organ. Nearly two hundred people, mostly poor Kansas farmers and their families, joined in, singing along and clapping whether they knew the words or not. The Matthew Miracle Salvation Show was kicking into high gear.

Latecomers slammed the doors of rusty pick-up trucks and hurried across the dusty field toward the entrance of the blue and white striped tent. A massive sign hung over the entrance, with a painting of a huge hand reaching down out of an incandescent cloud, touching a man. Where the extended finger met the man's head, his jet black hair was streaked snow white. **Matthew Miracle!** proclaimed the bold letters, **The Man Touched By God!**

Behind the tent, in a small, well-used Winnebago RV, the great man himself sat in front of a mirror, touching up his white streak with hair bleach. He hummed cheerfully along with the music filtering out the rear. "Bringing in the sheaves, bringing in the sheaves, we will go rejoicing, bringing in the sheaves." His was unique among salvation shows because he traveled alone. The help he needed to set up and tear down the tent, the choir and organist and ushers, were all local people that he'd hire in every town he visited. Most of them worked for minimum cost believing they were earning the good Lord's blessing–a sweet deal which enhanced his profits greatly. This choir sounded pretty darn good, which pleased him. He was expecting a large crowd; for two years the summer weather had been hot and dry with very little rain so the farmers would be looking for a miracle. And, of course, they'd be willing to pay for it.

"Hallelujah!" came the distant cry.

"Hallelujah!" came the cry from the crowd.

Looking at the stack of shiny brass collection plates, Matthew grinned to himself and pulled on his battery-operated, light-up jacket. "Hallelujah." He flipped the switch.

Ten thousand sparkling light bulbs spelled out VISIONS, and, in traditional Las Vegas style, the management had gone overboard in promoting the grand opening of the strip's newest spectacular review show. Massive roving spotlights, fireworks, a live orchestra and the red carpet treatment for arriving celebrities were just the beginning.

Cat Johnson, reporter for World Broadcast News wasn't happy to be there. As far as she was concerned, it was a fluff assignment and a waste of her time and talent. She hadn't gone through four years of college studying journalism to interview cap-toothed, silicone-enhanced egomaniacs. By rights, she should have been in Beirut or Bosnia, where the real action was. She should have been covering current events in Turkey, not some turkey event.

Her one-man crew, cameraman Roger Jackson, didn't appear put out at all. The twenty-two year-old African-American actually seemed to be having a good time filming a young blond starlet with gravity-defying breasts.

What's she got that I ain't got? thought Cat. Okay, her hair is long and blond and mine is short and red, but I could fix that–she obviously had. Okay, she has supernatural dimensions that I don't, but I could fix that–she obviously had. Okay, I haven't had personal relations with half the movie producers in Hollywood, but I could fix that... Cat laughed to herself. Naw, definitely not worth it. She'd make it on talent and hard work or not at all. Absolutely not on her back.

A surge of cheers from the crowd snapped her out of her thoughts. A long, white limousine glided to a stop in front of the brass-railed red carpet, the rear door opened and Jordan Masters stepped out, lighting up the crowd with his two thousand-watt smile. Roger automatically positioned the camera so he had Cat in his sight as the movie star approached.

The reporter donned her "on-camera" smile, flashing her perfect white teeth. "And here he is, ladies and gentlemen, superstar of the year, Jordan Masters." She turned to greet the twenty-six year-old idol who stepped up beside her. "Mister Masters! Cat Johnson, WBN entertainment news."

The man stopped and looked her directly in the eye. It was the first time any celebrity had done that, and it caught her off-guard. "It's a pleasure to meet you, Ms. Johnson," he said, sounding like he meant it.

"Miss," she said, automatically correcting him. "Miss Johnson." She held out her hand.

"Miss." He smiled. "Call me Jordan."

"Call me Cat."

"Cat." His eyes crinkled as he took her hand in both of his. It was a gesture that was almost intimate. His touch was firm and dry, not sweaty like most people in the limelight. She felt a soft heat rush through her.

"Jordan, last night the network broadcast of your Oscar-winning performance in Dear Mister President garnered the highest rating of all time. How do you feel about that?"

He laughed. "I feel great!"

"Will there be a sequel?"

He shrugged. "Well, people really have taken to the character, and in the film he was unanimously elected to a second term..."

With a wink, he started to leave, but stopped and looked at her questioningly. She suddenly realized, to her dismay, that she was still holding his hand. Embarrassed, she dropped it. Jordan smiled once more, then moved on. She felt herself flush.

Roger lowered his camera and watched the man disappear into the casino. "What's he got that I ain't got, girl?"

She looked down at her hands, the warmth of his touch lingering. "Well..."

"He is the Sexiest Man Alive!" screamed the caption over a picture of Jordan Masters clad in black silk pajamas.

Lucretia Burton looked at the two-page spread of the blond-haired, blue-eyed actor and smiled to herself, thinking that the magazine's editors finally got it right with their annual choice. Without warning, something inside her suddenly let loose and there was a gush of liquid spilling over her thighs and across the plastic sheet under her.

"Awww, no!" She threw the magazine against the hospital wall in frustration, startling the Secret Service agent.

A young, dark-skinned nurse rushed forward, speaking with an East Indian accent. "Her water broke! Let's prep her!"

"No," shouted Lucy, "Not until he gets here!"

The nurse spoke as if reasoning with a child, "We don't really have a choice, ma'am."

"Don't tell me, you stupid cow! I–"

She was interrupted as the door burst open and two serious-looking Secret Service agents entered, eyes sweeping the room. The tallest one looked at the female agent already in attendance, who gave a discreet nod. He spoke into his sleeve. "Clear."

A moment later Wesley Burton rushed into the room, flustered and out of breath. He glanced down at Lucy with obvious impatience, then focused on the nurse. "All right, all right, let's get on with it."

He was an A-number-one jackass, no question of it, but the nurse didn't appear to notice. She was clearly awed to be in the presence of the President of the United States. "It's an honor to meet you, Mister President."

"Charmed." He kissed her hand, staring directly down her cleavage.

Lucy vented her outrage and raised her voice almost to a shout. "Excuse me!"

Two orderlies hurriedly wheeled her out of the room as the latest contraction slammed into her.

The scream sounded like someone's soul had just been ripped into pieces. Lisa bolted out of the galley, her heart contracting with fear. A bleached-blond near the wing exit was actually standing on her seat, screeching hysterically. A dozen or so others also appeared to be in near or total panic. One fat man's face was such a bright red that he looked as if he might explode while an old woman standing in the aisle was so pale that she appeared almost translucent. Lisa hurried toward her, searching in vain for the cause of the chaos. She saw no man with a gun, had heard no explosion. In fact, nothing appeared to be wrong other than the fact that a lot of the seats were empty. Her eyes automatically swept the rear of the aircraft, searching for the other passengers. Only one man stepped out of the toilet, looking as confused and frightened as she did. She spun toward the front of the jet and saw nobody there either. At that same moment she noticed that the seats were covered with clothes: dresses, pants, blouses, jackets, sweaters and more; white dress-shirts with ties still knotted around the collars, pants with belts buckled in place and zippers closed, pantyhose draped over the front edges of seats, their nylon feet still tucked neatly into shoes. Also, there was jewelry scattered around–necklaces, earrings, watches, bracelets and finger rings. Several pairs of eyeglasses lay on piles of clothing, along with one dark wig. Looking on the seat next to her, Lisa's stomach lurched. A pair of slickly wet dentures were leaving a dark stain on a light gray dress, surrounded by a necklace of imitation pearls. Lisa felt her sense of reality spinning out of control because looking at all the clothing and possessions strewn about made her realize that their owners, the rest of the passengers–nearly two hundred people–were nowhere to be seen in the aircraft.

Stan watched Katie ascend skyward, then swoop back again in a smooth arc.

"Higher, Daddy, higher!" she called, excitedly, "To the man in the moon!"

It wasn't one of those fancy redwood "play environments" with a slide, sandbox and built-in tree house, it was just a cheap, tubular-metal swing set, but she loved to swing, and he loved pushing her on it. He answered with his best imitation of Jackie Gleason in *The Honeymooners*. "To the moon, Alice!" He gave a gentle shove.

She giggled. "Daddy! My name's not Al–"

The swing returned empty. A pair of leg braces fell to the grass with a metallic thump. A small yellow dress floated to the ground, followed by a fluttering hair ribbon.

Stan stared at them, stunned, shocked, unable to process what had just happened.

The magician stood center stage, bowing to well-deserved applause. Jordan Masters clapped as hard as anyone. He loved good theater and this guy was not only amazing, he was funny. The applause subsided and the crowd grew silent with anticipation.

On stage, the magician straightened up. "And now, ladies and gentlemen, the greatest illusion of all time."

He disappeared.

Jordan gaped, not believing his eyes. The magician hadn't stepped inside a box or behind a cloth; there had been no puff of smoke, no flash of lights, no cover at all. One moment the man was there, the next he was gone. His empty tuxedo had hung in the air for a split second, then crumpled to the floor. It was the most surprising, unbelievable, totally impossible magic trick Jordan could imagine.

In the center aisle beside him, Cat Johnson's mouth dropped open. Next to her, the cameraman slowly lowered his Mini-cam and looked over the top of the eyepiece, perplexed.

Matthew Miracle stood in front of a tent full of fervent believers, holding them spellbound. Behind him was a huge frosted-glass statue of Jesus on the cross. Okay, it wasn't really frosted glass, it was molded plastic, but it had cost a fortune. Money well spent, because it was luminescent so when the lights were turned off near the end of the service it took on a life of its own. The awesome visage of the savior glowing in the dark always inspired the suckers into new levels of giving.

One hundred and fifty paper fans bearing his likeness (and website address) were waving in front of him, like a meadow full of giant butterflies. The pitiful breeze they tried to stir did nothing to lessen the stifling heat. He, himself, was sweating profusely, dripping with perspiration. That was the disadvantage of working in a tent instead of a rented hall–it could get as hot as hell–but rented halls cut into profits and the tent had come cheap, from a bankrupt circus. The owner had given him a sweet deal. Well, why not, they were both in the same business, weren't they? Besides, he could make the heat work to his advantage.

"Everybody stop fanning now, ya hear me? Stop aaaaaall movement. Noooo blessed breeze. Just heat. Feeeeeel that heat? Choking, smothering, burrrrrning heat. Is it hot? Gimme an A-men!"

"A-MEN!"

"It iiiis hot. It is veeeery hot." He paused, staring at the floor, letting it build until both the heat and silence were near unbearable, then he jumped forward, feeling the intensity explode from him and shouted, "But I tell you, children, what you are feeling is as cold as the sweet, icy water from a snowy mountain brook compared to the fires of Hell!"

"A-men!" shouted the crowd, "Hallelujah!"

"Do you want to burn in hell?"

"NO!"

"Do you want to roast in hell?"

"NO!"

He ran to the front of the front of the stage and leaped off, into the center of the crowd. "Do you want to be impaled on the spit of lies, spread with the sauce of lust, and slowly barbecued over the fire of evil?"

"No!"

"Say it with me! Satan stay away!"

"Satan stay away!

"Satan stay faaaaaar away!"

"Satan stay far away!"

"Get thee BEHIND me Satan!"

"Hallelujah!"

"Satan... you devil..." Eyes wide, staring at some imaginary, hideous foe, he backed onto the stage, holding out his hands and shaking his head as if to say, no, no, stay away! Suddenly, he stopped, planted his feet, stood his ground and, pointing a finger, roaring, "... you can just GO RIGHT BACK TO HADES!"

"Hallelujah! Yes, Reverend!"

He spun toward the crowd, "Say it with me, GO RIGHT BACK TO HADES!"

"Go right back to Hades!"

"Because you can't have me, Satan, no! 'Cause I am going with Jesus!" He pointed toward the sky.

"Hallelujah! Amen, Reverend! Glory be! Goin' with Jesus!"

He stretched both hands toward heaven, fingers splayed, and squeezed his eyes tightly as if a painful electric current were passing through him. "Close your eyes with me and pa-ray!" he shouted. "Say it with me! Say, Jeeeezus take me away!

The crowd clenched their eyes shut and shouted as one. "Jesus take me away!"

"Let him heeeear His children! Jeeeezus take me!"

"Jesus, take me!"

"Jeeeezus, take me to heaven!"

Matthew waited, but there was no response. Clenching his eyes and fists even tighter, he raised his voice to a scream. "Say it! Jeeezus, TAKE ME TO HEAVEN!"

Silence. What in the world? He opened his eyes, puzzled. A wave of dizziness, nausea and disorientation swept over him, as if a fist had punched him in the solar plexus. He found himself unable to take a breath. He rubbed his eyes, blinked like a man who had just taken a blow to the head, then tried to focus again.

The tent, with the exception of himself, was completely deserted.

The contraction peaked and Lucretia screamed with agony. Gritting her teeth, she shouted at the doctor, "Drugs would be good, here!"

"You're doing great, Mrs. Burton, one more push ought to do it."

She looked over at her husband with venom, "After this, you never touch me again."

The nurse grinned. "Don't worry, Mister President, they all say that."

Burton attempted a smile, but couldn't quite pull it off. Lucretia took some satisfaction in that. He knew that she never made idle threats. She had gone above and beyond her political duty. He'd never get near her in private again.

Another wash of pain swept through her, quickly building. She cried out, swearing loudly.

The doctor leaned in, the picture of confidence. "Okay, Lucy, this is it. Get ready to push. And... go!"

She gritted her teeth and bore down, feeling like she was being ripped in two.

"Okay I can see his head! You're doing great! Push! Push! Heeeere..."

Abruptly the pain disappeared, her abdomen deflated, and the baby was out. She let out a relieved gasp and shut her eyes, collapsing back on the pillow. But something was wrong. There was no sound of crying. Shouldn't the baby... ? She opened her eyes. The doctor's arms were empty. Both he and the nurses were staring at her, shock etched into their faces. The female Secret Service agent was slowly removing her dark glasses, her own face a mask of horror. The President of the United States, arguably the most powerful man in the world, backed away as pale as a ghost, hit the wall, and slid to the floor in a heap as his legs failed him completely.

Lisa turned and ran for the First Class section, tearing away the curtain between the two areas.

"Jennifer?" she called, her fear growing by the second. Moving forward, she tripped on something and almost took a head-first dive down the aisle. She grabbed a seat back to steady herself and looked down. Her feet were tangled up in a Flight Attendant uniform lying in a heap on the floor–shoes, pantyhose, underwear. On top of this pile glittered her friend's brand new engagement ring. Lisa's consciousness dizzied with confusion and rising hysteria. She desperately needed a clue as to what had happened. Not only was Jennifer missing along with half the people in coach, but so was the man with the lap top in 2-A and half-a-dozen other First Class passengers. Pandemonium reverberated throughout the aircraft. One overweight man was gasping and clutching his heart while his wife leaned over him, crying and screaming. She screeched at Lisa, begging for attention. "My husband is having a heart attack! Help him! Help him!"

A long-haired man dressed like a rock star grabbed her roughly by the front of her uniform jacket and shook her. "What is happening here?" he yelled in an English accent, "What's bloody happening?"

Damn! How the hell did she know? She yanked herself away. "Please, stay calm, sir!"

"Stay calm? Are you daft? The people are gone! Everyone's just bloody disappeared!"

What? She looked across the aisle at the man with the cigar clenched in his teeth, who nodded confirmation. He appeared to be the only one in the aircraft besides herself who was not in complete disarray, although his cigar was almost bitten in two. Something behind his eyes changed, and he suddenly stiffened, spinning and looking toward the front of the aircraft. Lisa felt the frosty cold hand of terror grip her. She ran for the flight deck, the man right behind her arriving at the cockpit door at the same moment. Lisa banged on the reinforced metal, identifying herself and shouting the pilot's name. No response. She called for the flight crew to open the door. Still no response. Her mind whirled. She could get the emergency key, hidden in case of an attempted take-over, but if she grabbed it now, she'd almost certainly reveal its hiding place. The man beside her seemed calm, unnaturally so. Could he have something to do with all this? If so, and he got into the cockpit, he could make things even worse. She desperately banged on the door again. "Gerald? It's Lisa, Gerald, open up!"

"You're going to have to unlock it," said Cigar Man. "Now."

The authority in his voice demanded to be obeyed. A wailing scream came from behind them and Lisa knew he was right, she didn't really have a choice. Things couldn't get much worse, could they? She ran back to the galley, shoving away clutching fingers, ignoring pleadings, and snatched the key from its hiding place. Running back to the cockpit door, she attempted to insert it into the lock but her hands were shaking so badly she couldn't even hit the slot. The man took the key firmly from her, calmly inserted it, and opened the door to the cockpit.

Lisa pushed her way through and stopped short, stunned beyond all reason. She felt as though she might be violently ill.

The cockpit was empty.

Jordan Masters, applauding wildly, turned to the man in the seat next to him. "Great trick, huh?"

The seat was empty, except for a pile of clothing. Puzzled, he looked around the crowd. Other people were staring at empty seats also. It appeared that the magician had not only made himself vanish, but dozens of audience members as well.

Behind him, he heard the reporter, Cat Johnson, ask her cameraman,

"Are you taping?"

"Oooooh, yeah," came the low-toned answer.

Suddenly a woman in the front row stood and screamed; a blood-freezing sound, the first of many coming from all sections of the auditorium. Jordan could feel the panic rising around him, like a wave swelling from the ocean floor. He stood and held out his hands. "Take it easy, everybody, please!" he called, loudly.

The rear theater doors suddenly crashed open as shouting, frightened people burst through, spilling across the carpet into the auditorium. Beyond the doors, the casino was a madhouse of screaming humanity, racing around, stumbling over articles of clothing strewn about the casino floor as they searched in vain for companions nowhere to be found.

The reporter jumped clear of the onslaught. "What the–?"

The wave broke and the theater audience exploded, pushing, shoving, climbing over seat backs, scrambling for the exit doors.

Jordan heard Miss Johnson cry, "Come on! Move!" as she grabbed her cameraman by the arm and shoved him toward the side emergency exits. That seemed like a damn good idea, so he followed, trying to escape the stampede to the rear as he sprinted through the doors and emerged into the casino proper. He pulled up short, gaping at the mayhem and the rising tide of screams. A red sports car had crashed through the massive plate glass show window, destroying a dozen slot machines. A twisted body lay mangled under the tires. People were on their knees, snatching up money and chips scattered across the carpet. The entire crowd was out of control, hysterically wailing, fighting, running. The cameraman, still filming, made his way toward the broken window, focusing on the even more frightening events outside.

Jordan followed, stupefied.

Stan Washington stood alone in his small backyard, clutching a pair of tiny leg braces, staring uncomprehendingly at his wife's clothing in a jumbled heap on the grass. Behind him, over a smaller pile of clothes, the swing, empty, still swung, back and forth, back and forth...

Matthew Miracle staggered out of the empty tent and moved through the dust of the field in a state of utter disbelief as he searched for his missing congregation. Row upon row of old vehicles remained mutely parked on the gray ground. Beyond the deserted dirt road a vast field of dry wheat stretched to the horizon. But no people. Not another single soul.

A half dozen Secret Service agents, guns drawn, burst into the delivery room along with the sounds of screaming, yelling, breaking of glass and general commotion coming from the rest of the hospital.

"What in blazes is going on?" demanded Lucretia.

Four of the men immediately surrounded the President, pulling him to his feet. The other two, plus the woman agent, spaced themselves around her. She looked hard at the shocked faces of the medical team, then propped herself up on her elbows. Nobody was holding a baby. Her baby had not been placed in her arms, nor anywhere else that she could see. Then she saw the umbilical cord, trailing out of her birth canal like a skinned snake and just... ending in nothing.

Her screams echoed down the hall.

The Las Vegas Strip was a war zone. Cars and trucks had crashed everywhere, fires were burning out of control, a fire hydrant was gushing water two stories into the air, and scores of people lay dead or dying.

Just what had happened here? Had some terrorist detonated a bomb? But even as the thought occurred to him, Jordan knew this was something much bigger; he'd just witnessed a man vanishing into thin air! Several people were pointing upward and his eyes were drawn to a balcony some fifteen stories up on the high-rise hotel across the street. A man stood on the railing, trembling and wailing. He closed his eyes and leaned forward.

"No!" Jordan screamed.

The man stepped off.

Jordan shut his eyes rather than see the body impact on the roof of the carport below. When he opened them, a pale, overweight man with a drinker's red nose and watery eyes was standing next to him. The man, bald and in his late sixties, spoke with a familiar Southern accent. "Jordan."

Jordan blinked, startled. "Uncle Ed?"

"Come with me, we don't have much time." The old man tapped his watch twice and walked away. Jordan automatically followed his father's older brother, too confused to think clearly.

The female reporter was standing in the middle of the street, calmly speaking into a microphone, taping a segment. "As far as we can deduce, hundreds of people have simply disappeared into thin air." His uncle approached her without hesitation, stepping between the woman and her camera. "Come with us, young lady."

Anger momentarily colored the young woman's face, but quickly changed to puzzlement when she recognized the famous politician. "Senator Masters?"

"If you want the story that will make your career," said the senior Senator from Mississippi, "come."

Miss Johnson didn't hesitate for a milli-second. "Lead on."

Before the small group could take two steps, a huge jet aircraft roared by, perilously low overhead. Jordan watched, appalled, as it sheered off one of the spires on the Excaliber Hotel and crashed with an ear-shattering explosion into the side of the New York New York Hotel and Casino. Even from two blocks away, they could feel the heat and concussion from the blast.

"Oh, dear God," mumbled the cameraman, continuing to film.

New York New York burned. Because its architectural design was a recreation of New York's famous skyline, it gave the eerie illusion that the great city itself was engulfed in flames. One of the towers collapsed and Jordan cried aloud as a horrific flashback of the events of September 11, 2001 overwhelmed him. He found himself barely able to draw a breath through his dry, constricted throat. He tore his eyes away, shifting his gaze to his uncle who was also fixated on the rising fireball. The flames reflected in the Senator's eyes gave an uncanny impression that the fire was actually burning within him.

"It has begun," whispered the old man

Chapter 2

Catherine Johnson felt very much like Las Vegas looked: in total chaos. The city was coming apart around them; crowds running, screaming, crying and dying; horns honking, sirens wailing, alarms ringing. Fires burning out of control and so much smoke billowing into the air that the usual sea of neon was practically obliterated. No authority was evident anywhere. Where were the police? The firemen? The one exception to the sheer bedlam was the elderly Senator Edward Masters, now calmly leading her, Roger, and Jordan Masters around the side of the building. She practically had to run to keep up, following blindly in a state of whirling confusion as the elder statesman's words echoed in her mind. *"If you want the story that will make your career, come."* Of course she had followed. It was enough to be in the company of the number-one box office draw in the world, never mind the extra added bonus of one the most controversial politicians in the nation. For her, there was never really any doubt, but where were they headed, and why?

She was surprised when he led them straight to the WBN News van they'd parked near a service entrance. Senator Masters threw open the side door and climbed into the back. "Let's go."

I'm sure we left that door locked, Cat thought.

The senior Masters pointed to Roger. "You drive."

Roger gently eased his camera into a foam-lined case in the rear of the van."Where to?"

"Just drive."

Roger gave the old man a hard look, his eyes narrowing. Cat shot him a *just do it* look, in return. Reluctantly, Roger shuffled around to the front of the van, mumbling in an exaggerated slave dialect, "You da bozz, bozz."

The Senator appeared to take no notice. He climbed in the back and sat serenely on the bench-like seat, crossing his hands on his lap. Jordan, who hadn't said a word yet, glanced over at Cat and met her eyes, clearly as confused as she was. She shrugged. He climbed in beside his uncle, sliding the side door shut. Cat slipped into the front seat as Roger slammed the driver's door and peered through the dirty windshield at the mad congestion blocking most of Las Vegas Boulevard. "Okay, so where is it, exactly, that you want me to drive to?"

"Away," answered the old man, "South, if you can make it. Into the desert."

"Hang on, here goes." He eased the van forward, driving over a strip of grass, across a curb, and toward the street.

Finally, Jordan spoke up. "What are you doing here, Uncle Ed? What the hell is happening?"

"I am not your uncle, Jordan Masters."

Jordan looked bewildered. "What? What are you talking about?"

The old man regarded Jordan for a long moment, then looked over at Cat. She could sense a holding of breath, a hesitation in him as though he was reluctant to continue. The moment passed and he changed. Literally, physically. His body began to transform, to deflate, as if someone was letting the air out. His jowls tightened up, the fat inside seeming to melt away, and the skin simultaneously shrank as well. His bone structure shifted, cheekbones becoming more prominent, chin lengthening. His bulbous nose thinned out while his pale, capillary-riddled skin darkened to a healthier flesh-tone. The hairs of his bristly gray mustache withdrew into his upper lip, like a child sucking up wet strands of spaghetti. His bald cranium actually crunched into a new shape, and silver-white hair began to sprout. The worst part was the metamorphosis of his former brown eyes. The color faded away, growing paler and paler until they were devoid of all tint, just orbs of pure, blank white, then slowly, soft blue irises began to emerge, growing steadily darker until they evolved into an intense gas-flame blue.

Cat slapped a hand over her mouth to stifle a scream.

Roger, watching in the rear-view mirror, nearly drove off the road. He slammed on the brakes, skidded to a stop, threw open the door and leaped out, staring back through the windshield, wide-eyed.

Jordan, frozen on the spot, was barely breathing.

Cat gawked at the stranger who was now a kind-looking, gray-haired, man of some fifty years. Her heart was pounding against her breast bone as though it was trying to beat its way out. Finally she snapped out of her spell and virtually dove into the rear of the truck, snatching up the video camera from its case with trembling hands. "Can you do that again?" she pleaded, desperate to get it on tape. "Please? Please?" *Unbelievable! What a piece of film! The first footage of... what was he? A werewolf? An alien? This was Pulitzer stuff!* While frantically manipulating the camera's controls, she yelled, "Roger, get back in here!"

"I ain't getting in there with that face smooshin' thing!" he called.

The stranger turned to the cameraman, his voice lower than before, with no traces of Senator Master's southern accent. "You are in no danger, I assure you."

"Roger!" Cat demanded, fumbling to get the camera rolling, pulling the lens to its widest possible aperture and propping it in a position that took in the entire interior of the vehicle. "Now!"

Reluctantly, Roger slunk back into the van, staring, wide-eyed at the gray-haired man. "Freakin, living, breathing, Mister Potato Head!"

"Drive!" she ordered, "Get us out of here!" She wanted this story as far away from any other media representatives as possible. She needed a controlled environment, all to herself.

"All right, all right," he muttered, "Keep your skin on!" Roger glanced over his shoulder at the metamorphosed man and shivered. "You, too."

As the van pulled out, Jordan found his voice, although it was not more than a whisper. "Uncle Ed?"

"No, Jordan Masters. I only simulated his appearance to expedite cooperation."

"Who are you?"

The man shifted slightly in his seat so he was facing both Jordan, Cat, and the camera. It was if he knew the importance of the tape and was providing his best angle. "I am Gideon. I am of The One."

"The what?"

"The One. Guardians of all." His voice was toneless and hesitant, as if he was translating from a foreign language. "The time for judgment of your planet has come. In accordance to... that which is... you have betrayed the trust. Your planet is without harmony. This must cease. Those judged worthy have been taken. The rest are to be eliminated."

"Excuse me?" said Jordan.

"In seventy-two hours Earth time all nuclear weapons on this planet will be detonated."

"I don't understand," said the actor.

"Well, tell me if I got it right," spoke up the photographer from the driver's seat, "You're the universe police and you're going to blow our sorry butts off the freakin' planet."

"Succinctly put," said the alien.

"Suck sink this, Gort," snapped Roger.

"You waste your hostility on me," said Gideon, calmly, "I am no longer One. I am apart. Separated. I am... in dissension... with that ruling, therefore am no longer..." he seemed to search for the phrase.

"Part of the establishment?" suggested Jordan.

"Yes," nodded Gideon.

"A gangsta," mumbled Roger.

"A revolutionary," corrected Gideon. "It is believed that most humans are beyond redemption. Some... us... we disagree. We must prove the conclusion wrong. If all weapons could be rendered unusable, perhaps we could persuade them to alter, soften the judgement. That is my mission."

"Look," said Roger, "I hate to seem ungrateful, but for a superior intelligence you ain't too freakin' bright. I mean, why tell us? Why don't you beam your little E.T. butt into the White House and tell The Man?"

"Good point," said Jordan.

Gideon looked at the actor, intently. "I monitored your broadcast. Jason Powers touched humanity. We share ideals."

Cat frowned. *Jason Powers? What the heck was he talking about?*

Jordan caught on before she did, eyes widening in disbelief. "Jason Powers?" he said, with a horrified look, "No, no, no, no! That was a movie! I was acting!"

Then it hit her: in Jordan's latest film, he'd played history's youngest candidate for President of The United States–a charming, idealistic politician who, insanely, decides to be completely honest with the American people, which, of course, makes him a hero. The character was named Jason Powers. "Dear Mister President?" she gasped.

"The movie?" exclaimed Roger, unbelieving. "And we *humans* are too stupid to live?"

Cat grasped the alien by the shoulders. "This man is not the President of the United States, Gideon. It was a film! A representation!"

"I was playing a role!" added Jordan.

"There was more truth in it than you understand," said Gideon, patiently.

"Look, the real President–"

"Would be ineffective."

True, thought Cat, Burton was the weakest President in recent history.

"So do your Mighty Morphin Power Martian thing," suggested Roger, "and make yourself look like him. Beam him outta there while you call the shots for awhile."

Gideon shook his head, negatively. "I, too, would be ineffective." He turned back to Jordan. "You have not been chosen haphazardly. Your family history–"

"Whoa!" cried Jordan, holding out two hands as if to block the words, "Hold it right there. Just because I lived in the White House when I was a kid doesn't mean I can bust in there anytime I want!"

Actually, thought Cat, *he probably could.* Not only was he an international film star, Jordan was the son of one of the most honored politicians of all time, who had been assassinated live in front of millions of viewers on national television. It was that personal connection in particular, thought many, that had made him so effective in his role as President and had catapulted his first major film to blockbuster status.

Gideon removed a thick, black, metallic medallion he was wearing around his neck on a leather cord. Cat noticed the swirly pattern etched into it about the size of, and similar in appearance to, a camera lens. He looped it over Jordan's head. "This will help."

Jordan instinctively pulled away from the alien's touch and reached up to remove the thing. "You don't understa–" His words were cut off as eight barbs, like needle-clawed legs of a spider, suddenly shot out of the medallion and pierced his shirt. Jordan screamed as the claws not only penetrated cloth, but apparently flesh as well. Blood welled up, instantly staining the tuxedo shirt.

Cat shrank back against her seat in horror.

"Ahhh! Get it off me!" Jordan screamed, clutching frantically at it, which apparently only elevated the pain.

Gideon firmly snatched Jordan's hands away from the device, showing tremendous strength, instantly halting the man's efforts. "You must never remove that!" he hissed, showing intense emotion for the first time. Jordan was shocked into silence by the ferocity behind the prohibition. He stared down at himself, wincing, as the red stain slowly spread across his chest.

Cat felt her stomach roll.

"Man!" said Roger, "Now that's what I call a locket!"

Gideon released Jordan's hands and stood, bending low under the roof of the van. He addressed both Jordan and Cat, seriously. "Go speak to your leaders. Act immediately." Without warning, he opened the side door and stepped out of the moving vehicle.

"Hey!" shouted Cat, with a surge of alarm. They were moving at least fifty miles-per-hour.

Roger slammed on the brakes. The van skidded forward, skewing to the side, raising a cloud of dust. The camera bounced off the seat and onto the floor with a crash. Jordan braced himself against the front seat and leaped out of the van before it came to a full stop. Cat followed almost immediately.

Roger hit the street a split second later.

They were on the far south end of Las Vegas Boulevard, miles from the strip, surrounded by flat desert vegetation, a few small cactus, and... nothing else. No gray haired man, no fat politician, no one-eyed-green-haired-flying-purple-people-eater. The alien had completely vanished.

Roger bent down to check under the van, looked up at Cat and shook his head. Jordan, in his blood-stained shirt, swiveled slowly in the middle of the road. Three pairs of eyes searched everywhere.

Cat knees suddenly gave way under her and she fell, grabbing the open van door for support.

Roger let out a low, eerie whistle. The theme to *The X-Files*.

Chapter 3

When Lucy Burton walked into the White House Crisis Management Center, she was sucked into utter pandemonium. Dozens of people rushed about in all directions, pushing roughly past her. Computer printers and FAX machines spilled out reams of paper while banks of telephones blinked red lights and rang incessantly without response. Men and women in business suits, sweat-stained shirts with loose-hanging ties, military uniforms, and even jeans and tee-shirts scrambled everywhere. Her husband paced before a massive wall of one hundred television monitors, each screen tuned to a different world broadcast, his staff crowding around him looking like the useless idiots she knew they were.

Her doctors had insisted she stay in bed after the unspeakable ordeal of the birth, but she knew they were more concerned with the emotional trauma than the physical damage. Ha. They had highly over-estimated any psychological injuries, the idiots. She'd never wanted the brat in the first place. It was to have been merely another pawn in her husband's political chess game. Most definitely that was her last concession to his idiotic game plan. From now on, whatever Lucy wanted, Lucy would get. What she didn't want, couldn't stand, was to remain in her bedroom any longer. She wanted to be where the action was and she'd do what she damned well pleased.

She was drawn at once to the world-wide broadcasts. On one screen an English journalist with a thick mustache reported from the center of Piccadilly Circus amid a jumbled mess of wrecked and burning automobiles. On another, a Japanese reporter spoke passionately of thousands of suicides, reactions to the unexplainable disappearance of their loved ones. In Moscow, people in long, dark coats stumbled heavily through the snowladen streets like panicked animals. In New York City, looters scurried like cockroaches, smashing deserted store windows and running mindlessly past the television news crews with stolen armloads of shoes, microwaves, CDs, watches, liquor and more. In Las Vegas, a blond starlet stood in front of a marquis that read: Visions, the Magical Spectacular! She was gushing, "Oooo, he said it was going to be the greatest magic trick ever!"

"Oh, give me a break," muttered the President of the United States.

Lucy had to smile. She focused on one monitor featuring a striking-looking man with intense, haunted eyes and jet black hair streaked with a shock of pure white. Something about him caught her interest. He didn't look confused like everyone else, but seemed to know exactly what was going on. The caption identified him as Matthew Miracle, Evangelical Preacher. "It is clearly the Rapture," he said, sincerely and intensely, "His followers have risen to join their Savior..."

"Oh, brother!" snapped her husband. "The religious nuts are going to be all over this!"

She turned, with a smirk. "Don't worry, if it really is the Rapture, then all the religious nuts will be gone!"

Chief of Staff Harry Weinstein, a severe, balding man with a pinched face and rimless glasses, didn't laugh. "That's not funny. Not funny!"

Burton turned to her, apparently annoyed at her presence. "Shouldn't you be in bed or something?" Without waiting for an answer he spun around and shouted at the room, "Come on, people! I need answers and I need them yesterday! Move it, move it, move it!"

The atmosphere in this room was indicative of the major panic spread across the globe. The answers he and everyone else wanted so desperately were not forthcoming. At exactly 10:07 PM, Eastern Standard Time, millions of people from every walk of life, from every country on the planet, had instantaneously disappeared. There had been no warning. No explanation of any kind. Wealth and power had been no deterrent; even the President's newborn son had vanished. The immediate result of these disappearances was total havoc and massive devastation. Countless driverless cars, trucks, motorcycles, boats, snowmobiles, subways, trains and airplanes had crashed. Unattended stoves, ovens, irons, blow torches, and heaters had started tens of thousands of fires, many of which burned out of control while congested streets blocked the path of fire fighters. Power and communications failed erratically. Looters found many stores, especially "mom and pop" businesses, deserted and vulnerable. Invalids were abandoned. Hospitals, most severely short-handed due to the disappearance of their own staff, were flooded with injured. Psychiatric facilities were already jammed with people whose minds snapped with the shock of having a loved one vanish before their eyes. Suicides, unchecked, proliferated at a skyrocketing rate. In one split second, ninety-nine percent of the population lost loved ones. No one could accept it. Never before in the annals of history had there been such an overwhelming, world-wide, internationally-shared feeling of crippling grief. The survivors were desperate for answers. Answers which no one anywhere appeared to have.

Across the room, a young secretary suddenly burst into tears. Someone put an arm around her. A young aide in thick horn-rimmed glasses timidly approached Lucy. "Excuse me, Mrs. Burton, I know this is unusual, ma'am, but there's someone here to see you."

"Tell them to take a hike."

"It's Jordan Masters, Ma'am."

That caught her attention. "Oh? Really?"

"Yes, ma'am."

A slow smile crossed her face. "Where is he?"

He was in the East lobby, pacing, smoking a cigarette. Wearing a rumpled tuxedo with the jacket buttoned, and it appeared he hadn't shaved, which only made him more strikingly handsome. When he saw her, he hesitated a moment, then tossed the cigarette away and hurried across the lobby.

"Mrs. Burton? Jordan Masters."

She took his hand between both of hers and squeezed softly. "Call me Lucretia."

"Lucretia."

There was something about his smile, something almost hypnotic–like a magnetic aura, or a kind of cosmic vibration emanating from him. His presence literally made her knees weak. "And all this time I thought that was merely an expression," she whispered.

"Pardon me?"

"Nothing."

"May I introduce Cat Johnson of WBN?"

Lucretia felt a flash of annoyance as another woman stepped forward, intruding on her moment. She immediately buried her rancor and shifted into "charming First Lady" mode, holding out her hand with a warm smile. "Miss Johnson, welcome to the White House."

"Thank you, ma'am, it's a honor."

Jordan seemed anxious. "Mrs. Burton, I realize we're totally ignoring protocol here but... we have to speak with the President. It's really important." He paused, then actually blushed. "I heard you might be a fan and–"

"And you used that to get to me so I could get you to him," she finished.

"I'm sorry, I–"

"Don't be," she cut him off by touching one finger to his lips. "I am a fan. Now I'm intrigued as well." Slipping her arm through his, grateful for the support but feeling even weaker at the intimacy, she steered him toward a low couch, feeling that if she didn't sit, she might collapse. "But how did you get here, Mister Masters?"

"I flew in from Las Vegas in my own private jet, Mrs. President."

She laughed. "Lucretia will do. It would only be Mrs. President if I were the President." She dropped her voice low so the reporter couldn't hear, "and although things might be better that way, such is not the case." She lowered her eyes, then gazed up at him.

He smiled and she collapsed onto the sofa's red velvet cushions. This was ridiculous, feeling like a love-sick school girl. Or maybe it wasn't Masters, maybe the doctors had been right, maybe the birth trauma had taken more out of her than she realized.

He sat beside her and took her hands. She felt an intense energy shoot up her arms, almost like a low-voltage electric charge. The feeling landed deep in her pelvis.

"Lucretia, we have something to tell the President, Ma'am, but maybe you should hear it first." He shook his head and sighed. "You probably won't believe it."

Then, unaccountably, she reached out and unbuttoned his jacket. He stiffened and began to pull away, but she grabbed the front of his shirt and pulled him back. In another impulse, she hooked her thumbs between the buttons and yanked the shirt open, revealing the pendant fastened to his chest. Oval in shape, it looked like black ice. In its center was a round raised disc with an intricate swirling pattern. Eight arms, like the legs of a metal spider, dug into his chest, piercing his flesh, which was red and oozing around the punctures. Lucy knew she should have been repulsed, but her reaction was quite the opposite. She felt drawn to it. Entranced. Stunningly beautiful, it was like an obsidian stone, the deeper she looked into it, the more the colors seemed to come alive. It had called to her. And she recognized, somehow, that this was the source of the energy that was effecting her.

"Or maybe you will," said Cat Johnson, behind her.

Chapter 4

Cat Johnson, ordinarily unperturbed by the stories she was covering, was both frightened and stunned by the events she had witnessed over the past twenty-four hours. It had all started with the moment she'd made simple physical contact with Jordan Masters. Only a handshake, yes, but somehow far beyond that, as though fate had linked them together in that moment, and the entire world had changed. Literally. The freakish ride in the van seemed to indicate that the three of them–she, Jordan, and Roger–were becoming a part of history and it both exhilarated her and scared her half to death. Afterward there had been the frantic attempt to get to Washington, D.C. All airports had been closed, except for emergency operations, yet somehow Jordan had managed to convince the authorities that it was necessary to allow him to take off from McCarren Airport in Vegas and land at Dulles near the nation's capitol, even at a time like this. The man's powers of persuasion were astounding. With an uncanny ability to use smiles, jokes, friendliness and obvious sincerity he could make a person feel not as if they were being persuaded but as though his wishes were precisely their own.

In mid-flight, forty thousand feet in the air, Gideon had reappeared. He'd simply walked in from the rear of the aircraft, sat down calmly as if it were the most normal thing in the world, and started talking. Again Roger manned the camera and again the footage was priceless. Unfortunately, she hadn't been able to convince the alien to repeat his morphing trick, changing from one physical form to another. Caught on film it would have authenticated their story, but he refused to "play games" and had dismissed the subject. She hadn't dared to push it. Before the flight landed, he quietly stepped away and disappeared again. Roger insisted on a search, but they turned up nothing. Cat hadn't really expected to find him; they'd seen the being change physically from one human shape into another and that was more than enough to convince the three of them that Gideon was the real thing–an alien from beyond the stars.

Their arrival in Washington and subsequent plan to gain access to the President had been insane, but somehow Jordan managed again to pave the way. At the threshold of the last obstacle, the White House itself, they were forced to leave Roger and his cameras outside the gate. Thankful that she also hadn't been barred admission, Cat was willing to concede the "no photographers" rule to gain their entrance. Under the circumstances, it was enough of a miracle that she and Jordan had been granted access to the inner sanctum, especially considering the current global crisis. She wondered whether the strange amulet around Jordan's neck had anything to do with their success. Somehow since he was tagged with the thing, Jordan seemed to affect people. Did the device emit some sort of an ultra-low frequency of sound that soothed others on a subconscious level? Or could it somehow magnify and project Jordan's naturally positive energy? Or maybe the weird thing was just plain outer space magic. In any case, Jordan now appeared to affect people unnaturally. Lucretia Burton's outrageous reaction piled on more evidence that the device could somehow be the source of Jordan's manifest persuasiveness.

After Mrs. Burton ushered them through a number of hallways and into an elevator, they emerged into a massive room that swarmed like a hive of angry, killer bees. Cat caught her breath and froze in place. Twenty-feet across the room from her stood the most powerful men in the nation, indeed the world.

"Wesley!" called Mrs. Burton, approaching at a fast clip, "This is Jordan Masters."

A thin man spun to face them. She recognized him as Harry Weinstein, the president's Chief of Staff. He glared at Jordan, anger clouding his face. "What is this man doing here?" he asked, loudly, to no one in particular.

"You wanted someone with answers, Wesley," the First-Lady said to her husband, ignoring Weinstein, "Mister Masters has them."

Weinstein stepped between them and the leader of the free world. "Mister President, we're in the middle of a world crisis here!" He seemed to notice Cat for the first time and his frown deepened. "Who are you?"

She felt as though she might faint and had to swallow hard before she could answer. "Cat Johnson, sir. WBN News."

If he had been angry before, the man now turned livid. His face flushed from red to an alarming shade of purple. "How did a reporter get in here?" he shouted.

Several men in dark suits with earphones moved quickly toward her.

"Wait!" cried Jordan.

Lucretia glared at her husband. "Wesley!"

Burton held up a hand, stopping the Secret Service men. "Let's give them a chance to speak, Harry." Weinstein looked like he was ready to explode, but stepped back. Burton gave him a quick, reinforcing nod and turned to Jordan. "You've got two minutes, Mister Masters and the clock is running."

Jordan took a breath and glanced over at Cat. She felt her stomach twist, but her eyes met his, urging him on. The room grew ominously quiet.

Jordan took a breath. "Mister President, there is an alien contingent known as The One."

"Excuse me?" said Weinstein.

"These are..." Jordan struggled with the words, "... very important beings. Powerful. Guardians of the universe–that kind of powerful. And somehow we've been judged as... too... messed up."

"We, who?" asked Weinstein, still frowning.

"We, the people of Earth," answered Cat.

"Not all the people," Jordan quickly added, "They've..." he looked uncomfortable saying it, "beamed up those they've decided should live."

A barrel-chested, silver-haired, five-star Admiral in full uniform exploded with expletive anger.

At once, the room broke into a cacophony of voices.

"Listen to him," shouted Lucretia, stepping forward.

The room quieted a bit.

"Please, it happened!" said Cat to the Admiral, whose name tag read: Chilton. "You can't deny that! We found out that in three days from today, next Wednesday, they plan to detonate all nuclear weapons globally! Then they will finish us off, repopulate, and start fresh."

"Mister President!" pleaded Weinstein, outrage and disbelief painting his face.

"Please listen to us!" said Jordan, focusing on the Chief of Staff now, "Look who was taken, sir. The simple. The non-violent. The children." He pointed first to the President then the Admiral. "Not the powerful. Not the warriors. If we do not disarm–"

"And where is this giant spaceship, son?" asked the Admiral, with the tone of a psychiatrist humoring a delusional patient, "Don't you think we would have noticed it?"

"Well, obviously," said Cat, "They have some kind of stealth technology. They... cloaked it or something. Like, like in *Star Trek...*" Even as she said it, she knew it sounded insane and inane.

"That's enough!" exploded Weinstein.

Jordan stepped in. "Look, we're not explaining this very well... we know it sounds crazy–"

"I knew your father, Mister Masters," said Burton, clearly out of patience, "and he was a great man, so I've made allowances, but we're very busy here."

"Mister President, I met this alien!"

"It's true! As God is our witness!" added Cat.

"Security, get these people out of here!" shouted Weinstein.

The Secret Service rushed forward.

"No! Please, look!" Cat started to reach into her purse to remove the video tape they'd shot, but found her hands roughly yanked away and the purse torn from her grasp. Clearly the agents had misunderstood the gesture, perhaps thinking she was going for a weapon. "No! Wait! Stop!" The agents completely ignored her pleas and hurriedly hustled her and Jordan out of the room. Just before they were dragged around the corner Cat saw Burton whirl on his wife. "Lucretia!" he shouted, furiously, "What's the matter with you, bringing those lunatics in here? Somebody escort the First Lady to her room!"

The ensuing language that issued from Lucretia Burton's mouth like a stream of black venom would have shocked the nation.

Cat and Jordan were escorted, none too gently, off the White House premises. Cat was angrier than a wounded tiger as the gates slammed behind them. Just how incredibly self-centered, close-minded and obtuse were these idiots who were running the country?

Roger, who was waiting for them anxiously, looked at the Secret Service agents with a frown. "I'm guessing it didn't go well, huh?"

One of the agents, a huge man with a shaved head, growled, "Consider yourselves lucky we don't throw your butts in jail!" They started to stalk away.

"Hey!" shouted Cat. "HEY! My purse!"

The agents stopped. The leader gestured to his smaller partner. Having found nothing dangerous in it, the partner tossed her handbag through the bars of the metal gate. Roger's precious video tape was still inside.

The tape flew across the room and Cat caught it.

"I can't run that!" snapped Maggie Brinks, snapping off the video player.

They were standing in the evening news producer's office on the twenty-third floor of the WBN building in Culver City, California. Brinks was a 53 year-old, hard-as-nails woman with severely-cropped jet black hair that Cat was pretty sure was a dye job. Her face was that of a much younger woman, but seemed constantly strained, the results of more than one cosmetic surgery, if the rumor mill was accurate. To be blunt, if Maggie smiled, she'd split her skin like a snake. There was no danger of that, however. The intimidating Ms. Brinks never smiled.

"Why not?" demanded Cat.

"That belongs downstairs in the entertainment department, Catherine, just like you do. Up here, we do real news."

Jordan, who had been sitting on the low, black leather couch, stood. "Ms. Brinks–"

"Mister Masters," she said, in a clipped, no-nonsense tone, "no disrespect intended, but if you need publicity for your next film there are better ways."

"Maggie!" protested Cat, "This was real! I was there!"

"Catherine, the man is an actor!" She glanced at Jordan over her shoulder. "No disrespect intended."

"His father was the President of the United States!" exclaimed Cat, "His uncle is a Senator!"

"Then why don't you contact the esteemed Senator?" snapped Brinks, "Why is that, Mister Masters?"

"I tried that," said Jordan.

"But... ?"

Jordan hesitated. "But..."

Brinks answered for him. "But the Senator thinks his nephew has gone off the deep end, doesn't he?" In a room already heavy with smoke she flipped open a lighter and lit yet another cigarette. "This may be the first time I've ever agreed with the drunken old pervert. No disrespect intended." With that she turned her attention to the papers on her desk. Cat and Jordan hesitated. "Don't let the door hit you on the way out," said Brinks, without looking up.

With no other options, the duo left the office. In the hallway, Cat shook with suppressed fury and frustration at yet another failure. She looked at Jordan. "Now what?"

He sighed, shaking his head, resigned. "We get the hell out of Dodge."

Chapter 5

Deep in an underground installation, thirteen stories below the surface of the earth, Lieutenant Jeremy Harris swiveled his high-backed, padded, leather chair away from the massive bank of electronic equipment, to face his partner. Jeremy was an nineteen year-old, open-faced, red headed, Iowa farm boy with pale skin and a spattering of freckles across his cheeks. He and Lieutenant Chase Thayer had only worked together for three months, but they knew each other better than most married couples. Sitting together in an eight-by-six room ten hours a day with little to do except run the occasional ICM Launch Readiness Drill, they'd had plenty of time to talk. Today's topic was the same one on everyone's tongue, discussed non-stop, everywhere for the past seventy-eight hours.

"This is, what? Day four? And they still claim to have no idea what caused it."

Chase was an old money Alabama boy, his charming Southern manner and refined accent part of his inheritance. His sandy blond hair and piercing blue eyes made him Launch Site 58's most eligible bachelor and earned him his nickname, Thayer the Player. His first name seemed uniquely appropriate, too. "My money's on chemical warfare," he said, in a smooth, southern drawl.

"Come on!" said Harris, "Who'd develop a weapon that nasty?"

Thayer simply turned and looked at him with one raised eyebrow. Jeremy looked around at the millions of dollars worth of instruments of destruction surrounding them and shrugged. "Okay, good point. But maybe it was some kind of... atmospheric anomaly. It didn't affect a single person working down here. Maybe it was in the air, some kind of a weird electrical discharge or something."

"And just how would that make people vanish, pray tell?"

Jeremy shrugged. "I don't know, but think how fragile the universe is. I mean, if you changed one atom in a water molecule, you'd have... hydrogen or something."

Thayer gave him another dubious look.

"Something like that!" he persisted, "People are mostly water, so maybe they got changed to gas or something."

"Well, somebody's sure full of gas, son," said Chase, with a grin.

"I don't know how you take it so damn lightly! The very thought of it gives me the heebie jeebies. What if the moment it happened, Laura and I had been making love? What if she had disappeared right from under me?"

He shivered, looking at the small, silver-framed photograph on his computer console. Nightmares of that very scenario had kept him awake the last three nights.

"The odds on that are not likely," said Chase, quietly, looking past him at the picture of the smiling girl with corn-silk hair.

"Why?" asked Jeremy, with a frown.

Chase shrugged. "I thought you told me she'd been... distant lately."

Jeremy felt his shoulders drop. It was true, his girlfriend of nearly a year had changed in recent weeks. She said it was the job, the long hoursthe pressure of knowing her boyfriend had the power to destroy a good portion of the world under his fingertips. It creeped her out, she said. But he suspected it was more. She'd withdrawn, not wanting to make love and the last few times he'd called she'd been unavailable. "True, man."

"Still?"

"Yeah. If I lose her... jeez. It's bad enough you leaving."

Chase had announced, four days ago, that he was dropping out of the program, transferring to a normal desk job. Jeremy couldn't believe it, Chase was the perfect profile for this job: 20 years of age, raised in a small southern town with old fashioned American "love it or leave it" ideals, no living family, no close friends to speak of. A loner, with no discernible conscience. Thayer the Player. Why would he leave before his tour was up and transfer to a desk job at half the pay? It just didn't make sense.

Chase turned to face him, an uncharacteristically, serious expression on his face. "Look, Jeremy, this world has gone completely to hell in the past few days and there's something I need to tell–"

That was as far as he got because at that moment the room was filled with an ear-splitting shriek. The alarm nearly caused Jeremy to wet his pants as the computer console suddenly lit up like a Christmas tree. LEDs instantly switched from red to green, every monitor screen lit up, a series of numbers flashed across the formerly tranquil panels. Chase, eyes wide and face pale, glared at his partner. "What did you do!?"

Jeremy stared at the board in disbelief. "Nothing!"

Chase snatched up the red telephone, which didn't require dialing. "This is Lieutenant Chase Thayer 656137811. We have a priority red situation!" He gasped, eyes glued to his main monitor, "Oh my God."

Jeremy followed Chase's eyes. The screen blinked in bright green letters, two terrifying words: Launch Mode. A computerized voice came through the four speakers in the room, completely surrounding them, like the spirit of death-to-come. "Entering DEF-CON 4, detonation in T-MINUS 60 seconds."

"Shut it down! Shut it down!" screamed Chase.

Desperately, Jeremy typed in commands, his fingers flying over the keyboard. "I'm trying!"

The thick, steel door behind them swung open and the massive figure of Brigadier General Ryan Leigh filled the doorway. Beyond him, in the main compound, lights flashed, sirens wailed and people ran everywhere. "What in Lucifer's name is going on?" he roared.

"Don't know, sir!" called Jeremy, desperately, getting no reaction from his inputs.

"Who initiated this action?"

"Nobody, sir!"

"Well shut it down, soldier!"

"We're trying, sir!" He looked over at Chase who was frantically keying in commands on his own unit, with apparently just as much futility.

The computer voice announced, "T-MINUS 50 seconds."

"Abort!" shouted the General, "I repeat, abort this launch! That's an order, Lieutenant!"

Jeremy banged on the keyboard with frustration. He thought he might throw up. "Negative, sir. It's proceeding on its own!"

"Oh, mama!" cried Chase, horrified, "General! We're not proceeding with launch, sir. Just detonation!"

With those words, Jeremy felt as though his blood had turned to liquid nitrogen. If the missiles detonated without launch–

"That's impossible!" the General bellowed, "This is not happening!"

But it was happening. "T-MINUS 40 seconds."

The General snatched up the red phone, shouting, "Patch me through to the Commander-in-Chief! Priority Alpha!"

A short man burst into the room, his eyes wide and dripping sweat. The armpits of his Colonel's uniform were already darkly stained. He didn't bother to salute. "It's not just us, General, it's happening system wide!"

The General blanched. A voice snapped his attention back to the telephone. "Yes, sir, Mister President, you heard correctly. Yes, sir, that is exactly what's happening. We don't know! Something is overriding us! The computer announced, "T-MINUS 30 seconds." then continued, counting every second in an insanely serene tone. "Twenty-nine, twenty-eight..."

"Less than half a minute, sir," said the General loudly, over the continuing countdown. He listened a moment. "Say again, Mister President." Something behind his eyes changed, from desperation to resignation. "Yes, sir, initiate. Yes, sir. No, sir, I don't think we do have a choice. God help us all, sir." He turned to Jeremy and Chase. "Light 'em up."

Jeremy couldn't believe what he was hearing. "Sir?" His voice had a involuntary quaver.

"Launch missiles, Lieutenant! Let 'em fly! Now!"

"Detonation in fifteen seconds," said the computer. "Fourteen, thirteen..."

He and Chase exchanged horrified glances then, in quick, synchronized movements–motions that they'd practiced a hundred times but never, ever thought they'd have to use for real–inserted launch keys and hit the buttons.

Jeremy immediately switched his attention to the computer schematics of the launch sequence.

"Go babies," urged the General, through clenched teeth.

"Seven, six..."

"Oh God," said Chase, in a low voice, staring at a computer simulation of Missile Silo 3, and a flashing orange alert. Jeremy's vision turned blood red, his fear blocking his senses completely.

"One of the silo doors hasn't opened," whispered his best friend.

"Three. Two."

His sight returned as an icy wave of numbness washed over him. He gave in to the inevitable. He reached for the framed picture of Laura... but Chase was already clutching it to his chest.

"One."

With understanding, came death.

Chapter 6

The cork exploded out of the champagne bottle and shot over the railing on the redwood deck, arcing to the green stretch of lawn below. An eight-foot stockade fence divided the manicured grass from a looming forest and beyond that, mountain peaks silhouetted against the moon. Foam bubbled from the bottle onto the wood planking.

Cat Johnson watched as Jordan poured two glasses of very expensive champagne, and recalled their arrival at the mountain retreat three evenings before. Her first look at this vacation home, as they drove up on the wide, white-graveled circular driveway, had overwhelmed her. When Jordan suggested they escape from the city to his "mountain bungalow," she'd pictured some rustic log-cabin, perhaps a one bedroom shack with an old wood stove to keep the chill out–certainly not a huge, 10,000 square foot, English-Tudor hunting lodge.

"Wow," was all she managed to say.

"You like?" He killed the engine of the old four-wheel drive Jeep he'd been driving when he picked her up and cast his eyes fondly on the place.

She shook her head in wonder. "I don't get you."

"What? What do you mean?" He got out of the car and walked around to the rear.

As she stepped out, she breathed in the fresh, cool mountain air with immeasurable pleasure. "Well, to be truthful, I pictured you at first as the Ferrari or Lamborgini type, then you show up in this!"

He shrugged, pulling their luggage out of the rear compartment. "I'm not really a flashy kinda guy. I'm more comfortable with Old Blue here. Sorry."

"Don't apologize," she smiled, "It was a pleasant surprise." She took her bag from his hand.

Without argument, he led the way to the front door. "Well then...?"

"Well, on the one hand there's the Jeep, and on the other hand, there's..." She trailed off as he unlocked the heavy, twelve foot high, carved oak door and swung it open. "This."

The interior of the lodge was breathtakingly elegant. A two-story foyer led past a sweeping stairway to a cavernous living room with a massive stone fireplace. Over the dark wood mantle was a taxidermy masterpiece of six pheasants in full flight. An antique piano, almost triangular in shape, sat on a raised platform. The rest of the room was furnished with equally exquisite and expensive period pieces. Several lovely tapestries covered the oak-paneled walls. Thick Turkish carpets were spread across the highly polished hardwood floor. It was the home of a multi-millionaire.

Jordan led the way inside and through a wide, winding hallway. "Actually, it's pretty simple. This is my parent's place. *Was* my parents' place. It was their Camp David, a retreat from the rest of the world. I keep it as a reminder of them." He stopped outside a room and grinned, "And, to be honest, it's not a bad place to bring a date." He threw open a set of double doors, revealing a huge bedroom beyond.

Cat looked past him. The focus of the room was a large four-poster bed. She tensed. "Uhhhh, Jordan..."

"You'll sleep here," he continued. "I'll be upstairs."

She looked at him, surprised. She'd been sure he'd expect them to share the room, and the bed.

He misread her expression. "Unless you'd rather have the master bedroom. This one's okay with me, either way."

"No," she said quickly, feeling herself blush, "No, this'll do just fine."

He smiled. "Well then... welcome."

Pondering the last three days as they stood on the deck, she wondered why he hadn't made a single aggressive move toward her. They had spent many intense hours talking, mostly about whether it was the end of the world, or wondering if somehow they'd been tricked into making huge fools of themselves. After a "quick trip" to the closest store twelve miles away, he'd demonstrated skills as a culinary gourmet, which was a good thing because cooking was not her forte. She'd learned that in his youth he'd had no particular interest in acting, had never taken a class, and had practically been dragged into the business–which made him feel guilty when he thought about all the desperately struggling actors out there. When she asked about the Secret Service agents normally assigned to members of a presidential family he'd explained that at age twenty-one he'd used his prerogative to dismiss them, uncomfortable with their constant, ominous presence.

In spite of his profession, he was by nature a solitary man. They took long walks in the surrounding woods, sometimes walking side by side for long stretches, silent, lost in their own thoughts and fears. But the entire time, as attracted to him as she was, and as interested in her as he appeared to be, he had not demonstrated any sexual attraction to her. At first she'd wondered if he was gay, but during the course of their conversations that notion was quickly dispelled. She, on the other hand, was immensely physically attracted, aware on an intense desire to hold him, make love to him, to reaffirm life in the most basic way. They might both die at any moment, why not go for it? She'd even attempted a seduction herself but he'd quite unmistakably deflected it. In the nicest way, of course, in fact so smoothly that it almost didn't seem like a rejection, but she knew it was. And now, time was almost up. Every stomach-churning minute of every tension-filled hour of the past three pressurized days she'd dreaded hearing word of inevitable unprecedented global catastrophe. The past few hours as the deadline rushed toward them had been nearly unbearable. She had brooded outside on the deck alone, staring at the field of stars looking so normal and eternal, feeling sick to her stomach, bitter at the stupidity of mankind's rich and powerful, waiting for it all to end. She thought about her friend Roger, too, hoping he'd been able to be with people he cared about during this hideous countdown.

And nothing had happened. Nothing. No change.

Jordan handed her a glass of champagne and raised his own in a toast. "Here's to midnight on the third day, come and gone."

She stared at him, unbelieving, and checked her watch. Could it be true?

Jordan looked at her with concern. "Hey, you okay?"

She drained the glass in one swallow, shivering. "Yes." She shook her head. "No." She tried to voice the thoughts that were tormenting her. The utter terror she'd tried so hard to bury, the tremendous relief now that it seemed to be over, how she'd never think of anything in life the same way ever again. Her eyes suddenly filled with tears. "I just can't believe..."

"Hey, hey." Jordan stripped off his soft, brown suede jacket and placed it gently around her shoulders. "It didn't happen. It was all some sort of huge mistake. That's a good thing."

She wanted desperately to believe that. "Think so?" she asked, in a small voice.

"I do." He slipped an arm around her and she leaned into him. They stared up at the stars together for what seemed like a long time. She didn't mind. She liked it there, nuzzled close, taking in the vanilla smell of him. Finally, he spoke softly. "Look, Cat, you may have noticed I haven't made a pass at you these past three days."

"Really?"

"There was a reason for that."

"Because it might have been the last three days on Earth?" she asked with sarcasm.

"Yes."

That really confused her. "Okay, you lost me."

"I know most people would have slept together just because it might have been the end of the world," he continued, seriously, "But what if it wasn't? When the three day ultimatum has come and gone and the world is still turning... where does that leave the relationship?"

She looked up at him. "You're saying you didn't want to sleep with me because the world might not end? Then you'd be stuck with me?"

He gave a small laugh. "No, because I didn't want it to be about the end of the world, I wanted it to be about us. About the *beginning* of something."

The enormity of what he was saying rushed through her like a hot, wonderful wind. "Oh, Jordan."

She melted like warm caramel, but somehow he caught and held her. She felt a magnetic strength and intense river of energy flowing just below his surface as he pulled her to him. Their lips met, bodies melding, passion a sweet tidal wave, expanding, avalanching. The kiss, unbearably beautiful, lasted forever, which was far too short. Cat felt herself becoming weightless and realized that Jordan had swept her up into his arms. He looked toward the house, then into her eyes, the question smoldering. She nodded, almost urgently. He started to carry her inside, then abruptly stopped. She looked up at the grin stretching across his face as he looked out across the horizon. "Look at that, a shooting star. That's good luck, my lovely one."

She glanced back over his shoulder, and a mind-numbing fear impacted every nerve in her body. She heard a crash of shattering glass and distantly realized she had dropped her champagne goblet onto the deck.

"What is it?" asked Jordan, concern and puzzlement crossing his face.

She felt sick. Physically, violently, gut-twisting ill. Her mouth immediately lost all moisture. Her throat tightened so that she could hardly take a breath. She could barely manage to choke out the words. "That isn't a shooting star, Jordan!" Rasping, watching another streak shoot across the sky, her voice rose several decibels. "Neither is that. Or that. Oh no. Oh no, no, oh no..." Dimly she knew she was losing consciousness, and almost hoped she was dying.

The streaks of fire that were shooting across the distant sky were man-made objects.

"Dear God in heaven," he whispered.

Chapter 7

Matthew Miracle drove his celestial blue 2000 Corvette Stingray convertible down some long, dark, empty road, name unknown, far outside of some mid-Kansas town, name unknown, heading for some distant destination, name unknown. Wanting to be alone to think, he had taken the most desolate route he could find, twisting and turning down pothole-ridden back highways, narrow gravel and dirt roads. Vast fields of wheat surrounded him, stretching as far as the eye could see in every direction and he pictured himself as a very small life raft lost in an ocean of grain. It was a fitting allegory because he was, indeed, lost. In the very worst way.

His life, his work, his very beliefs had all been a sham. Worse, an abomination. The truths, which he had thought to be lies, were truths after all. His superiority had been ignorance. His entire existence, to this moment, had been worse than useless. His total belief system had been shattered in one fragmentary moment. How great was God! How utterly useless and negative, had been this worthless man's life.

Suddenly the car bucked violently and the steering wheel was wrenched from his hand. At first Matthew thought it was a tire blowout, but then he realized, to his frightened amazement, that the car was actually airborne. It slammed down with a violent crash that would have tossed him over the door had he not been buckled to the seat, and the car spun across the gravel. He fought for control but lost as the vehicle left the rough road, flew over a ditch, and smashed into a fence post with a jarring crash. He sat there, stunned and terrified with the thought that God might be angry enough to reach down and swat him off the road. The engine died. So did the headlights. The silence was overwhelming. It was interrupted by a screeching whoosh as a large flock of crows flapped from a huge tree, as if startled by something. Matthew stared up at the dark birds blackening the gray sky and felt a sudden chill, anticipating God's appearance. It came in the form of a mind-numbing explosion. He screamed aloud. His car began to shake as a low, intense rumbling came from deep within the earth. The plastic, glow-in-the-dark Jesus on his dashboard was jarred loose and clattered to the floorboards. With trembling hands he unbuckled his seatbelt then slowly stood up onto the leather seat, leaning against the top of the windshield, searching the darkness. Huge pits opened in the ground. Massive clumps of soil were heaved aside or fell into the abyss below. Beams of orange light projecting from the dark earth, lit the clouds overhead. A wash of terror choked his mind. It all suddenly made sense–the wrath from below, the black birds–it was not God who had come for him, but the Dark One himself. The ground directly below the car would now open up and he would be swallowed into Satan's foul hell below. Massive demons were beginning to emerge from the fields surrounding him. No, not demons, large obelisks. Monuments, he realized a moment later–monuments to man's greed, hatred and stupidity, rising out of the earth, pointing toward the heavens–a special delivery from Satan's hell to God's paradise.

Seven nuclear missiles blasted out of their hidden silos, the intense, flaming backwash immediately igniting the dry stalks of grain in the field as they cleared the underground tunnels. Matthew felt a hurricane of scorching wind blast by him, so hot he could hardly breathe. He feared his lungs would sear and the liquid in his eyeballs boil as his hair begin to crackle. Moments later, flaming objects began to rain down around him. One hit the hood of his car with a thonk–a black bird that twitched a moment, then lay still, wisps of smoke trailing out of the hollow cavities where its eyes once had been. Matthew knew that he, too, would die. He clamped his eyes shut, bowed his head, and waited for his soul to be claimed. Instead, the intense heat passed.

When he finally allowed himself to look several minutes later, Matthew contemplated the world out there with crystal clear vision for the first time in his life. Now he understood his mission. Burned away were the doubts. He knew now with absolute certainty why God had put him there, in that place, at that moment. In the fire storm he had tasted but a tiny sample of Satan's evil, of the torture of burning in everlasting hell. It had all been planned. A lesson. A warning.

He faced what was to come. It had all been foretold.

Running his raw hands through his white-streaked hair, he stared up at the flaming sky with burning, flowing eyes, and spoke in an intense, reverent whisper, quoting words written thousands of years ago: the Book of Revelation 8:7. *"And the first angel blew his trumpet and fire mixed with blood poured down on the earth. And a third of the earth, and the grass, and the trees were burned up."*

Chapter 8

The explosion, which occurred 10,000 feet above the city, was of immense power. Within a millionth of a second it emitted a force of energy five times hotter than the center of the sun. In less than a thousandth of a second the fireball had grown to 440 feet, within ten seconds it was more than a mile in diameter. Along with the intense heat and light, a flux of radiation–neutrons and gamma rays–exploded from the weapon. A shock wave of compressed air, two and a half times as bright as our closest star's surface, ballooned outward. Inside this was a second shell of hot gasses, far brighter than the first, which, in turn, burst through, creating a light that, to a young honeymooning couple standing on a hotel balcony nine miles away, appeared 100 times brighter than the desert sun. The girl, who was turned slightly away, suffered flash blindness, and found herself unable to see. She was lucky, her vision would return. Her new husband, who was looking directly at the distant flash, was not as fortunate. Both retinas were seared in a millisecond. He would never gaze upon his new bride again.

The burst of heat and light, known as a thermal pulse, lasted for ten seconds. In a seven and a half mile radius around ground zero, the area just below the detonation, windows were blown out, numerous fires exploded into existence and thousands of people suffered horrific burns, their clothing bursting into flame or melting directly onto their flesh.

The couple, even as far away as they were, suffered instantaneously what appeared to be an severe sunburn. Even areas of skin protected by layers of clothing were affected. The girl, wearing a white blouse, was less burnt than the boy because light color always reflects a portion of the rays. The young man, on whose shirt was a swirly black design that absorbed the rays, was left with a distinctive pattern etched into his torso.

Ten seconds after the explosion, the pounding shock wave spread out for three miles, half the weapon's energy contained within it. When it hit the earth, a second wave, generated by reflection, joined the first wave and moved out along the surface. Winds of 150 miles per hour pounded into anything in its path. Buildings were pulverized. Human bodies, inner organs crushed and hemorrhaging from the sudden compression, became mere projectiles. Even at the edge of the conflagration twelve miles away the heat was intense enough to cause a newspaper to burst into flame. The wave was traveling faster than the speed of sound, so its victims never even heard it coming.

The fireball shot upwards at 300 miles per hour, drawing rushing winds and debris with it, expanding outward into a mushroom shape. Winds created by the shock wave abruptly reversed and rushed inward, following the air being drawn upward into the mushroom stem. These gales fanned the flames ignited by the thermal pulse and cold air rushed in from all sides, bringing fresh oxygen, resulting in a massive firestorm.

Twelve miles away, the blast wave remained powerful enough to shatter windows. Multitudes of victims were hit by shards of glass, shredding skin to the bone. Stoves were overturned, gas lines broken, and electrical circuits shorted out, all causing more incipient blazes that spread rapidly through the buildings now without windows or many doors. Igniting many chemical and petroleum products, the conflagrations caused the air to be choked with toxic gases: hydrogen chloride, hydrogen cyanide, sulfur dioxide, phosgene, and more. The situation escalated in intensity and deadliness, promising to devour absolutely everything combustible within an area of one hundred seventy-five square miles.

All of that happened within the first thirty seconds.

Within an hour, survivors began to suffer nausea, vomiting, diarrhea, thirst, and fever.

Soon, wounds would grow infected and refuse to heal, gums would turn reddish purple, hemorrhages would render the skin blotchy, and hair would begin to fall out.

Unspeakable pain. Harrowing torment. Heart-breaking, inevitable death.

Chapter 9

President Wesley Burton, looking as if he had aged ten years overnight, stepped to the podium and the few White House press corps still left to carry on immediately fell into silence. He stared grimly at his notes then looked up at the gathered reporters with red-rimmed eyes, his voice hoarse and strained. "At three-oh-four AM, Eastern Standard Time, all nuclear facilities inexplicably activated. Not just in the United States–globally. Although every effort was made, no government was able to override the launches and without exception we were left with only two choices: either to let the bombs detonate underground with some degree of containment or else to launch and destroy the weapons in the atmosphere." He sighed and looked down at his notes. "Nuclear explosions create a brief, intense burst of electromagnetic energy known as an EMP–electromagnetic pulse. In less than a millionth of a second this pulse reaches an intensity of up to fifty thousand volts per meter, which is collected by metallic conductors, causing overloads in electronic circuits." He looked up. "We knew that a weapon discharged in the atmosphere would certainly have this effect, but detonating them underground would have taken tens of thousands of lives of our loyal armed forces personnel who man our defense bases. I had a terrible choice to make and only seconds in which to make it. Ladies and gentlemen, as you are all well aware by now, I chose lives over technology. The result has been devastating. Radio, television, and telephones have all been severely damaged. Eighty-seven percent of all of our computers, which are especially vulnerable to EMPs, have been wiped clean. Power and utilities, sixty-three percent shut down. Transportation, which includes electronic transmissions of automobiles, is seventy-eight percent down. The estimated number on electronics and telecommunications loss is sixty-eight percent. That number is as mercifully low as it is due to the use of fiber optics, which were not affected. They are, in fact, the reason any of you can see or hear me today."

He paused and gazed wearily at the shocked faces, unnaturally silent. "Tragically, a number of systems malfunctioned. Lift-offs aborted, and guidance systems malfunctioned causing detonations at both subterranean and, worse, low levels. The results have been catastrophic beyond all imagination. Much of the former Soviet Union has been destroyed. Reports are coming in describing wide-spread damage in Europe. Paris, as we knew it, has been leveled."

The reaction throughout the gathered assembly of reporters was one of numb disbelief.

"In the United States, large areas of Montana, North Dakota, South Dakota, and Wyoming have been severely affected. Nebraska and Kansas as well. Due to the danger of radiation fallout, all travel to those areas is now strictly prohibited. I am declaring martial law throughout the United States, effective immediately. Details will follow and, of course, we'll keep you informed of all further developments as they become known."

Hands shot up all around the room. The President gave a half-hearted wave toward a well-known CNN corespondent. "Yeah, John."

"We now know what happened, Mister President" said the reporter, somberly. "What you haven't addressed is why?"

The President looked distinctly uncomfortable. "That is currently under investigation. Like last week's disappearances, we have no immediate explanation."

Again, every hand in the room went up, vying for the President's attention. Cat Johnson, standing on the edge of the crowd in a dark blue skirt and jacket, took a deep, fortifying breath and stepped forward. Without waiting to be acknowledged and breaking all rules of protocol, her tone urgent, she spoke before anyone else had a chance. "Mister President, what about reports that you were, indeed, given an explanation? That you were informed exactly as to the cause of the disappearances and that you chose to ignore a warning about the possibilities of this current disaster, as well?"

Cat knew every eye, and camera, in the room was on her. This was the moment of truth. Using his private jet and personal influence, Jordan had flown her and Roger to Maryland and got them to the White House where they'd bluffed their way into the press conference, flashing their press I.D.s and hustling past the guards. Truthfully, in all the confusion, it hadn't been as difficult as she had anticipated. The powers that be at WBN had no idea they were there. Her professional career, and Roger Jackson's, were balancing on the edge of a very dangerous precipice.

The President glared at her in immediate outrage, then, as she saw recognition come into his eyes, he stiffened. "Your information is completely inaccurate, Miss... ?"

"Johnson. Cat Johnson, World Broadcast News."

Cat watched as Wilton Moore, Burton's Press Secretary, stepped forward and whispered in the President's ear. Burton smiled smugly and nodded, turning his attention back to her. "Ah, the esteemed Miss Johnson," he said, his voice dripping with sarcasm, "From the Movies and Groovies segment." The other news people reacted as if the intruder had brought a stink into their room. "This is not a Hollywood movie, Miss Johnson, this is reality. We'd all appreciate it if we could stick to facts."

Cat felt herself grow hot. Her cellular telephone rang. She snatched it from her belt and spoke into it. “I'm busy.”

Maggie Brinks' rasping smoker's voice screamed back at her. “No, you're fired! What are you trying to pull, you stupid–”

“Hold on a moment,” said Cat as the room reacted to the unexpected appearance of the First Lady, who had just walked through the doorway. In a black Chanel suit, no jewelry, and a fashionably artful short haircut, she made a striking figure as she strode to the podium and unceremoniously shoved her husband aside.

The First Lady faced the cameras. “Miss Johnson is absolutely correct, people. Exactly three days ago, my husband, the President of the United States, was, in my presence, apprised of these possible consequences.”

Roger, agog, looked like he was going to drop the camera. The room turned into instant pandemonium. The Press Secretary blanched white. The look on the President's face reminded Cat of the famous picture of Lee Harvey Oswald when Jack Ruby had shoved a gun into his stomach and pulled the trigger.

Lucy Burton continued, speaking emotionally. “He was told exactly what happened to all of your missing loved ones, including my new-born child. And, ladies and gentlemen, he was also warned that seventy-two hours from the date of that same meeting a global nuclear detonation would take place unless all weapons were disassembled! But he and his entire staff chose to ignore this information and all of us have suffered the consequences! Millions, maybe billions of people are dead!” She shot a look at her husband that could only be construed as pure hatred. “I, for one, can no longer be a part of this unconscionable act of cowardice. I resign as your First Lady.” She turned to Burton. “And, as your wife.” With an air of injured, regal dignity, she left the room.

The place exploded in disbelief. Burton, his face a deep purple color, looking as though he might literally detonate, hurried after his wife. Cat, closest to the door, was the only person who witnessed what happened next. In the hallway, Burton grabbed his wife and violently spun her around. “You witch! You've destroyed me!”

Her eyes flashed dangerously, “You destroyed yourself! And half the Earth.”

“Just like a rat to desert a sinking ship,” he sneered.

Lucretia Burton laughed harshly. “Interesting species, rats. Tenacious, adaptable, almost impossible to exterminate...” she leaned in close to him, her voice turning dry-ice cold. “and often used in experiments. This one failed.”

She spun on her heel and walked away.

Shocked, but feeling vindicated, Cat brought the telephone to her ear. "Maggie? You were saying?"

All animosity in the News Director's voice had been replaced by rabid excitement. "Do you still have that tape, Catherine? I'll clear the six o'clock."

Cat felt an unprecedented power surge. "How would you like an exclusive with Jordan Masters, as well?" she asked.

Brinks sounded like she might wet her pants. "If you can do that, damn, Cat! The sky's the limit!"

Cat snapped the telephone shut, cutting the connection. "There are no limits, Maggie," she said to herself. "Not any more."

Chapter10

The rock dust from multiple nuclear blasts at surface level, the smoke from unquenchable forest fires and the soot from burning cities spread across the Northwest leaving a sky dirtied with ash. The impotent sun hung in the sky, a brooding, dark purple orb. Although it was June, a deep chill permeated the ugly atmosphere, as cold as any northern December. Nuclear Winter had set in.

In the WBN news studio Jordan Masters sat at a small make-up table, enduring the attentions of a pale, thin girl who was applying a base coat of make-up to keep the shine off his face under the lights. The sponge was cold. He found both it and the girl unreasonably irritating.

"I can't believe I'm doing Jordan Masters," she was saying, in a nasal voice, "You can bet this goes on my resume!"

Jordan stared at her in the mirror. Across the planet major cities had been obliterated, huge geographical areas had been rendered unlivable by radioactive fall-out, millions lay dead or dying from radiation poisoning, Hell on Earth, and this kid was thinking about her resume? Outrage began to build inside him like a pressure cooker.

Cat Johnson approached from behind. Looking flawless in a coral suit with calf-length jacket over a white silk blouse, it was clear she'd already been through make-up. "Ready, Jordan?" she asked, with a smile.

He yanked away the protective tissue the make-up girl had tucked around his collar and tie, and stood, eager to get away. "I'm a little nervous," he said softly.

She looked dubious. "You're kidding."

He shook his head. "This isn't a movie, Cat, this is the real thing." They started to walk down a long hallway toward the set. "I don't know how you do it. I mean, I saw you in Vegas, the world was going to hell in a hand basket and you just stood there, calmly reporting. It was..." he groped for the right word.

She stopped walking. "Cold?"

He shook his head. That wasn't quite it, it was more like– "Eerie."

She gave him a considering look. "Do you remember I told you my parents were dead?"

He nodded. "Yeah." She'd mentioned it when he'd offered to have her family join them at the lodge, but then she'd dropped the subject and he hadn't wanted to pursue uncomfortable memories.

"It happened in the '85 earthquake in Mexico City. I was eleven. Family vacation. The earthquake hit and they were trampled to death by people trying to get out of the building we were in."

"I'm sorry, Cat."

Her eyes went far away, as if replaying the scene on some inner movie screen. "It all happened so fast. The world shaking, walls crumbling, bricks raining down on our heads. I was swept outside by the crowd, my hand torn out of my mom's grip." He voice took on a hollow, haunted tone. "People were screaming, moaning, bleeding everywhere... and the only person who seemed still under control was a television journalist. Like a rock, standing in the middle of all this horror, calmly reporting. I was drawn to her. And I remember her words. 'El diablo era el panico.'"

Jordan looked at her, questioningly.

"The devil was panic," she translated.

A middle-aged man with salt and pepper hair and mustache stepped into the hallway. He wore a headset with microphone and his eyes had the familiar haunted, hunted look that so many people shared these past few weeks. "Miss Johnson? Mister Masters? Can we have you on the set, please?"

"This is Roy Robbins, our Director," said Cat, making the introductions.

"Pleasure to meet you, sir," said Jordan.

"The pleasure is mine, Mister Masters." He turned and led the way. "We're rolling the tape, now. As soon as it's finished, we'll cut straight to you."

They entered the studio. Three cameras and a boom mike were focused on a small, raised set consisting of two chairs and a few ferns before an artificial backdrop of a large window showing the Los Angeles skyline at night. Scattered around the studio were several people, most of whom didn't seem to notice their arrival because they were focused intently on a series of monitors about the room. On the screens Gideon's image talked in the van. "It is believed that most humans are beyond redemption," he was saying, "Some... us... we disagree. We must prove the conclusion wrong. If all weapons could be rendered unusable, perhaps we could persuade them to alter, soften the judgement. That is my mission." The camera work was shaky and the sound difficult to hear, but everyone in the studio–as well as around the world wherever people could still pick up television signals, Jordan suspected–was riveted by it.

They stepped up to the set and sat in matching red arm chairs, knees practically touching. Roger came walking across the floor at a quick pace, a smile on his face. He shook Jordan's hand. "Well, this is it. Good luck, bro."

"Thanks, Roger."

Cat looked out at the monitors. "Is anybody even seeing this?" she asked.

Roger shrugged. "Good question. Difficult answer. Satellites everywhere are completely freaked due to the blasts and half the broadcast tech worldwide was dusted. I'll tell you this, anybody who can tune in is. We gotta be jacking the highest ratings in history!"

"Not that it much matters any more, does it?" said the Director, looking depressed. "We'll be live in ten seconds, folks." His manner reminded Jordan of the dire seriousness of the situation.

Roger hurried off the set. The Director stepped back behind the cameras and held up five fingers. Four. Three. Two. One. The tape playing on the monitors concluded and he pointed at Cat.

She turned to the camera and took a beat to let the enormity of what the viewing audience had just seen sink in. "I'm Cat Johnson, and we are now speaking to you live, in the WBN studio in Culver City, with Jordan Masters."

Deep in the inner city of Washington DC, in a neighborhood that no well-dressed, cap-toothed junior congressman ever visited, three young men strode boldly down the center of the street as if it were their personal property. Dressed in low-slung pants which revealed the tops of boxer shorts, tee-shirts under leather jackets, high-top sneakers and baseball caps worn backwards, they were a trio of scruffy, battle-scarred jackals on the prowl. There was an air of danger about them, characterized by the desperate, lost look in their eyes and the ax handles they carried so blatantly. They rounded a corner and, in the darkness of the sunless day, the assortment of broadcasting televisions in a store window glowed like the Holy Grail. The store appeared deserted, without the usual metal security grate protecting it. One of the teens, Jimmy, stared. "Whoa! Look at all those TVs!"

His friends exchanged glances, then unceremoniously swung their ax handles, expertly stepping back as the sheet of glass shattered and rained down on the debris-laden sidewalk. They didn't grab the televisions and run as an onlooker might have expected. Instead, the oldest boy reached in to the largest set and simply turned up the volume. On the screen, Jordan Masters was talking.

"... the second time, Gideon appeared in my own Lear jet while it was in flight and no, I don't know how he got there. He told me that The One had visited Earth before."

The street kids watched with intense concentration. They weren't going anywhere.

Across the world, in Egypt, a young Arab soldier, Ahmad Ahwadi, stared at the small black and white television mounted to the wall in the Pizza Hut. He spoke just enough English to understand what the movie star was saying. "They had left signs, reminders, but we ignored them." Ahmad found himself turning to look out the door. Less than one hundred yards away from where he sat was the great Sphinx and a few hundred yards beyond that, the Pyramids of Giza–all of which, some said, in spite of the official explanations, could not have been made by man.

"We were chosen as guardians of the planet but we abused the responsibility. We've mistreated our fellow inhabitants."

"Animals?" asked the pretty interviewer.

The man nodded. "And people."

In the tiny room of a cheap motel, Matthew Miracle watched the broadcast on a television that was bolted to the bureau, which in turn was bolted to the floor. He'd turned it on with a remote that was attached to the bedside stand, which was also screwed to the floor. They hadn't nailed down the Gideon Bible, though, which lay open on his lap.

"Great teachers were sent down to try to save us from ourselves," said Masters, "but the lessons they taught were largely ignored."

Matthew clutched the Bible to himself, filled with such regret he thought he would drown in it.

In the burnt-out rubble of what had been until only yesterday one of London's finest five-star hotels, seven shell-shocked nuclear survivors gathered around a fire they'd built in the remains of the former lobby's large fireplace using broken shards of once fancy Queen Anne furniture. Some were badly burned, their skin an angry shade of crimson, some showed early signs of radiation poisoning, all had an empty, hopeless look in their eyes. One, a white-haired old woman with no teeth, clutched a transistor radio. The shivering group of strangers stood in a tight circle close to the fire, leaning toward the broadcast. "So we destroy our planet–land, sea, and atmosphere–making our once beautiful home almost uninhabitable." The man's voice was mesmerizing. Hypnotic.

In the living room of his small, empty house Stan Washington sat on the floor, surrounded by the cluttered mess that constituted the remains of his life. A pair of tiny leg braces rested across the seat of a miniature wheelchair. A bevy of photographs–all he could find–were on the floor surrounding him in a radiating circle like a protective spell. His and Brenda's wedding. He and Brenda on their honeymoon. He and Brenda at the County Fair. A copy of the first sonogram of their baby: a series of blurry lines that represented a dream come true. Brenda five months pregnant, radiant with heavenly expectations. And six months pregnant, and seven and eight months pregnant, glowing and looking like she'd swallowed a basketball. She'd never made it to nine. The next photo was of Katie in an incubator, born prematurely–a tiny, helpless little angel with tubes running into her. Another one of Stan holding her, new-born, she no larger than his hands, he with tears of wonder in his eyes. Another of mother and daughter coming home from the hospital, one of the only pictures of Katie without leg braces. A shot of Katie with a pink cake on her first birthday. And various other cakes on a succession of birthdays. A family portrait of the three of them together. Katie and mommy on a merry-go-round. Katie and Mommy dressed up fancy. Katie and mommy on a picnic. Katie and mommy dressed as angels on Halloween. His angels. Katie and mommy, Katie and mommy, Katie and mommy...

Also scattered around the room were a number of empty liquor bottles. In his fist he clenched another, half-full, and watched the television through blurry vision, trying not very successfully to focus on the words the man was saying.

"Destroying ourselves might be acceptable, but making the entire planet unlivable for the rest of its inhabitants would not be tolerated."

Stan gave his attention back to the photographs and lifted his bottle, toasting them, wherever they were. "Cheers. I love you." He drank as tears spilled down his cheeks.

Sitting stiffly on the soft leather seats of his luxuriously-appointed stretch limousine, the man with the jet black military flattop lit a cigar with his gold Dunhill lighter. Beside him, open to the article on Jordan Masters, was the *People* magazine he'd picked up on the flight from hell. He leaned forward, watching a tiny TV screen intently.

"Then why destroy so much?" asked Cat Johnson.

"Punishment," answered Jordan Masters. "If the warning had been heeded–and I would say making millions of people disappear in the blink of an eye was a pretty good warning–then maybe this nightmare wouldn't have happened."

"Bull hockey!" yelled General Charles "Chuck" Chilton, slamming a fist against the table.

President Wesley Burton and his closest staff were gathered in the oval office watching the broadcast on six different televisions. Every network still broadcasting was carrying it simultaneously.

"But it has happened and now it's time for us to pull together." continued Jordan.

"How do you mean?" asked Johnson, in her interviewer role.

"Look, I don't have all the answers. I don't know why I was chosen. I'm just an actor."

"One hell of an actor," growled Burton.

"In the tape," said Cat, "Gideon mentioned your family. Your story is quite remarkable."

Wilton Moore threw up his hands in disgust. "Aw, great, here it comes!"

The picture changed to a file footage exterior shot of Saint Paul's Cathedral in New York City, then to an interior of an overweight priest holding up a baby in front of the altar. Cat's voice continued over the images. "As a newborn baby you were found deserted on the altar of Saint Paul's Cathedral in New York City. Within days, you were world famous."

The images changed to a familiar young politician and his attractive wife, holding the baby in their arms, grinning, waving to a crowd. "Adopted by a charming young Senator and his wife, you entered into one of the most prestigious political families of the twentieth century."

The man in the limo blew a cloud of cigar smoke at the screen as he watched historical footage of President John Masters being sworn into office. "Less than a year later, that young Senator was voted President of the United States." The new President kissed his wife and young son. "It looked like the great American fairy tale come true, until..." The picture cut back to the reporter, who looked directly into the camera. "while running for a second term, tragedy struck."

The picture showed the President walking through a large gathering with his wife, waving to the crowd. Suddenly a huge explosion rocked the camera.

"Whoa," said Jimmy T, fixated on the Washington store-front television.

A dozen other people had joined the three boys. An old, African-American man looked at him. "That the first time you seen that, boy?"

"Hey, I wasn't even born when that happened."

"That's history, kid. I remember where I was that day, when we heard the news." As though the memory itself had the power to chill him, he shivered and pulled his coat collar more tightly around him.

On the TV, Cat continued, over images of smoke, fire, a stampeding crowd, Secret Service men waving guns, screaming, shoving, chaos. "A terrorist suicide attack killed twenty-four Americans, including President and Mrs. Masters."

The image abruptly went from chaos to a single, shattered, little boy standing by a grave in silence. A young soldier presented the little boy with an American flag neatly folded into a compact triangle. The boy tried hard to put on a brave face, but a single tear dripped down his face. The camera zoomed in for an extreme close-up.

"Hold it, hold it!" said Jordan's voice, over the picture, "Please."

Press Secretary Moore sat back hard against his chair. "Yes, please!" The presidential staff sighed as the picture switched back to Jordan Masters live in the news studio. "Look," he said, to Cat, "I know what you're trying to do. It's about credibility. But my parents have nothing to do with this. Maybe they were good people," he paused and shrugged, "But then again, who knows, maybe they adopted me as a political strategy to enhance their image, as some people have said."

Burton stared at the screen, hardly believing he'd heard that.

Jordan continued. "I mean, a cozy couple with a famous baby is a lot easier to sell to the public than a bitter marriage with a philandering husband." He shrugged. "Hey, we've all heard such rumors."

Harry Weinstein gawked at the screen. Anybody inside politics knew it was more than a rumor, but he was dumbfounded to hear it from the ex-president's son himself. "Well, I'll be a monkey's uncle."

"Next," continued Jordan, "you'll start gushing about my loving uncle who was also assassinated as he ran for office." He paused. "By the C.I.A., according to some theories."

"He's killing his own credibility!" said Burton.

Moore shook his head in awe, entranced by the virtuoso political manipulation he was witnessing. "No. No, he's not."

Jordan ran his hand over his face. "And then, there's my mother's brother who does somehow keep a clean record," he looked directly at the camera, "In spite of the fact that he's been involved in more scandals than the National Enquirer has room to report."

"That clever son of a witch!" exclaimed Weinstein.

His mother certainly was, thought Burton, dryly, *but only one in a long line of First Lady witches. Including the queen witch of them all, Lucretia.*

"My point is this:" concluded Jordan, with what looked like utter sincerity, "Good or bad, I am not my family. I have no desire whatsoever to enter politics. Understand that. There is no ulterior motive here. I am only passing on a message."

"So let's make it clear," said Cat, "This is not the opening move of some political chess game?"

"More like a bloody checkmate," mumbled Jameson.

"Absolutely not," answered Jordan, "I'm perfectly happy leaving it in President Burton's hands now."

"First thing he said that made sense!" yelled Burton.

Moore leapt to his feet, excitedly. "Okay, maybe we're not dead! Everybody move! Now! Come on, Mister President, our turn!" He ran out of the room, already scribbling speech ideas in a leather notebook.

President Wesley Burton stayed in his seat, watching Jordan's final words.

"Quite honestly, Miss Johnson, I don't think the world has time for lies, innuendoes and political spins anymore. This has been a terrifying experience for all of us, but for those of us still alive, maybe it's time we finally learned from our mistakes."

In the burnt-out lobby of the Ritz, the old toothless woman raised a bottle of eighty-dollars-a-shot Louis XIII brandy she'd dug out of a crumbled lounge bar and toasted the radio. "You bet your cute butt, baby." The others nodded in solemn agreement, and passed around the bottle.

The man in the limo hit a small intercom switch that connected him to his driver. "Paul."

"Yes, sir?" came the disembodied voice through a small speaker.

"WBN News Studios. Now."

"And cut!" said the Director.

On the interview set, Jordan collapsed back in his chair, his stomach in knots.

"Great job," said Cat.

He shook his head. "I don't know."

"Trust me," she said, touching his knee gently, "Great."

He looked at her, feeling a heat rise within, her touch sending shock waves straight up his leg. He knew she felt it, too. He leaned in close, about to whisper, when Ted Maxwell, the network anchorman, strode up onto the set. Nearly six feet tall in elevator shoes, his slight paunch disguised by an expertly tailored Hugo Boss suit, every hair of his hand-woven toupee lacquered into place, he was a nationally-known figure. "Thank you, Miss Johnson," he smiled, revealing unnaturally white, perfectly-capped teeth. "I'll take it from here."

"Excuse me?" said Cat, looking puzzled.

"I'm taking over."

Jordan saw Cat stiffen, a frown darkening her face. "What's going on?" She raised her voice, calling to the Director. "Roy?"

The Director hurried over from the production booth. "We've got the President on live satellite feed with a rebuttal, Cat. We're gonna let Ted handle it."

Cat looked at the anchorman, then at Roy, then out past the lights at the assembled crew. In the darkness, Roger shrugged, looking defeated. Jordan knew exactly what was going on. Politics. Ted's considerable ego was threatened by this competent, attractive newcomer. Cat shook her head. "No."

Roy appeared totally taken off-guard. "No?"

She looked him in the eye. "No."

Maggie Brinks shot out of the production booth, approaching the set at a brisk clip. "Excuse me? What did you say, Miss Johnson?"

"I said, no, Maggie. I brought you this, this is my story."

"Miss Johnson," said Ted, condescendingly, "you've had your moment in the sun, now why don't you leave it to the big boys."

The Big Boys? Jordan could practically feel the air around Cat heating up. Maggie jumped in, speaking with the tone of a parent dealing with an unreasonable child. "Cat, no disrespect intended, but a more experienced anchor person–"

"No!" said Cat, firmly. "Maggie, if I don't stay on this, I walk."

Ted snorted a derisive laugh.

"And I take Jordan with me," she finished. "No disrespect intended."

The laugh choked off.

Jordan saw the wide-eyed look of delighted astonishment on Roger's face and had to bite the inside of his cheek to keep from laughing. Suddenly every eye was on him. He caught himself and shifted his attention to the tension-filled group on the small stage. Every eye was suddenly on him. He met Cat's pleading gaze, identified with her vulnerability, and with a surprisingly intense feeling of loyalty, he met Maggie's gaze. "Absolutely. If she goes, I go. This interview is over."

There was a long, thick silence. Finally, Brinks shrugged, as if she'd had this in mind all along. She turned to the anchorman. "Sorry, Ted, you're out of here. No disrespect..." she cut herself off, lips tight, and walked stiffly back to the booth.

Cat exhaled quietly. Jordan winked at her. She broke into a smile.

"You go, girl!" grinned Roger.

The anchorman shot him a withering look. The cameraman shrugged. "Sorry, Ted, looks like you've been outgunned."

The network icon flounced out of the studio in a tizzy of fury.

"Okay, people," called the director, raising his voice, "we go in 4 - 3 - 2 - 1." He pointed to Cat. She straightened up in her chair and faced the camera.

"Cat Johnson here at WBN Studios with... the remarkable Jordan Masters." Jordan flushed, still not comfortable with such an accolade. "We go now live, via satellite, to the White House."

Jordan turned his attention to the monitors as the oval office came onto the screens. President Burton sat behind his desk, hands folded in front of him, looking controlled and determined. "Ladies and Gentlemen, some serious charges have been leveled against me and the office of the President of the United States. I'd like to set the record straight."

Burton tried to exude confidence. Why not, the speech Moore had turned out in a matter of minutes was brilliant. Looking directly into the camera, thereby into the eyes of every American, he concentrated on the words of wisdom that had carried him through a long and successful political career. *The most important thing in life is sincerity. If you can fake that, you've got it made.* He was a master.

The President of the United States kept his voice firm and reassuring, picturing himself as a benevolent father speaking to his children. "While it is true that Mister Masters did come to us with an explanation for the disappearances of three days ago, and we greatly appreciated the information, we also appreciated the other..." he referred to a list of statistics in front of him, "sixty-seven thousand nine hundred and eighty-two calls we received, all from people equally convinced that their theories were correct. Germ warfare, radiation, Jesus took them, the Devil took them, Elvis took them, they went to live on a comet, water dissolved them because they were witches..." Out of the corner of his eye he saw Moore grin, puffed up with his own cleverness. "and of course, little green men from Mars." He gave a small smile as if to acknowledge the absurdity of it, then set his notes down, a deep furrow forming on his brow. "As for my wife's statement," he took a wavering breath, "I'm sure you're all aware that our newborn baby boy..." he let his voice crack, as though he might choke up completely, then 'forced' himself to go on, "also vanished during the actual childbirth, at the fateful moment of the terrible world-wide disappearance. The mind and heart-numbing shock was understandably traumatizing. She seems to be willing to believe anything except that her child is gone. She is now at our retreat, under sedation." He lowered his eyes to the desk. "I, too, like all the rest of you, am grief-stricken. I hereby declare that the nation will go into a National Period of Mourning for the next three days. All flags will be lowered to half-mast. We can only pray."

There was a bit of commotion as an aide burst into the room and yanked the Press Secretary aside, whispering to him frantically. Burton tried to ignore them, focusing once again on the camera. "Ladies and gentlemen, please, consider Mister Masters' story: an all-knowing alien rebels against the other all-knowing aliens... all without them knowing." He shook his head at the absurdity of it. "We have enough problems without lending credence to ridiculous fairy tales such as this. There is no alien! There is no spaceship!"

Abruptly, the room around him broke into chaos. His Chief-of-Staff rushed directly to him and leaned in close. "Excuse me, Mister President, you're needed immediately." Burton was astounded at his behavior but his advisor allowed him no time to voice a protest. Instead, Harry grabbed him by the arms, literally lifted him out of his chair, and hustled him out of the room. He was sure the stunned looks on the faces of the news teams were mirrored by his own.

Back at the studio, Cat watched the monitor, totally baffled. She touched the tiny earphone she wore, hoping to hear an explanation of what had just occurred. There was only silence. She looked past the cameras to the booth. Roy gave her an *I have no idea what's going on, but you better say or do something* gesture. She turned to the center camera. "Ladies and gentlemen, there seems to have been some new development."

As Burton raced into the Crisis Management Center, all traces of the calm control he'd shown the American public were gone. Already wet with sweat, his heart beating a mile a minute, his stomach churned with acid. They had just informed him that a massive alien spacecraft had been sighted entering Earth's atmosphere. "How is it we never saw this before?" he screamed at Admiral Chilton.

"We don't know," said the Admiral, looking sick, "Maybe, maybe it was...cloaked."

Burton exploded. "You're not going to tell me Masters was right?"

The answer came in total silence. First the disappearance of millions, then nuclear accidents, now this. Burton felt suddenly drained of all blood, as if he'd just been sucked dry by some mighty, psychic vampire. "Then why uncloak now?" he asked, weakly.

"Because, Mister President," the General said, solemnly, "it looks like the thing is out of control."

On the bridge of the aircraft carrier USS Constitution, Captain Lorin Trudell and his officers stood around the radar screen riveted on the bright green blip, with utter disbelief.

"Look at the size of that thing," gasped Pendleton, the radar man, "It's a mile wide! Impossible!"

Trudell grabbed a pair of binoculars and ran to the side wing, looking into the sky. "Oh my God," he whispered.

The other officers joined him. They didn't have binoculars, but none were needed. The flaming object looked like the sun falling toward them. The men stared, all at a loss for words.

The Captain went inside and sank into his chair. He was proud of his position. He had joined the Navy at age eighteen, fresh out of high school and had worked as hard as any man, kissing more than his share of board-rigid butt. The Navy had been his life, leaving very little time for his wife, daughter and son. The kids were college-aged now, but their schools had closed last week. All students everywhere had been sent home to their parents, where they belonged at a time of crisis like this. Why hadn't all military parents been shipped home to their children? He looked around him. He'd fought hard for this chair. Now, he'd die hard in it.

"Sparks," he said, to the radio man, in a resigned tone, "Get my wife on the phone, please."

The call was never completed. The flaming titanic spacecraft hit the Atlantic Ocean with a massive impact, instantly causing a tidal wave of enormous size and ferocity. The last thing Captain Lorin Trudell saw was a five-hundred foot wall of white, boiling water rushing toward him at an inescapable speed.

Admiral Chilton pressed the telephone so tightly against his ear that the flesh around it was bloodless. "It hit the Atlantic Ocean off the coast of Delaware," he reported to the room.

"Thank God!" exclaimed Burton.

Chilton slowly hung up the phone, looking deeply troubled. "Mister President," he said in a choked voice, "I don't believe you understand."

Jordan had a deep, disturbing feeling that something horrible had occurred, but what? After the tragedies of the past few weeks, what could possibly happen next? He looked over at Cat, who appeared calm, except for a single drop of sweat trailing slowly down in front of her ear. He wanted desperately to reach out and hold her hand, but knew now was neither the time nor place. As soon as this was over, however, he'd take her in his arms and–

Cat suddenly became alert, her hand touching the hidden ear-piece that kept her in constant communication to the production booth. "We're back, ladies and gentlemen, live from the White House. President Burton is entering the room now."

Cameras on the monitors picked up Burton almost staggering into the oval office and virtually collapsing behind the desk. The leader of the free world was shaking and pale. He stared at the desk, then took a deep breath and looked up into the camera. "Ladies and gentlemen," he said in a strangled voice, "it seems Jordan Masters was right."

In front of the Washington D.C. television store, Jimmy turned to his friends, Jacko and Gomer. "What's that supposed to..." He trailed off as a low rumble, growing increasingly louder, caught his attention. The others had heard it, too. Jimmy watched Gomer's eyes go upwards and grow wide. He turned to follow his friend's gaze and his mouth fell open. A wall of water, three times higher than the tallest building, came rushing at them. It had cars, trees, entire buildings caught up in its froth. Jimmy screamed, turned to run, and the world ended.

Jordan stared at the monitors uncomprehendingly. It had all happened in a matter of seconds, flashing images, like a hallucinogenic nightmare. What kind of twisted phantasmagoria had they been looking at? One moment the President had been talking and the next the entire image had gone insane, spinning over and over as if there had been an explosion of some sort, then suddenly they were underwater, in a tornado. Then, for a flash of a moment, Jordan thought he saw the President again, but it was just Burton's head, floating independently, staring into nothingness. Then the monitor had turned to snow.

He looked around, disoriented, and saw the same shocked confusion on everyone else's face. There was absolute silence in the studio.

Cat Johnson was the first to regain her wits. She looked into the camera and cleared her throat. "Ladies and gentlemen, it seems we've lost our satellite feed to the White House. Just before we did, there was an abrupt turn of events..."

Jordan felt a strong hand squeeze his shoulder and turned to look into the gray eyes of a powerful-looking man with a black, military flattop and trim mustache. "Come with me, Jordan." His clipped tone of voice conveyed the unmistakable message that he was used to being instantly obeyed.

"Who–"

"We don't have much time." He tapped his watch twice.

It was a gesture that brought back immediate memories of Gideon's initial approach in the guise of his uncle. Not only that, the watch had a familiar design on the face of it–the same design as the medallion that had buried itself in his chest. Jordan stared up at the man, whispering, "Gideon?"

"We have to go now."

Jordan looked over at Cat, wanting to tell her what was happening, but the reporter was occupied, listening, pale and now openly sweating, as information apparently came through the ear piece she was wearing. He scanned the room. Nobody else seemed to be paying any attention to him or the man (alien?) in the dark blue suit, who had already started toward the door. Jordan got to his feet, unhooked his microphone and followed.

He almost reached the door when he heard Cat call, "Jordan!" He turned back. She was starting to rise from her chair, but then stopped abruptly, her hand flying to her ear piece. She listened a moment then, looking stunned, collapsed back into her seat. He watched, disturbed by the sick look on her face. She was mumbling something. It took him a moment to realize what it was. "El diablo era el panico." He glanced over at Roger, whose eyes met his with a *what on earth is going on?* look. Jordan shook his head and shrugged, he had no idea.

Having apparently collected herself, Cat sat up straight and faced the camera. Her voice had a small quaver in it, but otherwise was clear and concise. "Ladies and gentlemen, reports are coming in now of another cataclysmic event. It seems much of the North American east coast has been hit by an immense tidal wave."

In the tiny motel room, somewhere in Oklahoma, Matthew Miracle shut his eyes and quoted from the bible he clutched to his breast. *"Then the second angel blew his trumpet and something that looked like a big mountain, burning with fire, was thrown into the sea. And a third of the sea became blood, and a third of the living things died, and a third of the ships were destroyed."*

The USS Constitution sank rapidly into the depths of the sea. Trapped inside the destroyed ship, the battered bodies of the ship's crew and officers floated in the wreckage. On the bridge, the body of Captain Lorin Trudell remained strapped to his chair, the cord of a telephone tangled uselessly and forever around his wrist, descending deeper and deeper into the endless black abyss.

Chapter 11

The vehicle was long, black, and sleek, but somehow it reminded Jordan more of a hearse than of a luxury limousine. He stepped out of the soft leather interior onto the tarmac of the now almost completely deserted Los Angeles International Airport. Ten yards away a glossy Gulf Stream jet awaited, stairway in place. Jordan stared. He'd never seen a black jet with no exterior markings before.

His escort had ridden in the front of the limo with the driver, leaving Jordan alone for a frustratingly silent twenty-minute ride. Still silent, the man led the way toward the aircraft. As they boarded, Jordan paused inside the entryway to take in the interior. With deep carpets and polished wood, it resembled the interior of an opulent mobile home more than that of an aircraft.

Ten men of various complexions and costumes sat in leather chairs around the edges of the room, all focused quietly on a large television screen showing aerial images of a devastated city. Jordan was drawn reluctantly to the horrific images on the screen: buildings crushed in two, bridges turned into twisted metal, zoo animals drowned in their cages. Behind him, the man from the limo slammed the aircraft's door, an ominous sound like that of a prison gate closing. He pointed Jordan toward an empty chair, and went into the cockpit. A moment later, hearing the whine of the engines starting, Jordan buckled his safety belt. Ill at ease, he glanced surreptitiously at the other passengers.

It struck him that there were no women present. Only males in this mini-United Nations. One looked African, another like an Arab, two Asians, a Latino, an East Indian, and four either European or American white men. Their ages appeared to range from the early fifties to one oldster who couldn't have been under ninety. All were dressed impeccably, accessorized with expensive jewelry. All were concentrating on the newscast.

When Cat Johnson came onto the screen, Jordan was immediately galvanized. She looked shell-shocked, but determined. His heart went out to her. The situation well over her head, she nonetheless was handling it valiantly. Jordan could hear the grief in her voice as aerial cameras picked up a succession of graphic visuals of the wide-spread devastation.

"Washington D.C., gone. New York City, wiped out. Most of the east coast as far west as Pennsylvania and as far south as Florida... under water. Cuba... Cuba seems to have disappeared altogether."

Somewhere in the back of his mind Jordan realized the jet was rising into the ash-laden sky, but his emotions were reeling with the shocking news.

Cat continued. "Details are unclear, but it has been reported that the cause of the wave and earthquakes was the crash-landing of some sort of massive space craft." Her composure slipped and her voice cracked. "My God."

"God?" said a voice from the rear of the room, "I think God had very little to do with it."

Jordan spun his chair around and found himself staring at a striking female figure. Lucretia Burton stood insolently in the rear of the cabin. She aimed a small black remote control at the television and used it to mute the sound, but allowed the terrible images to remain. She touched another button on the remote and a long, oval table rose up out of the floor with an electric hum. The men, whose chairs were evenly spaced around the polished wood, swivelled to face it. Tentatively, Jordan did the same, facing the former First Lady.

"Mrs. Burton, please, would you tell me what's going on here?" he asked. "Who are these people?"

"Who they are, doesn't matter," answered Lucy. "What they are does."

"And that is?"

Lucretia started walking around, behind the men. "The world isn't run by presidents, Jordan. Nor by congresses, parliaments, dictators, kings, queens, or emperors. Certainly not by "the people."

Jordan scrutinized the men around the table. "You're saying *these* men?" Her silence was her answer. "Then why don't I recognize anybody? No offense, gentlemen."

The emaciated, old man spoke up. "None taken." His white hair stretched like cobwebs over a mostly bare skull doing little to conceal the numerous liver spots. He had sunken cheeks and teeth the color of old ivory, but in spite of his frail physical appearance, he exuded power. His eyes, though lumpy with cataracts, were sharply focused and his slightly southern-accented voice was unwavering. "Anonymity is, in fact, our most useful tool. There is a need for figureheads, of course. Take Lucretia, for example: a few years ago we had a young Senator in mind for the presidency, but he needed a young wife to complete the picture."

"You're kidding," said Jordan.

"Rarely," answered the old man, folding his hands on the table in front of him.

"Now poor Wesley is dead," said Lucretia, with an emotionless shrug.

"These are days of dire circumstance," continued the old man, "however, a unique opportunity has arisen for someone of singular charm and charisma. Someone the people already know and trust." He looked at Jordan, pointedly.

"You're out of your minds!"

"Are we?" He pointed to the television which was lingering on the tragic image of the Statue of Liberty half submerged under water. "Take a look at the world, Mister Masters. Mankind is on the brink of extinction. Only by coming together will we survive. And only with the right leadership can we hope to be united."

"If you're referring to me, I don't think so."

A grandfatherly-looking man in a gray suit spoke with an aristocratic British accent. "You don't really have a choice, young man. Look at your life: your adopted family, your incredibly lucky career breaks, even your recent film. It's all led you to this moment."

Jordan started to stand. "Are you saying you people manipulated–?"

Lucy Burton laid a firm hand on his shoulder. "Hear them out, Jordan."

He forced himself back down, feeling a knot forming in his chest.

The Old Man addressed a silver-haired Japanese man, clearly the youngest of the group. "Mister Tanaka?"

The Japanese man made a small bow. "The first order of business will be to establish a new financial order. As you know, the nuclear detonations in our atmosphere caused massive EMPs–electromagnetic pulses–that wiped out practically all computer systems globally. And most financial records."

A man sporting wire-rimmed glasses and a German accent spoke up. "It is, of course, a cause of major panic."

A grossly fat man across the table looked at him. "Solution?"

"A new debit system," answered the Japanese man. He reached beside his chair, set a metal suitcase on the table and opened it, removing a machine that looked like a high-tech View-Master. The others studied it with interest. "No more cash, no credit cards, no checks, no banks. No cash registers–every check-out counter will simply have one of these devices, connected to an international computer system."

The bearded man in Arabic robes and a turban spoke up. "I thought all computers were destroyed."

Tanaka shook his head. "Not destroyed, just wiped clean. The hardware–the system–is still in place, it simply needs to be reprogrammed. With this." He lifted the device to his eyes in demonstration. "A user simply looks into the retinal scanner, the transaction is entered and financial records are automatically adjusted." He set it down. "For added security, it'll read a small radioactive tattoo placed here, on the forehead." He touched himself an inch above the bridge of his nose.

"People won't like that," said a dark-skinned Latino man with a thin mustache.

"Very low grade radiation," added Tanaka. "No more dangerous than a luminous watch. And invisible. Do you see mine?"

"You have one?" asked the fat man.

The Asian spokesman gave a curt nod. "Hai."

Everyone studied the man's unblemished forehead. Any mark there was, indeed, invisible.

"Yes, but do you glow in the dark?" parried the ebony-complected man with an African accent.

Only Jordan did not chuckle.

The old man held up the device. "Theft is impossible because it can be instantly traced."

"And it's international," added Tanaka. "No more exchange rates or changing money."

The old man slid the device across the table to Jordan. "It's called "The Masters Plan."

Jordan stared down at it like it was an oozing slug. *The Masters' Plan?*

"How is it decided how funds are dispersed?" asked the German.

Tanaka smiled. "Everyone will be allotted the exact same amount."

The room was filled with protests.

The old man raised his hands for order. "Gentlemen, relax! We all understand the importance of a class system! But the official policy is everybody gets the same."

Everyone settled down, smiling and nodding their understanding. The Englishman smiled. "Since three-quarters of the world lives in virtual poverty, we're going to make a lot of friends fast."

The German grinned, revealing a gold-capped tooth. "Jordan Masters is going to make a lot of friends fast." He turned to Jordan. "What do you say, Mister Masters, are you ready to save the world? Or was all your talk earlier just talk?"

Lucretia put both her hands on Jordan's shoulders and squeezed gently. "We have been favored, Jordan. It's time to return the favor."

An Indian man dressed all in white spoke up. "This is a chance to unite mankind, good sir. Can you walk away from that?"

They were all focused on him now. The old man's gaze was unwavering. "Are you one of us, Jordan?" He slowly reached out and laid his right hand on the table, showing the unusual onyx ring he wore, etched with a unique design. The others all did the same, displaying matching rings.

"No," Lucretia said, reaching around and grabbing Jordan from behind.

"He is not one of us!" She clutched his shirt and yanked the material back, popping buttons and ripping the cloth away, exposing his bare chest. The men stared at the medallion that was attached to Jordan's puckered, scarred flesh with barbed prongs. An awed murmur went through the group. The design on the medallion was identical to the one on their rings.

"We," she concluded in a tone of reverence, "are one of him."

Chapter 12

The restoration of broadcasting technology was stipulated to be the number one priority. Rebuilding communication and the concept of a unified global village was considered to be of utmost importance. Within four months, nearly eighty percent of the worldwide audience was able to tune in the new, somber theme music for the World Broadcast Network's Evening News. Those with television in addition to radio were able to view the broadcast's opening images of men in white coveralls, heavy gloves and filtration masks walking down the streets of a burnt-out city, collecting dead bodies. Behind them, a behemoth dump truck full of corpses slowly followed. It was a grim sight, the equal of which hadn't been seen since the 40's black and white films of Nazis burying Jews in mass graves. It was followed by other disturbing images: the Washington Monument broken in two, the Eiffel Tower a bent mass of melted steel standing in a sea of charred ruins, looters in the streets of Moscow battling police, a destroyed nuclear plant, a hospital with dozens of occupied beds overflowing into its parking lot, a 75,000-ton luxury cruise ship broken in half on a beach, a massive Buddha with its head at its feet, the National Guard marching, Hong Kong at night–neon signs dark and still, and a playground full of swings, jungle-gyms, teeter-totters and slides but eerily empty of children. The title: World Broadcast Network Evening News was superimposed over the film clips. It faded and was replaced by another title reading: With Cat Johnson. The picture dissolved to a close-up of Cat, in a cream-colored suit with a coral blouse, standing outside the tall gray columns of a Chicago bank.

"Good evening Mankind, this is WBN News, I'm Cat Johnson. Today marks the fourth month since the 'Day of vanishing: the New Beginning.' To mark the occasion, Jordan Masters has announced that the plan for a new worldwide financial system that will benefit all of us will go into effect immediately. This technological marvel, called The Masters Plan, is the latest in a series of groundbreaking innovations that has given this charismatic young leader unprecedented popularity. His message of hope and change seems to have been globally embraced."

The camera pulled back to reveal Jordan standing beside her, wearing light gray slacks, a loosely-knotted blue tie and a white shirt rolled up at the sleeves. He spoke with characteristic sincerity. "The mother ship that was destroyed by Gideon and his followers was not unique, Cat. Another may follow. Will we be destroyed or will we put aside our petty differences as nations and religions and colors to stand together? This system unites the world economically. Money, I've noticed, seems to be pretty important to people." He grinned. "So it's a start."

"Can you tell us more about how it works."

"Simplicity itself," answered Jordan, moving a few steps to where Lucretia Burton lounged in a comfortable-looking chair. "Ladies and Gentlemen, the former First Lady of the United States, Mrs. Lucretia Burton." Next to her, a handsome male technician manipulated a unit that looked like something an optometrist might use to examine eyes. The large mask-like device swung out on a metal arm, and pressed against Lucretia's face. "Look directly into the lenses, Mrs. Burton," he instructed. "Here we go." He flipped a switch. Nothing appeared to happen and, a moment later, he pulled it away. Lucy looked up expectantly, a smile on her face. "Well?"

The man laughed. "That's it. You're registered. Next!"

Mrs. Burton directly addressed the folks at home. "Well? What are you waiting for, America?"

A group of eager people started forming a line behind them. Jordan grinned and spoke directly into the camera. "It really is just that simple, folks. The details of all this will be explained on a WBN News Special, tonight at six o'clock."

"And again at eight, and once more at ten," added Cat. "Exclusively on WBN."

"Now, to answer the question many of you have been asking." Jordan continued. "Every man and woman on this planet will be allotted an equal and generous amount of money. Of course your assets remain your own, and what you do with your credits, how you use them to further yourself, is up to you. But let no one say he or she has no opportunity. We're are taking nothing away. We're only giving. For the first time in history, every person truly will be created equal."

A cheer went up from the crowd behind him.

Cat smiled. "They say that death is the great equalizer. But for us, the living, that title seems to belong to Jordan Masters. Reporting live from downtown Los Angeles, I'm Cat Johnson, WBN News."

Roger lowered the camera and gave her a grinning thumbs-up.

"Ow, ow, ow!" snapped Lucretia, slapping the tattoo technician and holding her forehead. "That hurt!" She stalked out of the room.

Cat quickly turned to Jordan. In the past sixteen weeks she hadn't spent any time with him at all, seeing him only when covering his news conferences. She understood that he was now the key player in a whole new socio-economic political system, and she believed in what he was doing, but she desperately missed their personal relationship. "Jordan, could we talk?"

A large man with a jet black military haircut cut her off rudely. "Thank you, Miss Johnson." He stepped between her and Jordan. "Jordan, we need to move on."

"Excuse me, but–"

"We're running late, Miss Johnson, you'll have to forgive us."

Jordan seemed flustered. "Can you give us a moment?"

"We're late as it is, sir. We have to go now." He took Jordan by the arm and moved him gently but firmly toward the door. "Thank you again, Miss Johnson," he called over his shoulder. "We'll be in touch."

"Jordan?" She heard a touch of desperation rise in her voice.

He looked back at her, hesitating, but then the man propelled him out the door where his attention was immediately taken by the outside crowd which cheered as if he were a rock and roll star.

Cat shot a look of frustration over at Roger, who shook his head and shrugged. She ran out in pursuit just in time to see Jordan being hustled into a black limousine. Inside the vehicle, waiting, was an ancient-looking man. He looked past Jordan, focusing on Cat, his eyes burning. His unwavering gaze locked onto hers until his mirrored window slid shut and she found herself looking at her own frustrated image.

"Jordan Masters is no great leader! He is an actor playing the role of a great leader. Ever wonder who writes his scripts?"

Stan Washington watched the preacher from the back of the crowd. The speaker was somewhat scruffy, with a stubbly beard and longish hair, but there was something about him. He had charisma, charm, and spoke with such sincerity that it was nearly impossible to walk away. *Heck,* thought Stan, *appearances could be deceiving;* he, himself, wasn't exactly looking his best these days. He shaved only irregularly and hadn't had a haircut since Brenda and Katie had disappeared. He'd worn the same shirt for over a week now.

It had been four months since Brenda and Katie had disappeared. Four months, two weeks, three days, seventeen hours. Stan had remained at home for almost three weeks, lost in a liquor-induced oblivion, drowning in a deep well of self-pity. One night he dragged himself off the floor and out of the house, not because he wanted the fresh air, but because he was out of booze. His car's electric ignition had been fried by the EMP, so he walked the two miles to the nearest liquor store. He fully intended to buy a bottle, return home, down the whole thing, then use his old service revolver to put an end to his abject loneliness and misery once and for all. The store, to his bitter disappointment, was closed. He briefly considered heaving a trash can through the plate glass window and helping himself to a bottle or two but then he thought about the poor schmo who owned the store. Maybe he'd lost his family, too. Maybe he, too, was barely hanging on to his sanity, and the destruction of his property would be the final blow that pushed him over the edge. Stan only wanted to end his own suffering, not add to someone else's, So he turned away from the store and kept walking. And walking, and walking. Why go home? The only attraction the place held for him now was the siren call of that loaded .45. The pictures on the walls, the closets full of frilly dresses and fancy patent-leather shoes, the pink bedroom with white, baby elephants dotting the wallpaper, the bed he'd shared with Brenda but hadn't been able to bring himself to sleep in since she'd vanished... too many memories, all of them agonizing beyond words, reminders of what had been wrenched away from him. So he kept walking. Away.

The first night he was startled by a large pack of dogs running across a nearby field. He had already heard tales of domesticated animals, their masters having disappeared, crazy with starvation. He wasn't sure if they would attack humans yet, but that day couldn't be far away. Hiding in an abandoned car until they were gone, he concluded that walking might not be the safest way to travel. He would have to find a working vehicle.

Cars weren't difficult to locate–they were scattered along the roads every couple of miles or so–the trick was to find an early model without an electronic ignition, one that was still drivable. Thousands had crashed into trees, poles, or other cars when their drivers vanished, but some had simply veered off the road with minimal damage.

Stan spotted an old four-wheel jeep sitting in the middle of a field, out of gas. He surmised that when the driver disappeared–leaving his old cowboy boots, jeans, jockey shorts, pearl-buttoned shirt, and cowboy hat behind, on the front seat–the thing had rolled across the field about thirty yards, stopping on its own since there was no more pressure on the gas peddle. It couldn't turn itself off, however, so had remained idling until it ran out of gas. Luckily, unlike many of the other cars Stan had checked out, the driver had evidently not been using his headlights or the radio so the battery still held a charge. With four-wheel drive, the Jeep was ideal because frequently the highways were so jammed up with wrecked cars he knew that sooner or later he'd have to go off-road to get around.

Figuring it was worth the trouble, Stan hiked back a mile or so to a badly damaged truck that had crashed into a signpost. He figured either the impact had killed the engine or its standard transmission had stalled out when its driver's foot abruptly released the clutch, but in either case, the gas tank was full. The sign on the door read: GREEN THUMB & SON. Two nearly identical sets of white, grass-stained overalls lay across the seat in the cab, one larger than the other. On the bibs were stitched the owners' names: One read simply: SENIOR, the other, JUNIOR.

The rear of the truck was filled with gardening equipment. Using a pair of rose pruners from a metal toolbox bolted onto the bed of the truck behind the cab, Stan cut a length of garden hose to siphon gas from the vehicle into a near-empty gas can sitting next to the two lawn mowers strapped in the rear. For good measure he filled a watering can as well, then returned to the Jeep. Supplied with gas, it started on the second try.

Stan drove it back to the gardening truck to drain its remaining fuel, keeping the hose for future use. It certainly wasn't stealing since both vehicles were clearly abandoned and he doubted the former owners cared anymore about earthly transportation, but Stan couldn't help but wonder about Senior, Junior and Cowboy. Where were they? Wherever they were, were his beloved Brenda and precious Katie at the same place? Had they been whisked away to another planet where the aliens held them prisoner in cages like zoo animals, performing unthinkable experiments on them? Or had they been aboard the spaceship that crashed into the ocean? Most people seemed to believe the latter and mass memorial services had been held throughout the world, mourning the dead.

Stan could not accept the idea that they might be gone forever. Like the family of a soldier missing in action, he refused to give up all hope. It was hard enough to deal with the fact that he hadn't been able to protect them. Katie had almost literally been snatched right out of his arms! What kind of a man couldn't protect his wife and child? Why had they been taken and not him? Thinking about it twisted his heart into such knots that only the mind-numbing effects of alcohol could ease the overwhelming agony.

He drove west, for no better reason than that was the direction he could go the furthest before hitting an ocean. He had some money, but what good was it? Cash had become easy to come by, he discovered. Piles of it laid around in the purses and wallets from the Taken–but most folks no longer valued paper money. Bartering seemed to be the transaction of choice, one useful product in exchange for another, either that or the amount of cash charged was so outrageous that it was laughable. Stan didn't care, he didn't need much except basic food and shelter and they weren't hard to come by now. Cars weren't the only things that had been abandoned.

Observation of a house for a short time, Stan discovered, was an easy way to establish whether it was occupied. The smaller the house, the more likely it was to be empty because a lot of folks were packing up their stuff by the truckloads and moving into larger, deserted homes. If a place appeared desolate, Stan would knock on the door. If anybody answered, he'd apologize and move on, but if nobody responded, he'd bang louder, then try the knob. If locked, he'd check the windows. If the place was secured, he'd move on; he had no desire to frighten some poor home owner who walked in to find a giant black man in his house, or to be thrown in a jail cell somewhere. If the houses weren't locked, however, he'd go in and quickly check them out.

The signs of desertion were clear and easy to spot. First and foremost, there were the tell-tale clothes: small piles of material–underwear inside pants or pantyhose in skirts, socks neatly tucked in shoes, jewelry or glasses within rolling range–easily identifiable as belonging to The Taken. A few of these little altars of personality scattered about was tantamount to a "Vacancy" sign. Dead pets were also a frequent, and disheartening, indication. He buried more than his share of dogs, cats, and birds. Sometimes there was no evidence of occupation at all. Perhaps the owners had been out on the town that night, catching the latest sci-fi or horror flick at the Roxie with no idea that real life was about to take a turn more warped and twisted than any plot they could have been watching. Were they visiting the dentist, spending their last few hours on earth miserable? Or maybe at work when it happened, miserable again? In any case, if not clothes, food was usually a tip off. Especially bread. If Stan found fresh bread, he am-scrayed outta there, but if he discovered what looked like a science experiment in a Wonder bag, it was indicative that the owners had been gone for some time, and had left quite unexpectedly. As the days wore on, even the food in refrigerators that were still running began to rot. Eventually, his diet consisted mainly of pasta, rice and canned goods. Now and then he got lucky and found fresh produce in somebody's vegetable garden if the insects–all of which seemed to have survived just fine, thank you–hadn't done a number on it.

In his trip across country, Stan skirted around the ruined urban areas, staying in a wide variety of homes, studio apartments, small town-houses, condos, houses of all sizes and even one Victorian mansion where nobody, as yet, had exercised their squatter's rights. For entertainment he simply wandered from room to room, studying the furnishings, books on shelves, clothing, jewelry, wine, pictures in albums and on walls, knick-knacks, awards proudly displayed, CD collections, video libraries, and small, secret items tucked away in drawers. Love letters in an old shoe box hidden on a closet shelf, diaries under mattresses, well worn teddy bears–all told fascinating tales infinitely more interesting than any old TV show or movie. He'd sit for hours trying to figure out what the Taken's lives were like. What set them apart? What made them the chosen ones? What did they all have in common?

The Bibles, for one. He'd first noticed it in the second and third house he visited. Bibles laid on the coffee tables in both. In another apartment the Holy Book was on the kitchen counter. Intrigued, he found himself playing detective, searching for them nightly, at every stop. Almost without exception, every home he stayed in had a Bible, sometimes more than one. Not neglected, covered with dust and tucked away on the shelf of some forgotten bookcase, but out in plain sight. On desks, bedside stands, coffee tables, fireplace mantles and the tops of toilet tanks. Many were well worn and dog-eared. In some were marginal notes, hinting to intriguing insight into the owner's frame of mind.

It got Stan to thinking about Brenda and how she had tried to talk him into reading the book. So, late one night, in honor of her memory, he sat down in front of the fireplace in a small Texas ranch house and gave it a shot. Not knowing where to start, he opened it at random. Daniel begat Solomon, begat Rachel, begat Ross begat Chandler, begat Phoebe or whoever. Who cared? He tried another section, but the words didn't make sense; it was like reading some foreign language. Frustrated, he hurled the book into the fire and found a bottle of Jack Daniels instead. There was no God. There was no heaven, no hell. There was only this life, which had been heaven and was now hell. And there were wife-stealing, baby-snatching aliens. And there was good Tennessee whiskey. While it lasted.

Six weeks later, a fortnight ago, Stan had been sleeping off yet another hangover, using a park bench to take advantage of the warmth of the mid-day sun, when a voice invaded his subconscious. A low voice. A sincere voice. It pierced the haze of his drunkenness and found a desperate, defeated man. He shut his eyes, squeezing his fists against his ears, but the words relentlessly echoed in his brain. He tried to ignore them–a lot of what the voice was saying he'd heard a long time ago from Brenda, more than once. He'd resisted listening in those days, too, pushing her words aside, regarding her beliefs to be a crutch–a false hope to help her through a harsh life, a weakness in a world where lack of strength meant death. The Bible was a white man's book of fairy tales or legends and myths–perhaps good for helping little children sleep but, for a thinking adult, self-delusional. Sometimes her dependence on the book had even angered him, jealous of the respect and attention his wife paid to it.

But all those houses, with all those Bibles...

At first, returning to the park every day as a getaway retreat, he'd tried to pass off the itinerant preacher's words as the usual ravings of a fanatic. But after the cataclysmic events of the past fourteen weeks, he found that attitude impossible. For nearly two weeks this guy, Matthew Richards, had been preaching daily to a rag-tag crowd here, and his outdoor congregation had quadrupled in that time. Sure, people came and people went, but Stan had noticed a steadily growing number of core believers attending every day. Much to his surprise, he realized he was one of them. Little by little, he listened, paying closer attention not only to the words but to their meaning.

"God created all men equal, not government!" cried the preacher. "Don't you see? Every time you make a purchase you're checking in with them! Where you are, what you do, everything you own–they'll know!"

Absolutely right, thought Stan. Without cash, every single purchase, down to a stick of gum, was registered somewhere in the new system.

"But the alien came to him!" yelled a woman in the crowd, "The savior Gideon!"

"There is no alien! People did not get sucked up into a space ship! These are lies! They returned to their God! Look at the signs!" He held up his worn Bible. "Our water is undrinkable, the sun and moon have been blotted out! These things were prophesied!"

"Then why didn't you get called to heaven, preacher man?" called a harsh voice.

Many in the crowd seconded that question.

Miracle's eyes went dark with shame. "Because, my friends, I was a fake. I did not believe the truth. I was a false prophet. I heard, but did not listen."

Stan felt his stomach twist into a tight knot.

"But I do understand this truth: Jordan Masters will take us to where we have never been before."

"Good places!" shouted the woman.

"So it would appear," answered the preacher, quietly.

"Then what's your problem, mister?"

"Appearances," said Matthew Miracle, simply, "can be deceiving."

Chapter 13

A year passed. The changes were radical and global, accepted almost docilely and without political protest by the planet's remaining inhabitants whose only thoughts were to survive and restore some semblance of comfort. They clung to anything that would help them accept their pain, ease their deprivations, and solidify lives turned so upside down that their hearts and souls still remained numb as they struggled to retain what sanity they could in the face of the disasters that had almost extinguished life as they had previously known it. The world without children was a bleak place. Without the playfulness, the innocence, the hope for the future, desperation ran high. The children had represented joy in life, inspired moral values. Perhaps setting examples for them kept the world a softer, more honest and happy place. With only adults around, attitudes became harsher, tempers shorter, reactions more violent.

The new world leader, Jordan Masters, offered hope. His meteoric rise to unprecedented power was unique in the annals of history. Thanks largely to the wholehearted endorsement of highly respected former First Lady, Lucretia Burton, the only survivor from the White House, the people of the United States welcomed his leadership with open arms. Other world leaders soon followed her lead, pledging loyalty to the new ideals of the charismatic young man. Masters had not been voted into any particular office through any official governmental process, was not a President, dictator, king, sultan, nor an emperor, but he appeared to have the inside track on the alien invaders. The only life preserver available, the vast majority clung to the hope he represented. Except in the United States, he had not actually replaced any country's titled leader, but had managed to bring them together in an unprecedented show of unity against the common world enemy, the malevolent visitors from space. In less than a year Masters had managed to unite all the nations of Europe into one federation, a feat any political analyst would have sworn completely impossible.

Today's news was even more amazing.

When the new, upbeat theme music for the WBN Evening News played, the original opening images of world events had been scrapped in favor of a hopeful outlook. Gone were the horrifying pictures of death and destruction. In their place were only positive images: cities being rebuilt, Jordan Masters waving to a crowd of fans, relieved people registering for the new banking system, Jordan Masters sitting on a tractor wearing a hard hat, Jordan Masters dressed in black, surrounded by thousands attending a memorial service for the lost, Jordan Masters shaking hands with various world dignitaries, a young couple getting married, and Jordan Masters speaking to a distinguished-looking crowd of scientists. A new, brighter, logo flew in: The WBN Evening Report, with Cat Johnson. The logo dissolved to Cat. Her hair, now longer, had been chemically brightened and cut in a new style. She looked sharp and professional thanks to an excellent European tailor.

"Good evening Humankind, this is WBN News. I'm Cat Johnson. Tonight, in spite of the continuing darkness of this nuclear winter, the world celebrates a new light. As you all know, following Jordan Master's inspired leadership these past ten months almost two hundred nations have agreed to join together in a new United World Coalition. If that feat is considered incredible, then today's historic event must be nothing less than a miracle."

The picture cut to video footage of two men, one Arab and one Israeli, sitting at a table surrounded by dignitaries under a tent in the middle of the desert. Between the two former adversaries, smiling broadly, was Jordan Masters.

Cat Johnson's voice continued. "On the border between their countries today, thanks to the efforts of this remarkable statesman, a peace treaty was signed between Israel and Syria, representing all Arab nations."

On film, the two men signed the paper. Jordan held it up as the other men applauded. Amazingly, the two Middle Eastern leaders actually stood up and embraced each other. The camera zoomed in on Jordan Masters, who faced it directly. "To honor this historic occasion, I'd like to announce the construction of a new World Center to be located right here in the Middle East. What better place to represent rebirth than in this newly united region, bringing ancient cultures together in beauty and dignity?"

Documentary footage of construction on Saddam Hussein's palace was shown. The compound was an unlikely cross between traditional Arabic and modern styles of architecture.

"In 1989," said Jordan, over the film, "reconstruction was begun on an ancient, historically significant site, a remarkable creation that was miraculously left unscathed by the Invasion. We have pledged to complete the construction there, to fulfill the dream of uniting all the people of Earth. The new World Center, in Babylon."

"How do I look?" asked Jordan. He was never completely comfortable watching himself on camera, and he knew that practically everyone on earth would be witnessing the event, one of histories greatest achievements.

"Excellent," said the old man, Frederick A. Marco.

"Dynamic," said the man with the cigar, Derek Steele.

They were gathered in the sumptuous viewing room of Marco's palatial estate, watching the newscast of events filmed earlier in the day on a screen that stretched across an entire wall.

Lucretia leaned close to Jordan and whispered, "Sexy."

Jordan looked at her, startled at flirtation, then smiled in spite of himself. The past year had been one wild ride. The men he had met on the jet flight that fateful day had been true to their word: the real power had not resided with presidents, congresses, parliaments, dictators, kings, queens, or emperors. These men were the actual power behind the power. Jordan, himself, wasn't sure of how they'd managed to persuade so many to follow him, but they had. A few had balked, but after personal meetings with him they, too, had almost all acquiesced. On each of those occasions Jordan had felt an electric, almost sexual energy vibrating deep within his chest and couldn't help but wonder how much the implanted alien device influenced people's minds. On the rare occasion that a country's leading official refused to cooperate, the person quickly fell from grace, grew deathly ill, or even disappeared altogether. He found it disturbing and more than a little disconcerting how life had become a roller coaster ride without a seatbelt: he had no control over it, so he just held on for dear life. He truly believed he was doing a great thing in unifying the world, but it had all happened so fast that he was still reeling.

"However, not everyone seemed pleased about the announcement," continued Cat Johnson, still broadcasting, "Evangelist Matthew Richards, with his ever-increasing number of followers, had this to say."

A close-up of Matthew Richards filled the screen. His hair was now shoulder length and his beard had a white streak that matched the one in his hair. He read from the Bible: *"The beast forced all people to have a mark on their forehead so that no one could buy or sell without this mark."* The television camera angle changed to show that he was standing in front of a packed crowd at the Hollywood Bowl in Los Angeles, California. *"And all who worship the Beast, their names will not be written in the Lamb's book of life!"* He shifted his gaze toward the crowd, eyes burning with conviction, his voice sounding like thunder. "Will you give up your everlasting souls?"

His head exploded, shooting sparks and smoke.

Jordan spun around, his heart pounding. Lucretia, standing beside him with a smoking gun in her hand, shot the television image twice more. She whirled to face him, her fury almost a physical presence. "He turns man against man and then calls *you* the Antichrist!"

Frederick Marco turned to Steele. "Tell Cat Johnson we don't want that man getting any more air time.

"Yes, sir."

"We can't do that!" protested Jordan, "It's legitimate news."

"We *can* do it," said Lucretia. "She'll do what we tell her; she owes you her career." She tossed the now empty gun to Steele and pointed at him with a finger. "Only positive stories from now on. In fact, I want everything approved through this office."

"Yes, ma'am."

Jordan opened his mouth to argue but Marco laid a hand quietly on his shoulder. "Put it out of your head, Jordan. Think of good things. Think of the new world we're building. Think of..." he broke into a smile, "the new Babylon."

The construction was completed within a year.

An ultra-modern steel and glass city rose up out of the desert like a Phoenix from ashes. Resembling something out of a futuristic sci-fi movie, one almost expected to see flying cars whizzing by the towering gold spires that dazzled in the Middle Eastern sunlight. The city was the impressive result of the unique combination of calculating visions, power, and unlimited financing. In the center of the gleaming metropolis stood the crowning architectural achievement: a huge golden palace/compound–headquarters for Jordan Masters and the New World Government.

Other than political dignitaries and media superstars, few outsiders had ever been invited to the inner sanctum, so Roger Jackson was not prepared for the overwhelming effect of the place. He stood next to Cat on the wide pink marble steps, gazing up at the immense structure in awe, wondering how a snot-nosed street kid from the projects had ended up here.

He had been twelve years old, when his mom had hooked up with Dung. Dung was a fat, hairy, abusive drunk who wore the same crusty jeans and black leather vest all the time, which is why he stank, which is why Rog had always thought of him as Dung instead of his real name, Doug. Roger had never understood what his mom had seen in the walking pile of scum because as far as Rog could tell the man was as black inside as he was outside. There was no doubt he had hated Roger from the moment he laid eyes on him, clearly jealous that "his woman" had to share any of her time and attention with her son. He would cruise into the tiny fifth floor walk-up apartment, slam the door behind him and demand a beer. If Roger didn't "snap to!" he'd find the steel toe of a pair of fifteen double D's halfway up his butt. Hey, looked funny in cartoons, but in real life, there was nothing funny about getting kicked in the rear, it hurt like the blazes. Roger found that his only defense against the big man was humor. If he could make the man laugh, it dissipated the perpetual anger, so Roger used jokes and smart aleck remarks like a shield to deflect the hurt and pain. It had become a lifetime habit which, to Roger's way of thinking, wasn't a bad thing. There was only one other thing about Dung that hadn't been bad, as far as Roger could tell. He was a thief.

Okay, okay, it wasn't good. It was wrong, and the people in the ghetto neighborhood where they lived and Dung "worked" couldn't afford to lose their stuff anymore than he and his mom could. A part-time cocktail waitress job at Moxie's didn't exactly put their family in the 50% tax bracket. Roger had wanted to get a job to help out, but his mom had insisted his job was going to school and doing homework, so they didn't have a lot of extras. No big deal, neither did anyone else he knew, but that made Dung's "job" even worse because he was usually victimizing people no better off than they were. There had been one good thing about Dung being a thief, however. The video camera.

Roger had first seen it when he came home from school one Friday afternoon. Laying on the torn couch cushion with a bunch of other junk Dung had boosted from some unlucky schmo, an open, black metal suitcase lined with gray foam rubber held a video camera and accessories. Normally Roger tried to ignore the stuff Dung brought home, avoiding even a glance at it, as if he could distance himself from the crime. He couldn't turn the creepo over to the police because the man would certainly get out in a matter of hours and his young life would be over there and then. So, instead, he stayed as far away from "Dung's stuff" (which was almost always somebody else's) as possible. But this camera–this shiny, package of Japanese electronics–called to him. It beckoned. He did want his head to stay attached to his neck, however, so he walked away from it and locked himself in his bedroom. Half an hour later, he came out, standing inside his doorway, looking longingly across the apartment at the camera. It was so... cool. From the twin snoring noises–one thin and reedy, the other sounding like a Saber-tusked Rock Beast from the planet Zark–he could tell his mom and Dung, who both worked the night shift, were asleep in the other bedroom. Moving cautiously and silently, he sat down on the couch next to the camera, not planning to touch it, just itching to examine it closer. It was an early model, the kind that loaded an entire full-sized VHS tape. In addition to the power cord, it had a battery pack with charger, which meant that not only could you use it at home but you could take it "to go." Double cool. He wondered if the battery was charged. Without touching it, he studied the buttons. It looked simple enough to work, even had a thing marked Auto-Focus. Man, the thing did everything for you, no skill required! He listened again, able to hear the chainsaw noises from there. Heck, he could probably have heard the big pig snoring from Utah, half-way across the U.S. of A.! It wouldn't hurt to pick it up, would it? Maybe look through the viewfinder? What harm could it do?

He went for it.

The battery was charged. The camera clicked almost imperceptibly and a tiny TV camera inside lit up. Roger was fascinated. He held the eyecup against his eye, peering through it at the room beyond. Everything was black and white, like on *I Love Lucy*. Looking through the camera, the old, ratty apartment didn't look nearly so bad. He could zoom in on the pile of dirty dishes or pull back to reveal the entire room, including the "new" color television that Dung had provided a few weeks back. He wondered, if he plugged directly into the television and filmed the screen, would he get a picture of the television on the television on the television on the television, into infinity? And how many of them would he be able to make out? He zoomed in on the overflowing ashtray on the coffee table. In an extreme close up, they looked almost surreal. He pulled back and panned across the room, past the ancient air-conditioner that hadn't run as long as he could remember, across the old lamp... and almost screamed aloud as he landed on a close-up of Dung's scowling face. He quickly lowered the camera, feeling his stomach turn into ice water.

"What are you doing, butt face?" growled the big man.

"I... uh..."

"What do you think you're doing?" he repeated, louder. Meaner.

"I was just–"

"Touching my stuff." He said it the way the average person might have said "torturing kittens" or "eating dog poop," like it was the most heinous crime in the world.

Roger quickly turned off the camera and laid it back in the foam-lined case, yanking his hands away like it was red hot. "Sorry, Doug, I didn't hurt it, I just wanted to see–"

"See what? What having two broken arms was like?"

"Oh, leave him alone." My mom appearing in the hallway behind Dung, trying to look past his massive pile of jellyfish flesh. "I'm sure he wasn't hurting it."

"It's mine. Nobody touches my stuff."

"Gimme a break, Doug, you told me it was a piece of junk. You told me the guy at the pawnshop wouldn't even give you anything for it because everybody's buying those little half-sized ones now."

He whirled on her. "Maybe I wanted to use it myself!"

Her voice took on a derisive tone. "Yeah, you told me what kind of movies you want to make and I told you forget it, pal! Ain't gonna happen. Some two-bit thief like you comes in here and steals it and the next thing ya know I'm all over the internet!"

"Hey, I don't mean to burst your bubble, but you ain't no Baywatch babe, chicky!"

"Oh, yeah?" Suddenly her tone changed, becoming both little girlish and sexy at the same time. "You come back in here and I'll show you a few tricks that prissy white girl never even dreamed of." She pulled him toward the bedroom. Roger knew that she was running interference for him, and was grateful. Very grateful.

Dung shot him final look, scowling. His mom leaned over and whispered something in Dung's ear. Roger didn't know what she said, but it seemed to surprise the heck out of the big guy. He grinned, a lascivious look. Not the kind you want to see someone give your mom. On the other hand, his mom didn't seem to mind. "And that's a better offer than you'd get from any pawn shop, bubba," she added, aloud.

He looked at her a long moment then, completely out of the blue, laughed and turned to Roger. "Okay, it's yours, kid."

Roger looked at him, blankly; absolutely, positively, one-hundred percent sure that he had heard wrong. "What?"

"It's all yours." He pointed a stubby finger at him. "Don't say I never gave you anything." Turning to follow Roger's mother into the bedroom, he took two steps then abruptly spun back. "Hey! You take any good movies..." he thrust his hips forward and back a few times, in an overtly sexual motion, "I wanta see them." With that, he disappeared into the bedroom.

Roger grabbed the camera and got out of there before Dung realized that he had done something nice and changed his mind. And before he could overhear whatever it was his mom had promised.

The camera had changed Roger's life. His mom's sacrifice that day (the equivalent of throwing herself on a hand grenade, to Roger's way of thinking) saved him. It gave him a way to deal with the increasingly difficult existence in the projects. In much the same way that watching violent television shows doesn't affect people, Roger found that when he watched the world through the camera he was able to distance himself from the painful realities of everyday life. The inner-city neighborhood he lived in was a cesspool of drugs, sex, violence, and raw emotions, but through the lens everything seemed surreal. At first he pretended that he was shooting some *NYPD Blues*-type action/cop drama. Eventually, his life became a never-ending documentary. He retreated into a make-believe yet excruciatingly real world. He became well known in the neighborhood as "Camera Man" and his relationship with the camera lasted long after his mom's with Dung had ended.

There were two local gangs fighting over territory in the hood, the Diablos and the Blood Angels. Six years later, Roger had still managed to avoid joining either gang by convincing both that he was the official historian of the area and had to keep himself neutral in order to be allowed access to both groups, as well as the cops, the emergency crews, the shop keepers, and the rest of the neighborhood. He'd shot a few videos with both of them, editing them in camera with a quick-cut NYPD Blue style, making the gangs look cooler and tougher than they actually were. Of course, in the video he showed to the Diablos, the Angels always looked like idiotic dweebs and vice versa. He was the only kid he knew who hadn't been forced to pick sides in the turf wars.

One night, Roger was shooting a pick-up B-ball game when all sanity broke loose. A low-rider full of thirteen year-old Diablo shooters came careening around the corner, guns blazing. The players, Blood Angels, scrambled for weapons as bodies burst open with blossoming red eruptions. They didn't have a chance. Perhaps the shooters were familiar with the tall, thin figure with the camera pressed against his eye, or maybe it was just fate, but when the shooting ended Roger was the only person still on his feet. He had stood in the midst of the killing field, witnessing the entire event unfold through the lens, filming the carnage. He'd seen one boy's eye explode at the same time the back of his head disintegrated; saw another pitch forward, his back arching inward. One went down, clutching his throat, trying to hold back the blood that bubbled between his fingers. Another, screaming and crying like a baby, had been holding his crotch, his baggy jeans quickly growing wet and red. No tough guys here. Roger recorded the sound of automatic gunfire, the screech of hot tires on pavement, the yells and screams of panic and pain. It all seemed as unreal as a cheap movie and for some unknown reason it had never occurred to Roger to hit the concrete himself. He just stood there, until he was the only one standing. He got it all on film. The horror. The blood. The terrible, haunting screams.

Later, some man in a wrinkled, brown suit stood over him as he sat trembling in the corner, leaning against the rusting fence of the ball court. The man was staring at the video camera in his lap. Roger, thinking the man was a cop, handed the tape over. Turned out, he wasn't. He was a reporter for the local news.

The film was a sensation. Roger spent a lot of time with the cops, but even more time with the reporter. Eventually, he mentioned that he had other tapes; an entire library of them. The reporter watched them, edited them, won a documentary prize of some sort. Roger won the prize, too. The news station hired him, and eventually hooked him up with another young newcomer–a woman he'd immediately, and secretly, fallen in love with. One terrifying and unbelievable turn of events had led to another, and here they were, him and Cat.

Inside the palace, the lavish opulence matched the exterior. The high ceilings, marble floors, sweeping staircases, crystal chandeliers, antique furnishings, velvet drapes, and gilded picture frames holding famous works of art were almost overwhelming.

Cat was wearing a calf-length tan skirt, a cream blouse, and high suede boots. She'd removed the skirt's matching jacket due to the overwhelming heat outside. It seemed hot everywhere on the planet, these days. Once the ash and soot that had darkened the skies had partially cleared, it was discovered that the ozone layer and atmospheric gasses had been seriously damaged. The radiation, absorbed and reradiated with a longer wavelength, caused a Greenhouse effect allowing temperatures around the planet to rise an average of ten degrees, resulting in even more chaos: ancient melting ice created floods, long-standing bodies of water had run dry.

"Holy cow," mumbled Roger.

"Impressed?" asked Cat.

"No, I mean just that: holy cow!" He pointed to a life-sized golden calf, encrusted with jewels. "Hard to believe they built this place in only ten months."

"I could live here."

"You'd like to."

"Excuse me?"

He raised one eyebrow. "I've asked it before and I'll ask it again: what's he got that I ain't got?" He couldn't understand her fixation with Masters. Sure the guy was handsome, rich, famous, powerful... but there were more things to life. Like unending loyalty. Like a man who would walk through the worst neighborhood in hell for you. Like a man who knows your every manner, habit, and fault and loves you anyway. Cat must have caught the seriousness in his voice, because she suddenly looked uncomfortable. He quickly added. "Except for those ugly old paintings. He's got them." He pointed to three large, framed canvasses hanging on the wall: a Renoir, a Van Gogh and a Picasso.

Cat laughed.

Wanting to ease the awkward moment further, Roger pointed behind her, expressing his amazement. "Who *is* their decorator?"

A huge gilded statue of Masters, two stories tall, stood in the center of the vast hall. They approached it. A jeweled, etched plaque at the bottom read: Our Savior.

Roger looked up at the visage. "That's a little creepy."

As if it heard him, the statue suddenly opened its eyes and moved, looking down. Roger screamed as the giant sculpture reached toward him with one massive metal hand. The hand swept past, barely missing him, rising as the statue spread its arms in a welcoming gesture. Masters' voice echoed through the large hall. "Welcome to the World Center. Built for all mankind." The effigy continued to move until it resumed its original position, frozen in place once again.

Roger, too, remained unmoving. Frozen. His heart pounding like the bass in a cranked-up lowrider.

Cat approached the animatronic statue, a smile forming on her lips. "It's like the Pirates of the Caribbean." she said, sounding pleased.

"More like the Haunted freakin' Mansion!" he burst, swallowing the sour taste that had risen in his throat.

"Impressive, isn't it? It's programmed with greetings in every language." They turned. A powerful-looking man in a steel gray suit came down the wide, sweeping staircase.

Roger thought perhaps they had met before, but couldn't place the face. Embarrassed by his fright, he strutted around the rear of the statue. "It got a big string in the back you pull or what?"

The man ignored him, going straight to Cat. "It was a gift to our leader from his lady."

Cat looked stricken. "His lady?"

"Ms. Baylock. Welcome to the World Center, Ms. Johnson. I am Derek Steele, at your service. Follow me, please."

He turned, without acknowledging Roger, and led the way up the wide steps. Cat, looking stunned, followed. Gathering up his heavy cases of camera equipment, he mumbled to himself, "And how are you, Mister Jackson, can I help you with anything? Why no, thank you, sir." He glared back at the eerie statue. "Except maybe a place to change my underwear!"

As Cat followed the man upstairs, her heart and mind were racing. Baylock? Who in the world was that? She'd never heard of any woman Jordan was involved with. And why did she even care? Roger had asked a very good question: what was it about Jordan Masters? Cat spent hardly any time with him in almost two years, yet still was haunted by his presence. It was incredible what he was accomplishing for the world, she acknowledged, but her interest went much deeper. It went back to those three long days and nights just before the nuclear detonations, when they were the only two people in the world who truly believed in the warnings from Gideon. To the long walks and intimate conversations they had shared during that intense time when they both believed the world might end. To that heat-filled moment when he had swept her into his arms and kissed her. Unfortunately, in the next instant, everything had changed and they had both been caught up in a whirlwind of fate, swept apart by circumstances. She understood that they were both doing important jobs, indispensable work, but she yearned to renew their private relationship.

They followed Steele down a long, carpeted hall and stepped through an intricately-carved doorway inlaid with gold, onyx and jade.

Jordan sat behind a massive rosewood desk in an expansive office, signing papers. He was wearing white silk pants, a pink, short-sleeved shirt, was tanned and as boyishly handsome as ever. Lucretia, looking coolly-elegant in a sandy-colored jersey dress with dolman sleeves and a large brown belt with hammered-brass fittings, was standing next to him, shouting into the telephone. “I don’t care what country he thinks he’s leading. You tell him if he wants to meet Jordan, he comes here like everybody else!” Her voice turned syrupy. “Then send him a box of Cuban cigars.” She hung up and winked at Jordan. “Nothing rarer than a Cuban cigar these days.” She looked up, noticing the new arrivals.

Jordan hit his feet, grinning, and hurried around the desk. “Cat!” He swept her into his arms. “Man, it’s good to see you!”

Strong emotion washed over Cat at this long overdue reunion. She marveled that, after all this time, his presence could evoke in her such a powerful reaction. Her voice sounded strained. “Jordan.”

He kissed her on the cheek, lingering close, his warm breath on her earlobe as he whispered, “How long has it been?”

“Three years,” she said, her knees feeling weak. Then added quietly, “Two months. Fourteen days.”

Jordan looked into her eyes. “Too long. Much, much too long.”

Lucretia stepped between them, neatly separating Cat from Jordan. “Miss Johnson. So nice to see you again,” she hissed, her voice clearly indicating that it was anything but.

If Catherine had fur it would have stood on end, but she managed a smile. “I can’t tell you what a pleasure this is, Mrs. Burton.” She kept her voice cool.

Lucretia gave her an equally chilly smile. “Baylock. I’ve gone back to my maiden name. Do call me Lucretia.”

Cat felt like she'd just heard fingernails dragged down a chalkboard. Roger stepped forward with a grin and held out his hand, congenially. "Nice to meet you, Lucretia."

She turned away, ignoring him.

Jordan jumped in, clearly trying to cover her rudeness. "Roger, my man!" He grabbed the cameraman's hand and pumped it, checking out the white linen suit and teal shirt. "Nice threads, amigo! Come a long way since that wild ride in your van, haven't we? It's so good to see you. It's good to see both of you! Come! Sit! Have a drink!" He pointed to a well-stocked bar, behind which the man who had met them downstairs was waiting.

"What's your pleasure?"

"Water, if you don't mind, please," said Cat.

"Got any Louis the 13th Brandy?" Roger asked, with a grin.

The man gave him an icy look.

"Bud Light?" he muttered.

"So," said Jordan, sitting on a red velvet couch, and pulling her down beside him. "What brings you to my neck of the desert, gorgeous?"

Cat looked at him, confused. "You summoned us."

Jordan mirrored her confusion. "Summoned you? No I didn't." He glanced at Lucretia questioningly. "Did I?"

She was about to answer when a soft voice came from the doorway. "I did." Cat turned and was stunned to see Gideon walk into the room.

"Gideon!" exclaimed Jordan, clearly as surprised as Cat was to see the alien alive and well. "My God! We thought you'd gone down with the mothership!"

"My comrades brought the ship down, but I was not aboard," said Gideon.

Jordan strode across the floor and threw his arms around the silver-haired man.

"Where in hell have you been for three years!?" snapped Lucretia.

"We could have used your presence," added Jordan, pulling away.

"You needed to act on your own," said the alien, with fatherly patience, "And you have made wonderful strides, I'm proud of all of you. But now, you must come with me."

"Where to?" asked Jordan.

The alien smiled. "To the next level."

Chapter 14

Within the hour, the entire entourage was 41,000 feet in the air, streaking through the sky. Gideon was being his usual enigmatic self, refusing to answer any questions about their destination or the reason for the sudden trip. He explained, when pressed, that he hadn't been aboard the mothership when it had gone down, but that all of his compatriots had been. He was now alone in his stand against his kind. Alone, that is, except for the people of Earth.

In the small galley, Cat opened a brushed-aluminum refrigerator door and stared at the contents in amazement. The compartment was filled with bottles of Coca-Cola. "Oh my gosh!" she gasped, "Are these what I think they are?"

Jordan stood in a doorway behind her. "The real thing. Help yourself."

Reverently, she selected one, popped the top and took a long drink of the frosty liquid. "I'd forgotten how good these were. Nobody's seen one in years."

"Really?"

Cat leveled a measuring look at him. "You know, I can't decide if you're just being smug or if you really didn't know. Either way it's frightening."

"What do you mean?" he asked, growing serious.

"You're either out of touch with the real world or you're living above it. Neither one is a good quality in a leader, Jordan."

"I see."

Cat suddenly felt defiant. "You gonna have me fired for saying it?"

"Excuse me?"

She gave hem a steely-eyed look. "'Jordan Masters got you hired, he can get you fired.'"

"What?" He looked perplexed. "What are you talking about?"

"I'm talking about the fifth amendment, Jordan." She had been absolutely furious when all coverage of Matthew Richards and his teachings had been banned from the airways.

Jordan's face suddenly registered realization. "I see. Well, first of all, the U.S. Constitution doesn't even exist anymore, it was swept out to sea and now it's a half mile under the ocean somewhere."

She stared at him, appalled by his words. "I can't believe you just said that! Can I quote you on that?" She held up a hand. "Oh, no, of course I can't! That might make the great dictator Jordan Masters look bad!"

"And secondly," he said, forcefully, "the world has changed, Cat! The old rules don't apply! Everything is different now, or hadn't you noticed?"

"Just how much is becoming very clear by the minute," she answered, stiffly.

"Look, Catherine," he said, in an imploring voice, "certain kinds of stories don't help anybody. Focusing on the negative is counter-productive. We're trying to unite people, can't you see that?"

"Using censorship?"

"Does a parent let his children watch pornography?" asked Jordan, raising his voice. "No, he guides them! Limits their exposure so they form a positive personality."

"We are not children, Jordan!"

"Okay, maybe you're right. I don't know." He collapsed against the wall, suddenly looking bone weary. He stared at the floor for a moment and when he spoke, his voice was filled with doubt. "I don't know everything, Cat. I'll tell you something; I hardly ever sleep anymore. I lay awake, staring at shadows, letting the day play over and over in my mind. Did I do the right thing? Did I make the right decisions?" He shook his head, slowly. "I don't know!" He looked up at her. "You can't begin to imagine what it's like. I mean everybody everywhere is looking to me for the answers. And I..." He shrugged. "I just don't have them."

In spite of her anger, Cat felt bad for him. Her voice softened and she touched him gently. "You've accomplished miracles, Jordan. People do appreciate it."

He had, it seemed to her, an almost childlike need for her approval. His manner brightened at her touch. "I get these ideas, Cat. They come to me in the early hours of the morning, like the sun rising and filling me with light. Extreme, radical plans, so different from anything done before. Crazy ideas that..." he smiled excitedly. "That work! I'm just an actor, Cat, an actor. But maybe that's why I was chosen. As a... presenter of these ideas." His eyes took on a distant look. "Truth be known, Catherine, I'm not the one calling the shots here. It's all coming from above."

She studied him, wondered if he was referring to heaven or an alien space ship.

Steele's voice came through the intercom, interrupting her thoughts. "Buckle up, people, we'll be touching down in Tel Aviv in ten minutes."

Cat returned to the main cabin just in time to hear Roger ask, "Why Tel Aviv?"

"Patience," said Gideon, from across the aircraft.

Roger stared at Gideon, then leaned close to Cat and whispered. "That guy creeps me out."

Over his shoulder, Cat saw Gideon turn towards them and gaze at the back of Roger's head, as if he had heard the comment. Impossible, he was far across the cabin. Then again, he wasn't human. Who knew how sensitive his hearing might be? She'd have to warn Roger against making any disparaging remarks, even in a whisper.

At that thought, almost as if she had spoken it aloud, Gideon shifted his gaze to her and nodded seriously. A feeling like centipede legs ran up her neck and she involuntarily shivered. After an uncomfortable moment, he relented by breaking eye contact, and gazing serenely out the window. Cat shivered again, more violently this time.

Ten minutes later the jet's wheels lightly touched down on the hot tarmac of the newly re-built Tel Aviv airport. The landing was so smooth that Cat couldn't even distinguish the moment when the wheels hit the ground. Ten minutes after that the pilot, Steele, stepped out of the cockpit and lit up a cigar. Cat surreptitiously observed the self- assured looking man, unsure what to make of him. Was he a pilot, a bodyguard, an executive assistant or something else? He spoke only rarely, but it was clear that behind those eyes his mind was sharply focused. He seemed to take everything in, but expressed an opinion about nothing. He clearly served the others but not in a subservient way–more as if it were his choice. And he definitely treated her and Roger as his subordinates.

He stepped into the galley and poured himself a generous scotch.

Gideon, who she noticed had never buckled his seatbelt, rose and crossed to the main cabin door. Twisting the large handle, he said, "Prepare yourself, Jordan."

"For what?" asked Masters.

Gideon turned to him, smiling. "For anything."

He pushed the thick door open.

The cool quiet of the aircraft interior was immediately dispatched by the loud roar of a crowd and the intense desert heat. It was almost a physical blow, and Cat found herself retreating as if assaulted by a roaring, oven-hot entity.

Jordan, on the other hand, seemed drawn to the heat and sound. He moved to the doorway as if in a trance. At the instant he appeared, the volume of cheers grew so loud the jet seemed to vibrate.

Lucretia broke into a wide smile.

Jordan gazed outside, looking confounded. "How'd they know I was coming?" Then he abruptly turned to the silver-haired alien. "Ah, it's time," he said, with realization. "It's time the world met you, isn't it?"

Gideon shook his head firmly, "No, Jordan. This is your moment."

Jordan opened his mouth to protest when his mentor raised a hand to halt him. "Your moment," he repeated firmly.

Jordan's face clouded.

"However," said Gideon, grasping Jordan affectionately by the shoulders. "I will be standing by you, my friend."

That said, his body began to grow, chest widening as if taking in a massive breath of air, back broadening, neck thickening, and arms lengthening. His face began to shift, the skin bulging and pulsing as if a multitude of beetles were scurrying about directly below the surface. His hair rippled like seaweed caught in a riptide and sucked into his scalp until only a half-inch remained all the way around. Color bled into the follicles, darkening the tone to a deep black. His nose spread, his lips thinned, and the tip of his chin seemed to pull into itself, squaring off. His skin tone altered as if an interior sun had eclipsed, and a five o'clock shadow appeared as black whiskers poked through the pores on his now square jaw.

Cat stared, agog. Even though she had seen a transformation like this once before, she still found it wholly unnerving. Especially the eyes.

Just like the last time, Gideon's blue irises faded away until his eyeballs were solid white, looking like tiny hard-boiled eggs in his sockets. A moment later they faded back in, steel gray, staring at an identical visage only a foot away.

Derek Steele gawked at his exact double.

Cat could hardly believe it herself. Except for the clothes, it was impossible to tell the original from the clone.

Gideon reached out toward the immobile aide and plucked the cigar from between his lips, clenching it in his own teeth. When he spoke to Steele, even his voice was a perfect imitation. "Wait here." Without further ado, as if what had just occurred had been the most ordinary thing in the world, the alien stepped out the door of the aircraft. Another clamor arose from the gathered crowd anticipating from his descent that their idol was about to appear.

Lucretia moved up close behind Jordan, pressed her breasts against his back and whispered in his ear. "Let's go, baby. Turn on that Masters magic." Distracted, Jordan glanced over at Cat, clearly self-conscious about Burton's obvious intimacy. Cat held his gaze, clearly letting him know that she was not only disappointed but disgusted by the way he was allowing himself to be manipulated. He seemed to want to say something to her, but before he could find his voice, Lucretia gave him a little nudge toward the door and the moment passed.

As he stepped hesitantly out onto the metal ramp, the crowd let out a great roar of approval. Jordan smiled and proceeded down the steps.

Lucretia buttoned her low-cut blouse high to the collar, reinventing her appearance for the very conservative people of this region. Checking herself in a mirror, she smiled ever-so-slightly at the reflection, shot Cat a frosty look, then followed Jordan out, waving like royalty.

Cat turned to Roger. "Ready, amigo?"

Roger, clearly freaked out by all of this, grabbed Steele's drink from his hand and drained it. "Wait here," he said to the man, returning the empty glass.

The pilot, still paralyzed with shock, did not respond. As still as an oil painting and as pale as a cadaver, he continued to stare at the spot where Gideon had transformed.

Roger hoisted his television camera and, trailed by Cat, exited the aircraft into the vivid heat of the moment.

Astonishingly, the airport was blanketed with people, tens of thousands–on the ground, in the windows, on the roof. Screaming, waving, whistling, applauding, and holding banners bearing Jordan's likeness. A band consisting of primitive animal hide drums, tambourines, and a number of unusual woodwind and stringed instruments, played energetic music. Two dozen women in colorful Israeli costume danced. A group of children in white and blue school uniforms proffered bouquets of yellow flowers. A platoon of soldiers stood at attention.

It appeared that most of the Tel Aviv police force had been brought out to keep control.

Roger filmed, as Jordan and Lucretia worked the cheering crowd, shaking hands, high-fiving, winking, hugging and, yes, even kissing babies. Following close behind, Cat overheard Jordan say to Lucretia, "This is great, but why are we here?"

"I think we're here to make a speech," she said, pointing to a high wooden platform that had been built in the middle of the tarmac. Gideon/Steele was standing on it, gesturing Jordan over.

Masters and Baylock made their way up and stepped out onto the stage, in full view of all The cacophony of screams, shouts, whistles and applause was so loud that Cat wanted to cover her ears. Jordan approached a bank of microphones and tapped one. Assured that the microphones were in full working order, he lifted his arms. "Thank you, good people! I'm overwhelmed by your welcome!" The crowd roared again, pleased to be appreciated. Jordan grinned with more confidence, stepping a bit closer and raising his hands again. The cheering dropped by a few decibels. "To paraphrase a classic," he started, "It was the worst of times, it was the best of times..."

That was as far as he got. Unexpectedly, the air was ripped by sirens. The people, at first, seemed confused. Then grew uneasy, until outright panic gripped them.

"What the heck is that?" asked Roger, looking up from his camera.

"Air raid?" asked Cat.

"Air raid?" he repeated, incredulously.

"No, no," she corrected herself, "It can't be an air raid. We have world peace, right?"

Roger swung his camera skyward, looking through it, sweeping the sky. Cat saw him tense.

"What do you see?"

"Just some black specks... let me focus." He adjusted the long lens, using it like a telescope. "Uh oh."

"What?"

"Someone didn't get the no war memo."

Within seconds, the black specs were close enough to be identified with the naked eye as jet fighters and bombers. All at once a bright pin-prick of light flashed from one of them and moments later a huge ball of flame exploded on the far side of the airport. The crowd screamed and ran, pushing and scrambling for cover as more missiles impacted all around them. Lucretia screamed, staring at the onslaught, wide-eyed.

Jordan turned to Gideon. "What's going on?"

The alien looked up at the sky, calmly. "Russian fighters. A final power play."

Cat ducked as an explosion ripped through one of the terminal buildings, blasting windows out in a storm of deadly flying glass. She could hear screams of pain and anguish.

Jordan stared at Gideon, incredulously. "You knew? Jesus Christ!"

Gideon's eyes flashed with fury. "Do not use His name like that!" he snapped.

Jordan turned toward the stairs. "We've got to get out of here!"

Gideon grabbed him by the back of the shirt. "No!" He jerked him backwards. "Stand your ground! Do not leave this platform!"

"I'll be killed!"

"Do as I say!" roared the alien, "Stay!"

He turned and leaped off the stage, landing easily next to Cat, fifteen feet below. Now alone on the stage, Jordan and Lucretia seemed frozen with indecision.

A missile rocketed through the air and demolished a nearby row of parked airplanes. A ball of flame rose sixty feet into the air, Cat shut her eyes and threw herself onto the ground as the heat thundered over her. The real Derek Steele dashed down the steps of the Gulfstream and bolted across the tarmac just moments before the jet was hit by an incoming rocket. As his personal transport exploded, Jordan screamed out, reeling in pain. Cat looked up to see a long piece of shrapnel imbedded in his chest, like a sword. Jordan stared down at the metal impaling him, then his eyes rolled back in his head and he collapsed on the stage. Cat screamed. Lucretia threw herself down beside him. "No!" she cried, yanking the shard of sharp metal out of his chest. Frantically, she tore at his shirt, popping buttons and ripping the fabric aside, staring wide-eyed at the bubbling wound. She pressed her hands down over it, trying to staunch the flow of blood. Jordan tensed, let out one last, wet breath, fell still, and the blood stopped flowing. Lucretia cried out in anguish and collapsed on him.

Cat found herself unable to breathe, her mind unable to accept his death. Dead. Jordan was dead.

The medallion embedded in Masters' chest suddenly pulsed with a blinding light. Lucretia was nearly thrown backwards. The medallion began to glow–increasing in brilliance from a bright yellow radiance to an intense, deep red. Lucretia seemed to be attempting to pull away, her body vibrating with the effort, but something apparently held her in place as if an intense electrical current was running from Jordan's body into her.

Cat screamed with horror at what happened next. Lucretia aged. Her skin paled until it was almost white, small lines appeared around her eyes and her dark hair became streaked with gray. The change wasn't extreme, and over the normal course of ten years wouldn't have been noticed much, but taking place in an instantaneous transformation it was terrifying. Somehow, in some manner well beyond her comprehension, Cat understood that the medallion was drawing life force out of Lucretia and feeding it into Jordan, reviving him. The blood on Jordan's chest bubbled as if boiling, turned brown and quickly dried to a cracked crust. The wound beneath it closed, leaving only a pale, jagged scar. Suddenly he arched his back and gagged. His eyes flew open. With a spastic heave of his chest he threw Lucretia aside, rolled across the wooden platform as if being attacked by invisible hornets and leaped to his feet, shrieking and clawing at the medallion which now shone blindingly white hot.

Cat watched in stunned disbelief as the resurrected man raked his skin with his fingernails, gouging bloody furrows in the flesh, apparently trying to tear the medallion from his chest. The sky above grew ominously dark as storm clouds appeared from nowhere into the previously clear sky. Stupefied, she stared at the boiling clouds, reminding her of time-lapse films she'd seen. Her attention reverted to Jordan as his scream grew in intensity. Lucretia scrambled across the stage on all fours, distancing herself from Jordan whose body began to glow, incandescence enveloping him entirely. Sparks of electricity arced between his fingertips.

Cat stared, aghast.

The medallion's center suddenly irised open, like a camera lens, and a light beam of fire-red energy shot out into the sky. A jet fighter streaking through the boiling clouds burst into a spectacular fireball. Jordan, jerking like a puppet on a string, spun in the direction of another incoming jet. The light beam caught it too, and the aircraft disintegrated into a firestorm of debris. Jordan continued to jerk and twist as if wracked by spastic convulsions and, with each move, another aircraft was torn from the sky.

People stopped running, transfixed by the amazing scene playing out before their eyes. Standing on the raised wooden platform, glowing, arms spread, fingers splayed, back arched, a seemingly unending scream issued from Jordan's mouth. Mesmerized, unable to move, Cat was unable to discern if his wail was one of fury, agony, or ecstasy. The energy discharge gave the eerie illusion that it came not from him radiating upward, but rather that it was a beam from heaven descending into him. An area of light around his head glowed just a bit brighter than the other light emanating from his body, giving a distinct halo-like effect.

As the crowd watched, they reacted in awe, calling aloud to each other, staring, pointing with wonder at the spectacle on the stage. Standing next to Cat, Gideon shut his eyes with what looked like pure ecstasy. "Now," he whispered.

The medallion released a tremendous pulse of energy, the likes of which Cat had only seen in films of a nuclear explosion. The backwash hit her like a clap of thunder reverberating through her body. Not so much a physical sensation, but an emotional, metaphysical one. The warm rot of worm-infested corpses, the nervous itch of child molesters, the putridness of rotting flesh, the painful electric rush of thrill killers. She felt the suffocation of unbearable loneliness, the burning coldness of torturers, the rabid hunger of selfishness, the utter fearful despair of abused children, the desperate, violent weakness of rapists, and the barren emptiness of pointless death. It drove her to her knees, almost out of her mind, gagging.

At that moment, the entire remaining enemy forces simultaneously exploded like the spectacular finale of a monstrous fireworks display. The sky rained fire onto the surrounding desert sands.

The crowd, most of them collapsed on their knees or prone, was rendered mindless into silence. Cat felt her gorge rise and fought for self-control. Her heart pounded so hard she feared it might seize up.

The energy beam imploded back into Jordan's body. He collapsed on the wooden planks, barely conscious, pale and soaked in sweat.

The gathering, perhaps five thousand people or more, were virtually motionless, like a painting. Like Cat, many were physically sick; some had fainted. Cat blinked, trying to restore her blurry vision. Through her tears she suddenly saw Gideon, who had moved near her into the shadows under the stage, begin to age dramatically. The visage of Derek Steele melted away, hair sprouting like weeds and turning nearly white, a long beard growing, skin loosening and remolding itself, and his body shrinking until the black coat, which had been too tight moments before, now hung like a sackcloth on him. It was not Steele or Gideon who stepped out from under the stage, but the image of an ancient Rabbi. The old man hobbled up the steps of the stage, until he was in full view of the crowd, then slowly bowed down before Jordan, head touching the wood.

Lucretia was the next to move, clearly taking her cue from Gideon's new persona. She, too, fell at Jordan's feet. Derek Steele, among the crowd below, immediately knelt as well, hands raised toward Jordan reverently.

Others in the gathering also began to kneel.

Jordan, looking like he'd endured a holocaust, stumbled to his feet.

As he rose, most of the silent throng genuflected before him. He seemed to focus on them then for the first time and stiffened, gazing out at the supplicating masses. Cat stood and watched him anxiously. At this moment the true nature of the man's character should show itself. How would he react?

Something in Jordan's eyes changed... and he broke into a smile. Cat could not bear it. It was the smile of a predator, the reaction of a man who has been given the power of a God–and found it to his taste. *He is lost,* she thought. She turned away, feeling like something jagged and rusty was twisting through her heart. With the exception of herself and Roger, who was still filming as if on a movie set, almost all of the thousands present were bowing down to Jordan as if he were a deity.

Their god stepped forward to the front of the stage, thrust his arms toward the sky, and stood triumphantly before them.

The crowd went wild.

Chapter 15

"And the whole world was amazed and followed the beast."

Matthew Richards stood on the huge Las Vegas stage, reading from the Book of Revelation to an assembly of nearly three thousand. In a pair of faded jeans, black tee-shirt, and old, worn cowboy boots, his appearance was a far cry from the picture he'd presented in the battery-operated jacket of the old days. Matthew "Miracle" no longer existed. After his epiphany he had found the name repulsively pretentious so he'd reverted to his given name, Richards. Here were no gospel choirs, no music directors, no hand-held fans bearing his likeness, nor collection plates of any kind. There was no bigger-than-life, glow-in-the-dark, molded plastic Jesus–just a plain, solitary man backed by a large red banner whose bold white lettering read: *Witness. Understand. Believe. Everything depends on it.*

"The dragon had given his power to the beast and they worshipped him asking 'Who can make war against him?'"

The crowd reacted with amens, and calls of support.

Matthew lowered his Bible and looked out over his flock. "Times have been hard," he said, quietly.

More than one called out their agreement. "Very hard. And I'm afraid, brothers and sisters, that I can only tell you that they will grow worse. It will take all your faith to survive. But you must. Because as bad as life on this earth gets, as wickedly, stinkingly, unbearably bad as it will become... that is but a fraction of how good it will be when it's over."

The crowd raised their voices with amens and hallelujahs.

"Take heart in the knowledge that we are not alone. See those people with the cameras? This message of hope is being telecast to hundreds of thousands of followers across the internet." He looked back at the banner above him, raising his hands to it. "Witness the events we are living! Read your Bible so you can understand! And believe! Everything depends on it!"

In an extravagantly decorated bedroom, Lucretia sat on a massive four-poster bed, dressed in a green silk negligee, watching the broadcast on a large internet television. To remedy some of the damage caused by the incident in Tel Aviv, she had dyed her hair blond and restyled it to achieve a more youthful look. Only the small lines around her eyes remained as reminders of the sudden aging she had gone through. Jordan emerged from the bathroom, wet hair tousled, still warm and damp from a shower, a towel wrapped around his waist. She raised her eyes from the monitor, her gaze drawn like a magnet from his handsome face to the medallion that Gideon had attached to him, now permanently fused to his body. Thick clumps of scar tissue had surrounded the prongs that dug into his chest, the black metal and flesh grown together since the incident in Israel.

"That man is dangerous," commented Jordan, his eyes fixed on the television.

"I ordered him silenced," Lucretia said, muting the sound with a remote.

"What?"

"You said it yourself, Jordan, he's dangerous."

"You can't just..." he hit the bedpost. "Blast you, Lucretia, when you give orders like that you undermine the principles we stand for! Somehow, people always find out, and how does that make us look? Nothing can stop me now anyway. You saw the unearthly power I have. The power of God!" He touched the device bonded to his pectoral muscles. "It filled me, overwhelmed me, exploded from me!" He stood at a set of French doors that led to a balcony, looking out at the futuristic city below. "For a long time I doubted, but no more. How else can we interpret this? I must be the chosen one. There is no other explanation, Lucy, the devil himself couldn't have stopped me. I myself couldn't have stopped me!"

"Jordan, those people are saying you *are* the devil himself!" she cried, trying to get across to him the seriousness of the threat the preacher represented. "And it's not just that one man either, there's an entire underground network of those people."

He turned back to her. "You make it sound like a war."

"It is a war!" she practically shouted. "These religious nuts preach disharmony! They meet in secret places, beaming their poisonous downloads from undisclosed locations and we can't track them because they refuse to register!" The frustration of it made her nearly rabid. "They have no money, yet somehow the bastards survive!" Her voice dropped in tone, filled with hatred. "Worse, they infected three of our own."

Jordan stared at her. "Who?"

She could see that he was as shocked as she had been to learn this. The idea that even one, never mind three, of the ten men she had introduced in the black jet that fateful day could turn against him was unbelievable. It certainly attested to the dangerous power the poison-preaching preacher held. "Chen, Nichols and Rodriguez," she spat. Their names left a bad taste in her mouth. "But don't worry about it, they've been cut off. Which is exactly what we have to do with Richards."

Jordan seemed to consider her words. Finally, he spoke quietly. "We don't want to create a martyr, Lucy."

She nodded in agreement. "He'll simply disappear."

Jordan still didn't sound convinced. "He's only one man."

She crossed the room and leaned close. "It's a start." She pulled his towel away.

He smiled briefly at her action, then his eyes became distant. He broke away from her and stood naked and silent in front of the television, watching the preacher and his followers. When he finally spoke, his voice hardened to a tone she had never heard before. "You're right, it is a war."

He went to the bed, picked up the television remote and, handling the device like a gun, pointedly clicked off Matthew Richards.

The gesture said it all.

"Good night, Reverend. I'll lock up after you leave."

"No, Jacob, don't. Keep the doors open, no one must ever be turned away from God's sanctuary."

"But people come... they steal things."

"If they come to steal the silver," Matthew Richards said with a smile, "give them the gold as well. And thank the Lord you had it to give."

"Yes, Reverend."

"Call me Matt." With a smile and a wave, he exited the theater and walked through the deserted casino, his footsteps quiet on the blackened carpet. The place still held the thick, cloying scent of smoke. Most of the craps and blackjack tables, wheels of fortune and roulette, and endless lines of slot machines had been removed, but numerous damaged pieces remained, scattered around the building like neglected gravestones–burned and broken reminders of man's desire for a quick and easy fix. A large pile of destroyed slot machines were heaped against one wall, smashed open, coins long stolen. Far beyond them, at the other end of what had been the hotel lobby, the shattered tail section of a 747 aircraft lay rusting in the moonlight which spilled through an opening where the roof once had been. Matthew shuddered at the sight, imagining what the horror of that night must have been like for the people in this building. The presence of death still hung heavy here. Then again, the presence of the black horse was heavy everywhere.

He pushed aside a dark curtain and stepped through a shattered glass door into the building's rear parking garage. It was the safest, least conspicuous way to enter and leave. Exiting the front door, one would walk directly into the bright lights of "The Strip," which hadn't taken long to resume business. It confounded Matthew, because many essential businesses had been destroyed by the holocaust. Some of the services folks had relied on during their former everyday lives had disappeared altogether, never to start up again, yet the Vegas casinos, although somewhat scaled down, had reopened and were dealing cards within months of the terrible conflagration. *A telling comment on the state of the world,* he thought

Matthew found it odd, broadcasting these days out of a casino theater surrounded by vice, but he had been drawn to Vegas for that very reason. Why go fishing in sand dunes? It made more sense to go where the fish were. Besides, fact was, even before the disaster the city of Las Vegas had more churches per capita than any other city in the United States, so finding an appropriate location had been an easy task. He'd started in a sizable building in the northwest part of town, called Canyon Ridge Christian Church. He selected it partially because it didn't look like a traditional church. Not that he had anything against stained-glass windows and pulpits, but he was trying to reach the masses. He didn't want preconceived prejudices against any particular religion to stand in his way. Plus, being inconspicuous was highly desirable and that building, on the outside anyway, looked more like a brown warehouse than a church. Within months, however, he'd outgrown the building's capacity of twelve hundred, even with four daily services, so he'd searched for a bigger venue. The huge showroom at one of the abandon, damaged casinos had fit the bill perfectly. With a capacity of 6000, only two services were now needed.

Working out of this space had the added bonus of throwing the world government authorities off his scent. If discovered, they would be shut down as "revolutionaries" in a New York minute. Matthew both resented and regretted having to hide, and found himself balancing on a razor's edge as he attempted to keep himself and the message available to all, yet avoid being silenced by the powers that be. The casino showroom had been an inspiration. For the past month they'd managed to stay in a single location–the longest they'd ever gone without having to pack up in the middle of the night and slip away after a tip that a raid was imminent. Apparently, so far, nobody had thought of searching for a religious service on the Vegas strip.

"Excuse me."

Matthew spun around, startled by the voice behind him. A dark-haired man with a dirty face had stepped out of the shadows of the parking lot's third level.

"Reverend, my wife has been hurt, could you help us?"

Matthew relaxed, then was filled with concern. "Of course."

The man quickly led him around an old RV parked in the corner. "We were coming out of the service when some hooligans jumped us."

As Matthew rounded the end of the large vehicle, he saw a blond woman lying on the ground, moaning. He quickly went to her and knelt down. Suddenly there was a blur of movement and Matthew felt a fist slam into his face. He staggered backwards, stunned, unsure what had just happened. The woman rose to her full height and tossed aside the blond wig, not a woman at all, but a thin, wiry man.

The man looked at his partner. "Hooligans?"

The first man shrugged and laughed, as a third man stepped out from behind an overflowing, putrid trash dumpster. Matthew opened his mouth to speak and the man kicked him in the stomach. Unprepared for the blow, the air exploded out of him, and he dropped to his knees, unable to breathe. He saw the second kick coming at his face and tried to block it with his forearms but the blow rocked him and he fell over onto his shoulder, his cheek impacting hard against the cold cement. He saw blood dripping and realized his nose was bleeding. Rolling into a fetal position, he managed to get enough breath to rasp out, "I have nothing of value."

The voice that answered was colder and harder than the cement. "We ain't lookin' to steal, Liar Man."

Matthew heard the smooth snik of a switchblade knife opening. The other two men grabbed him by the arms and dragged him to his feet. He felt an overwhelming sadness. He looked at them through blurry, swimming vision. "If you do this," he said sincerely, "you will surely go to hell."

The misguided souls simply broke into grins. The leader raised his knife and stepped forward.

"Too late..." said a deep, growling voice from the rear of the RV. A huge African-American man stepped out of the mobile home, his eyes as black as coals. "Hell just came to them."

There was a moment seemingly frozen in time as all the men sized up the situation. Then the newcomer struck. Matthew barely saw the man move, but suddenly the hood with the knife flew into the side of the dumpster with a solid crash, slumping to the floor, senseless. Facing their attacker, the two men released their grip on Matthew, who slid to the floor, his legs unable to hold him. The black man moved like a tornado. One of Matthew's captors swung a ham-like fist, but his target had vanished and was suddenly standing behind him. There was an unpleasant crunch and the thug started screaming in agony, staring down at his leg which was now bending the wrong direction at the knee. There was a whirl of movement, a wet thud, and the screaming abruptly stopped. The third hoodlum snatched at his jacket pocket, producing a small black pistol. The black man spun, like a cyclone, whirling around the gunman's body, capturing his wrist in an iron grip as he went. He kept turning, passing behind the attacker, jerking the other man around in a tight circle. As the man with the gun swung around, Matthew's defender suddenly reversed his own path, twisting the wrist inward and down. The man's body going one way, his gun hand, wrist and forearm, the other, his arm broke with a loud snap and his feet flew out from under him. He landed on his back with a bone-jarring crunch. Matthew's deliverer was now in possession of the gun. The man on the ground made an attempt to rise, but the speedy giant struck like a rattle snake, slamming the man in the forehead with the heel of his hand. The blow propelled his head backwards, where it hit the cement with a solid thud. His body went limp and he lay still.

Matthew started to rise when the man against the dumpster threw a knife which spun end over end toward him. There was no time to react and the knife buried itself in his chest with a thunk. He fell backwards with a surprised cry, landing hard on the cement again. "No!" shouted the black man in a fury, swinging toward the attacker and cocking the gun in one smooth, deadly motion.

"No!" cried Matthew. "Don't!"

The man with the gun, hesitated, quivering with barely checked rage.

Matthew looked down at himself and pulled the knife free. There was no pain, no blood. "That is not the way, brother," he implored. "Look, I am unharmed! I'm okay! See?" He spread his arms to show. For a moment he feared the man would pull the trigger anyway. "Dear God," he hastily prayed aloud, "We ask Your forgiveness for these men, for they know not what they do. I thank you for allowing no harm to come to me and pray you afford my attacker the same favor in spite of his transgressions."

The murderous look in the giant's eyes flickered, and he glanced over at Matthew, hesitantly. Matthew gazed back at him, silently pleading, hoping that his vocal prayer held meaning for this man. Against the dumpster, the knife-thrower stood frozen, like a soldier caught in the headlights of an enemy tank, his face dripping sweat and his breath coming in ragged gasps. Abruptly the large man uncocked the gun and flipped it end-for-end, catching the barrel in his massive fist and holding the grip of the pistol out to the man with the knife. The hoodlum stared, unable to comprehend the offer for a moment, then grinned wolfishly and grabbed for the gun. Again, the black man struck so fast that Matthew almost missed the action. With a blur of movement, the hood's head snapped back and he slumped to the ground, unconscious.

The giant rescuer spoke hoarsely, fear showing in his eyes for the first time. “Are you really okay?”

With a shaky smile, Matthew reached into his inside coat pocket and took out the Bible that he had placed there. Almost three-quarters of the pages were pierced where the blade tip had buried itself in them. “Yeah. Look.” He held out the book and let out a relieved laugh. “I’m fine, praise the Lord.”

The stranger nodded and mumbled, “Praise the Lord.” He made some quick movements and the gun he was holding seemed to disassemble itself in his hands. With an angry grunt, he threw each piece a different direction then, without a word, picked up the three unconscious men one at a time and unceremoniously threw them into the reeking garbage dumpster.

“Thank you,” said Matthew, still sitting on the cement floor, stunned by it all.

The man approached until he was towering over Matthew, and held out a massive paw. Matthew took it and felt himself being lifted to his feet as if he weighed nothing. Without letting go of his hand, the man said, in a surprisingly gentle voice. “Stan Washington.”

“Matthew Richards.”

The large man smiled. “I know.”

Together, they walked down the steps, out of the parking garage, into the garish brightness of the Las Vegas strip.

They walked in silence for a period, both lost in their own thoughts. Matthew waited patiently, figuring that his companion would talk when he was ready.

It didn’t take long.

“I was at your service, Reverend. I’ve been following you for quite some time now.”

“I thought you looked familiar.”

“I saw those three men come into the meeting tonight. There was something about them. They slipped in after it had started, sat alone in the back, never spoke to anyone else. They didn’t belong, ya know? I mean, I’ve seen people wander in and wander out, and I’ve seen folks hear the word and ignore it, but these men had a different agenda. They kept eyeing the television crew, watching the exits, examining the crowd, but never seemed to be listening to the message. As they left the building, I followed. When they hung out near the exit, I figured out they were up to no good, so I hid in that old, RV and watched.”

“I’m grateful. You were very... efficient.”

“Special Forces training. Navy SEAL. When I got married my wife wanted me to go civilian. She said we shouldn’t bring a child into that kind of life. I figured she was right. She was always a lot smarter than I was." He paused, gathering his thoughts. "Once I was out of the military I realized that I was only trained for one thing, didn't know much else, so I taught martial arts." The man shrugged his massive shoulders with a small smile. "I guess it's a good thing I kept training."

Matthew returned the smile. "God works in mysterious ways."

Stan shook his head sadly, a note of bitterness creeping into his voice. "He took my family from me, Reverend. My wife, my precious baby."

Matthew had heard this story time and time again in the past few years. "Your wife believed in God."

"Yeah. She tried to get me to listen, but I was too damn stubborn. By the time I realized she was right..." His voice choked up and he stopped walking, staring at the ground.

Matthew stopped and faced the big man. "You must believe you'll see her again, Stan. We've all been given a second chance."

"I don't get it though, Reverend, a man like you–"

"I was no different, my friend, believe me," said Matthew. He sighed, his mind returning to the past. Perhaps if he shared his story, it would help this man understand.

"I wasn't always the person you see before you, Stan. My journey started when I was eleven years old. My mother..." he took a breath, amazed at how difficult it was to tell it, even now. "There was a... drunk driver. He drifted over to the wrong side of the road and hit my mom head on. This was before airbags were popular. She hit the steering wheel, went through the windshield... snapped her spine." He paused, reliving the anguish he'd felt upon hearing the news. "There was nothing the doctors could do. She was paralyzed from the neck down. She... she never rallied like you hear some people do. She never even tried." Again, he trailed off, surprised by the bitterness he still felt. He shut his eyes and quickly asked God's forgiveness for that. A moment later he went on with the story, telling it as quickly as he could. "After the accident, she didn't do much except watch TV all day. Soaps, game shows, talk shows, court shows, the shopping network... and then she discovered religious shows. You know the ones: Las Vegas-style productions with full orchestras, pearlescent-robed choirs, special effects, and white-haired, pompadored, southern-accented, holy rollers." He paused a moment. The words, the memories of himself they conjured, made his heart ache. "She loved those shows. She was hoping for a miracle, I guess..."

He thought back, remembering her laying in her bed day after day, hair unwashed, smelling sour, enamored with some Bible-thumping fool strutting around on a million-dollar stage like a Mick Jagger of the Born-Again

Crowd. He had felt such contempt. "I didn't get it, Stan. How could she have faith in God after what happened to her? It just didn't make sense. I could not, for the life of me, understand." He felt the bitterness rise in him. "Neither, apparently, did my dad. One day he just... left."

"I'm sorry," said Stan, lowly.

Matt told about the day everything had changed. A bird had flown into his mother's bedroom window with a solid thunk, leaving a powdery wing mark on the glass. His mother had completely freaked out and screamed for him to run outside and check on the creature.

"The bird was dead, Stan, but I couldn't tell her that. Emotionally, my mom was a mess, the slightest little thing could set her off. She'd fly into a rage, or hysterical laughter, or a fit of tears and depression. I knew that if I told her that bird was dead I was risking a reaction that would be all out of proportion." He sighed. "So I went back upstairs and told her that it was only a broken wing and that I would take it to the vet to get fixed. You wouldn't believe her response. Hysterical tears of relief. You'd have thought I'd told her of some miracle cure for her paralysis or something."

A grizzled man with dark eyes suddenly lurched out of the shadows, grabbing Matthew by the shoulders. Stan tensed, but Matt stopped him with a gesture, recognizing the newcomer's face from attendance at several of his services.

"Reverend, I'm a believer, Reverend, but I got no money. I got no food. Without the mark..."

"I know my friend, it's the same for all of us. Go to the old Lucky Dice Hotel. Tell them I sent you. They'll take care of you."

"God bless ya, Reverend!"

"And you, too."

He watched the man hurried away into the darkness.

"How do you do it?" asked Stan.

"Do what?"

"Feed those people. Most of your followers aren't registered."

"That's true, but some got the mark before they saw the light. They help us out as best they can, for small, specialized purchases here and there. As for the rest of it, God provides. Have you any idea how big the drug industry was? The marijuana fields in Northern California, among others? Many of those people are now with the movement. They no longer grow mind-altering crops, but vegetables, fruits and grains. And they had a covert distribution system already in place."

"Christians?" asked the big man, incredulously.

Matthew smiled. "Some. Others are just plain anti-establishment and hate the idea of big brother watching over us all. Anything they can do to stick it to the authorities!"

Stan grinned and nodded. "God provides." He grew serious. "So, go on with your story. Please."

Matthew's thoughts returned to his childhood. This was the first time he had ever shared his full history with anyone and he was unprepared for the strong emotions and memories the recollections evoked. "That bird, Stan," he continued, "that bird became a third member of our family. Every day I had to give reports on how it was doing. How the vet was working gratis because it was the "Christian" thing to do and how, no, my mom shouldn't call to thank him because he had said he had thanks enough by doing the Lord's work. How the bird grew stronger and stronger until one day, weeks later, the tape binding the injured wing was removed and I gently carried it out of the vet's office to a nearby park–"

"Wait a moment," said the other man, looking confused. "I thought the bird was dead."

"It was, Stan," he said. "This was all fantasy. I made it up as I went along. Sitting on the edge of my mother's bed, describing how worried I was that the poor thing might not be able to fly but what a heartwarming sight it had been to see it winging toward the sun in full glorious flight... and so on." He felt himself flush with shame.

"As the spring came and went I told her about the bird's entire life: how it met a mate and the two of them flitted happily about, how they'd made a nest in low branches of a leafy apple tree, how I climbed the tree a month later to discover three tiny light blue eggs, how the eggs hatched one day." He shook his head. "I even described the tiny hairless chicks with huge heads, you know? How they grew and soft brown feathers formed, how she nudged them out of the nest until they learned to fly on their own. And of course the next year, they were back. And the year after that." He stopped and faced the big man. "And you know what, Stan? I discovered that I was really, really good at it! I was a natural, improvisational actor. I was a brilliant story-teller. I could make her believe! You see, Stan, that bird showed me a lot about myself and about people. My mom didn't need the truth, she needed to hear that the bird had survived happily in a way that she couldn't; that it was leading a full and satisfying life even if she never could. To me, the lesson was obvious: people didn't need reality, reality sucked! What they needed were illusions of hope!"

"Reverend–"

"I know, I know, Stan," he said, softening, letting him know that he realized the insanity of it, "but at the time I really believed that." He gave a bitter laugh. "And having seen my mom's evangelism shows–having been forced to sit beside her hour after hour–I knew exactly how to feed people their illusions. So I dyed a white streak in my hair, bought a light-up coat, and created Matthew Miracle–preacher and gold mine extraordinaire!"

Washington stared down at him, focusing on his white-streaked hair and beard. "That isn't natural?"

Matthew couldn't help but smile as he touched his hair with wonder. "It wasn't, Stan, but I haven't touched it up in years." He remembered his astonishment at finding that, even after he quit coloring it, the white streak remained, growing in naturally with the rest of his hair. "Think God is trying to tell me something?"

Stan seemed to be having a hard time grasping the story. "I don't get it. You're saying you were a..."

"Fake is the word you're looking for, Stan."

"But you knew the Bible!"

Matthew nodded. "Ohhh, yeah, like an actor with a script, I studied it 'religiously.' Hey, I also studied the Koran, the Bhagavad Gita, and the Book of Mormon. I was an equal opportunity con man, I'd take money from anybody." He grew serious. "But knowing and believing are far from the same, my friend. I never personally believed. Until that day in the tent. When it happened."

"What happened?"

Matthew related the shock he felt upon opening his eyes and finding himself alone in the revival tent, his congregation having vanished. "They called to Him and God answered, Stan. At that moment, for the first time in my life, I understood the truth and I knew that I had been so, so wrong."

Stan reached into his tattered coat and pulled out a worn piece of paper. He silently offered it to Matthew. The preacher took it: a 5x7 photograph of a beautiful woman with cafe-o-lait skin, and an adorable little girl with laughing eyes. He looked up in time to see the big man wipe away tears.

"They were my whole world, Reverend."

The pain in his voice broke Matthew's heart. He put an arm up and around the massive shoulders as best he could, and the two men continued walking through the ruined city in silence.

Chapter 16

With a low rumble, a massive corrugated steel door slid open, spilling bright light into a dark, empty warehouse. Gideon led the way inside, followed by Derek Steele, Mister Tanaka, Lucretia Baylock, and four Arab soldiers–the group's personal elite guards. Jordan Masters took up the rear pausing to study the exterior of the dilapidated building and wondering impatiently why Gideon had dragged them out into the middle of the Iranian desert to see such a run-down facility.

He picked his way cautiously across the cracked and stained cement floor, letting his eyes adjust to the darkness. Through high, wired windows, dim beams of light dancing with swirling dust motes provided the only illumination. "What is this place?" he inquired, "And why are we here?" As usual, Gideon had been his uncommunicative self, providing no answers during their newest expedition.

The alien crossed the hanger-like room to a door made of old wooden planks and pried one of them loose. He pulled one aside. Behind it, to Master's surprise, was an electronic keypad lock. As Gideon punched in a code, responding tones echoed faintly through the cavernous room. With a hiss of compressed air, the door slid smoothly aside, revealing the interior of an industrial-sized stainless-steel elevator. Jordan exchanged glances with Lucretia, whose eyes shimmered with expectation. The rest of the group seemed more curious than wary as Gideon led the way inside.

After the eight of them followed, Gideon pushed a button, the door whispered shut, and the unit slowly descended. In twenty seconds, it glided to a stop and the doors opened.

Jordan stepped out of the elevator, but the sight that greeted him brought him to a halt. They were in a huge underground laboratory, surrounded by stainless-steel fixtures, air filtration systems, glass partitions, and state-of-the-art pre-holocaust equipment.

"What the...?"

"It's a chemical plant," said Mister Tanaka, with wonder. "Abandoned but apparently still in pretty good shape."

"Completely operational," said Gideon.

"I don't get it," said Masters, impatient to get on with it.

"Rebuilding a nuclear arsenal would be futile," said the alien, walking further into the lab, "No doubt my species would detect and neutralize them, just as before. However, non-radiation devices are not so easily discovered. With my help, a chemical weapon could be manufactured that would not affect humans, but would be lethal to my kind."

An uncomfortable feeling crept over Jordan. "Why would we need to do that?"

Gideon faced the group, solemnly. "Because, my friends, The One have sent another ship."

Deep in the city of Istanbul, a worship service in a damaged, abandoned mosque had just concluded. The domed building was lit only by candles throwing dancing shadows across the walls, making the scattered, gold tiles flicker like stars. The windows, once breathtaking works of stained-glass art, were blacked out with thick tapestries.

Since the attempt on his life in Las Vegas, Matthew had not only left the city, but the country as well. In an effort to be closer to the arch-enemy, the Revered Leader of the United World Coalition, Jordan Masters, he had moved his operation to the far side of the planet. The danger in this location was greater and it was immensely difficult working in a foreign society, but he had faith that God would protect them as He had done for so long.

In spite of Matthew's reassurances, Stan Washington had insisted on accompanying him, taking up an unofficial, self-appointed duty as Matthew's "guardian angel." It was a position he felt he had been born for. Everything in his life, his imposing physical presence, his intensive training, and his new-found beliefs had brought him to this place. Each and every day he studied the Bible with his friend, and found his own outlook on the world to be continuously evolving. It was almost as if the Bible was a mystical book– but not in the usual way. Like, it had magical properties that only revealed its message to those with open minds and hearts. Stan had attempted to read the Gospels before, staring at the strange indecipherable phrases couched in obscure language. But once he opened his heart to God, the meaning of it all had filtered through to him. The teachings began to fulfill him in ways he could never have anticipated. It was a truly supernatural odyssey that he was honored and proud to experience.

They had been in Turkey for only a week, but already the group of followers had grown to over two hundred souls. It amazed Stan, considering that they had arrived in the country with only a small core group of twelve. Many of their new congregation had only a rudimentary command of English, yet they seemed to understand what their guru was teaching. Another testament to the power of the word.

He leaned against a tall, marble column, listening to the group nearest him as they exchanged thoughts on Matthew's most recent talk, to which they had just listened. "Jordan Masters was an adopted child," the pastor had said. "No one knows his origin. The child just appeared at a most convenient time and was immediately adopted into what was to be one of the most influential families in world. Whose child is he really?" Stan pondered the question. Was Masters the devil's son, or just some poor jerk being played for a patsy? He had done so much good for the world right after the Great Cataclysm, bringing the human race in its agony together as never before, but although he had been a kind, loving suitor and an attentive fiancé prior to consummating the marriage, would he turn into a violent, abusive husband? Was his benevolence real or just a tool to manipulate those who could propel him into a position of unstoppable power?

Stan's thoughts were interrupted when Matthew led a large muscular man across the floor to meet him. The man was nearly as tall as Stan, with a weight-lifter's body, square jaw, and eyes the color of blue glacier ice. Hair blond and close-cropped, unshaved, moving like a jungle cat–the man immediately reminded Stan of the sergeant who had headed up his SEAL training, but this man didn't seem nearly as hostile as his old Sarge. In fact, he seemed a bit beaten down.

Stan introduced the newcomer. "Stan, I'd like you to meet Vladimir Koskov. He was stationed nearby with the Russian Army before the Change, and stayed on in the area. Vladimir, meet Stan Washington."

The two men sized each other up. In a different time–in the world as it had been–they would only be looking at each other over the barrel of a rifle, in battle. This day, however, Stan could smile and hold out his hand. "Nice to meet you, Vladimir."

"Call me Vlad, please," the Russian said, in heavily accented English. The dry, powerful grip was accompanied by a gap-toothed smile. Some good things did come out of all of this mess.

"Vlad has some questions. Luckily, he knows our language pretty well," said Matthew.

"Uh huh. Questions about what?"

"About being a Christian. The Bible. God," said the Russian.

Stan was taken aback. "Whoa," he said, holding up his hands in a "stop" motion, "I'm not the one to talk to. Matthew is–"

"You're exactly the one to talk to," interrupted Matthew.

"But I don't know–"

"You know what's in your heart, Stan." He pointed to the banner which hung on the wall. *Witness. Understand. Believe. Everything depends on it.* "That word witness doesn't just mean stand by and watch, you know."

"Yeah, but–"

"Vladimir and you are alike in very many ways. I think you could help him more than I could." He turned and walked away, a smile on his face.

Stan watched him go, then turned to the big white man. They stared at each other for an awkward moment.

"Outflanked," said the Russian.

That made Stan laugh. "Yeah." He shoved his fists in his pockets. "Truth is, Vlad, I'm kinda new to all this myself."

"You were a soldier, too," stated the man, studying him with a professional eye.

"Yes. Navy SEAL."

The other man nodded. "Good training."

"The best."

"Second best."

"Oh?"

"SPETSNAZ."

"Ah, figures." The SPETNAZ was the Russian equivalent of the SEALs. "How long?"

"Eight years."

"Long time."

The man shrugged, then grinned. "I like to blow things up."

Stan burst into laughter.

"How long for you?" asked Vladimir.

"I quit after four."

"Why?" He pronounced it "vye."

Stan felt his throat tighten. "My daughter was born." He told the other soldier a little about how Brenda had urged him to resign, how it turned out to be a good thing he did because he was then available to help out with Katie's special needs. They talked a bit about family. Vlad was unmarried and his parents had both passed on which is why he had remained in Turkey after the Cataclysm. Having no one to go home to, he hung around, living hand to mouth, studying English and Turkish to keep his mind occupied. Cautiously Stan mentioned Brenda's religious beliefs, and how he had scorned them.

"And yet, now you believe these things?" asked the Russian.

"Yes, I do," answered Stan, proud of the way it felt to affirm his new outlook so positively.

"I have trouble with it," said Vlad, with a shrug of his rock-like shoulders.

"With what?"

"With God. With Jesus Christ. With the Bible. Religion. You know, with all of it."

"Ooookay."

"How did you get there?" asked Vlad, abruptly.

"Hoo boy." Stan scratched his head. "Man, that's a complex question!" He thought about it, not quite sure himself. "I guess," he started, hesitantly, "I decided to walk the walk."

"Walk the walk?"

"Walk in Jesus' footsteps." He looked at the other man's puzzled expression. "Okay. okay, let me back up. Like I said, I'm not very good at this. Have a seat." He sat on the floor, cross-legged. The other man settled down, too, folding his body like a Swiss Army knife. Stan ran a hand over his head, trying to get his brain working. "Let me start at the beginning. Question one, from me to you. Do you believe in God?"

The soldier shook his head, seriously. "I don't know." His eyes glazed over a bit, focusing far away. "I've seen so many... things."

"Yeah," Stan murmured, as some atrocities he'd witnessed flashed through his own mind's eye, "I can relate." He tried a different approach. "Okay, uh, do you believe in Jesus? I mean, it's pretty obvious he existed, right?"

"Maybe. Some say he was the son of God, but many say no. Maybe he was, maybe he wasn't."

"Okay," said Stan, conceding that point for now, "But even if he wasn't, he was a great teacher, right?"

"If he existed at all. I found out my mother believed it, in spite of government forbidding it, because I discovered an old Orthodox icon and prayer book hidden under her bed clothes after she died. But she didn't tell me. I think she was protecting me. So I grew up ignorant with a very bad attitude toward people who had religious beliefs."

Stan couldn't help but grin.

Vladimir frowned. "What is funny."

"You." Stan held up his hand before the man could take offense. "And me. We are so much alike, it's scary. And it's becoming very clear why Matthew introduced you to me." He watched the shadows dancing across the floor. "All right, my friend, I'm going to tell you how I came to be a believer. I started with Jesus, and the lessons he taught. No..." He paused, regrouping his thoughts. Finally, he looked up, meeting the other man's patient gaze. "Did I believe in God? No, not really. Was Jesus the Son of God? Not necessarily, no. Did Jesus ever exist at all? I wasn't even sure of that! For all I knew, some writers made him up. Maybe he was a compilation of a number of teachers. Maybe he was just a smart guy with some radical ideas. Maybe all the miracles he did were exaggerations or misinterpretations of what really happened or just plain stories invented by the early church authorities to make him seem more magical or mystical or something and build up their following."

"I have wondered these things."

Stan nodded, then leaned forward to emphasize his next point. "But, for me, none of that mattered."

"Why?"

"Because even if I was foolish enough to ignore all the evidence that he did exist I couldn't ignore the fact that the *teachings* that are attributed to him exist. There is no doubt of that."

"I'm not sure I follow."

"I'm a fact guy. I like them hard and clear. So even if I'm not sure God exists, or that Jesus was the "Son of God," or even that Jesus walked this earth, I cannot argue that there are no lessons that Jesus gets credit for. There are, of course, many. That's an inarguable fact. Right?"

The other man nodded. "Da."

"Okay then. Step two. Are you familiar with those teachings?"

"A bit."

"Good, same as me, at that time–a little bit. So I asked myself: if I, personally, lived my life following those teachings, would I be a better person? The answer was–"

"Yes."

"You bet your babushka, yes! Absolutely, yes. And, if *everybody* lived their lives following those teachings, how could we go wrong? Would the world be a better place?"

Vladimir nodded seriously. "Da."

"It sure would, my friend. It would make all the difference. So, to follow the examples of Jesus Christ makes sense, doesn't it?"

"Da."

"Exactly the conclusion I came to."

Vladimir looked back at him, thoughtfully. "And that is all there is to it?"

Stan grinned. "Naw, not even close. But it's a start. The rest, I truly believe, you'll have to discover for yourself."

Vlad started to retort, but was cut off by a loud commotion at the front entrance to the mosque. The door was kicked open and three Arab soldiers shoved their way in, shouting, brandishing weapons and pushing a bloody man before them. Stan spun around and saw the guard he had posted outside collapse on the floor, breathing raggedly and moaning, clearly in pain. The soldiers were wearing the red uniform of the United Coalition Army, but the long cloths of their Ghutrah headgear was wrapped around their faces, as if prepared for a sand storm, revealing only their eyes.

Stan leaped to his feet, but froze as one of the soldiers fired a blast into the air with an Uzi. "Nobody move!" cried the man, in English colored by a thick Arab accent. He walked slowly into the room, eyes suspiciously scanning the frightened worshippers. "This is an illegal gathering. You have all been found guilty of dissension against the harmony of mankind. The punishment is death." With no more of a warning, he swung his weapon toward Matthew and fired, point blank. Matthew was blasted backwards off his feet. Stan, in utter horror, screamed, "Noooo!" drawing out the word in anguish. The other soldiers cocked their automatic weapons and swung them toward the crowd. Stan was about to rush them, damn the consequences, when an authoritative voice shouted from the rear. "Wait!"

The soldiers hesitated uncertainly, as a tall man stepped forward, throwing back the hood of his burnoose to reveal raven black hair cut in a military flattop. In American English, he asserted, "I am not here to worship with these dogs. I am a spy, an undercover agent sent by Masters himself!"

The team leader looked at him long and hard, then scanned the rest of the crowd. "Are there any others here who will denounce this congregation?" He repeated the question in Turkish. Then in Arabic.

Two other people, one male and one female, hurried forward, badly frightened. "Mercy, please," the woman screamed in Turkish, "We are not with them! We're on your side!"

Then a small man in a filthy turban scuttled forward on his knees, hands clasped in front of him. "Me too! Oh, Allah, spare us, I beg you."

The head soldier considered the four people through hard, slitted eyes. Finally, he nodded. "Go then! Get out and never speak of what is about to happen here."

The tall man strode out the door anxiously followed by the others. One of the three soldiers shut the door firmly and stood in front of it. The leader turned back to the group of gathered worshippers. "So you are all willing to die for your beliefs?" he sneered.

Stan stepped forward, his eyes hard and unwavering. "We are."

As the spies ran from the mosque, they heard the sound of automatic weapons fire and screams. Derek Steele paused, looking back. He had not, in fact, been sent by Masters. He had infiltrated the new group of heathens on his own initiative and had been planning to gain favor by bringing the information to his boss. A smile of cruel satisfaction crossed his face as he hurried into the night. Once again, Masters had been a step ahead. Excellent.

Inside the mosque, the Arab soldiers finished spraying the shrieking crowd with bullets.

Stan stared down at himself, then over at Vladimir, in shock. They were unharmed. He looked up at the others. It seemed no one had been killed or even injured. Was it a miracle? Had God's hand stopped the bullets?

The leader lowered his weapon and turned to Stan. "It is good that you would die for your beliefs," he said, "Because we do not wish to worship with non-believers."

To Stan's utter astonishment, Matthew rose up from the floor. The preacher went up to the enemy soldier, facing him with a smile. "Ahmad, my friend."

The lead soldier unwrapped his face covering, revealing a swarthy-skinned man. He grinned, revealing yellow teeth. "Matthew!"

The two men embraced. Ahmad turned to the stunned congregation. "I apologize for the dramatics, my friends, but we had suspicions that this gathering was being infiltrated. I doubt those spies will return."

Stan stared at the guns, comprehension dawning. "Blanks?" He and Vlad exchanged stunned glances.

"Indeed," said the soldier. He sent a man outside to make sure the spies were gone, and explained to the crowd in Turkish what was going on.

Matthew approached Stan, looking ashamed, speaking in a low tone. "Stan, I'm sorry, I apologize for not warning you about this, my loyal friend, but–"

Stan held up a hand, cutting him off. He fully understood that part of the test had been for him. He took no offense, in fact, would have insisted on it had the roles been reversed. "No need, Matthew." He confronted the Arab. "And who are you, if I may ask?"

"This is Ahmad Ahwadi," said Matthew, putting his arm around the man, "a good man who used to laugh but no longer does."

Stan nodded, seeing his own pain mirrored in the soldier's eyes. "I understand." They embraced, in brotherhood.

Ahmad's fellow soldiers unwrapped their faces as other members of the congregation stepped forward to welcome them. After the introductions were complete, Ahmad addressed Matthew somberly, concern etched deep in his face. "I am afraid, Matthew, that I bring very, very bad news."

Chapter 17

Midnight.

A middle-aged soldier leaned his rifle against the corrugated steel wall and nervously rolled a hand-made cigarette. Packaged cigarettes were extremely expensive because only one company continued to manufacture them, and it was half-a-world away in the southern region of the United States. The tobacco he was using wasn't even real. It was an unsatisfactory mixture of other leaves and herbs, but it did have a redeeming feature–a pleasant touch of hashish. Of course, if he got caught smoking it he was in big trouble, but there was no one to be accountable to out here in this God-forsaken desert outpost except the other guards. If they noticed, the worst that would happen is they would demand some of his potent mixture for themselves in return for keeping silent. He tucked the dry paper between his lips, fished a thick wooden match out of his shirt pocket and struck it on the rusty hinge of a door.

"Don't you know, smoking is bad for you?" asked a soft, low voice from behind him.

The soldier didn't understand the language, but he knew he'd made a terrible mistake. He dove for the rifle, but his world was reduced abruptly to darkness.

Stan caught the unconscious man before he hit the ground. That was number three, the last of them. He flashed a small penlight three times. A dozen other men, all armed and dressed head-to-toe in black, wearing masks, appeared over a sand dune and silently rushed the building. Stan yanked open the door and the soldiers burst inside, brandishing weapons with sound-suppressers. The small group of workers inside, dressed in gray jumpsuits, were caught off-guard and quickly subdued.

The gigantic warehouse was just as Ahmad had described it, except that now the interior was piled high with large metal barrels. Stan stared at the black, yellow and red labels on the canisters. "Dear God," he said, in a choked voice. The logo on the barrels was a human skull with lion's teeth and long, flowing hair, wearing a gold crown. Beneath it read: APOLLYON.

"Apollyon," whispered Ahmad. "Destroyer."

"Somebody grab an empty one of those barrels," ordered Stan. "The world needs to see this."

One of the soldiers obeyed as Stan followed Ahmad to the false door and opened it, revealing the security access panel.

"Are you sure you know the correct sequence?"

Ahmad nodded. "I paid very close attention both times we visited here. Of course, there is always the possibility that they changed it."

Stan felt his stomach clench as Ahmad punched in a sequence of numbers. The panel beeped twice and the elevator door opened. Relieved, Stan herded his small task force inside. As they descended, he silently prayed for the success of their mission. So far, no one had been killed. He wanted to keep it that way.

The elevator door opened and they streamed into the underground laboratory, at this moment in full operation. Aiming their weapons at equipment, not people, they opened fire, badly frightening the dozens of workers in white biohazard suits who had, moments before, been busily absorbed in their work. A small, portly man with a thick mustache stepped forward, shouting in Arabic. Stan couldn't understand a word he said, but it appeared his name was Riza Kumir, and he was the one in charge. "We don't want anybody hurt!" Stan barked. "Get your people out now!

The Manager stared at him, perhaps surprised to hear English.

Ahmad stepped forward and raised his voice to the room, shouting in Arabic. Again, Stan couldn't understand what was being said, but he saw the reaction it caused. The workers all stared at Ahmad with abject disbelief. Ahmad shouted something else. Nobody moved, they just exchanged perplexed glances, then, in a cacophony of loud voices, began to argue with Ahmad and each other.

Impatiently, Stan removed his sound-suppresser from his weapon and fired a loud burst in the air, shattering acoustic ceiling tiles. Pieces rained down on Kumir, who covered his head and cried out in alarm.

A scientist in a small glassed-in chamber, startled by the sudden violence, backed into a rack of glass vials which fell to the floor and smashed on the tile. He stared at the tubes, his face a mask of horror, then broke and ran for the air-locked door. He never made it. His body suddenly jerked as if hit with an electric jolt. He stumbled and reeled, clutching his head and screaming. Suddenly, a circular sign in the same shape as Jordan Master's medallion appeared on his forehead, erupted and burst, spraying blood across the glass walls. Ugly festering boils broke out across his face and blood oozed from his nostrils, ears and tear ducts. He dropped to the floor writhing and screaming, then abruptly stopped moving or breathing.

Stan watched it all with repulsion.

Panic erupted as Kumir and his workers bolted, screaming, for the elevator.

Ahmad stepped up to the thick glass, peering in at the dead man. "Harmless to humans, huh?"

"Matthew was right."

Ahmad nodded solemnly.

The elevator doors closed and the facility's workers headed topside, escorted by several of Ahmad's loyal troops.

Stan turned to the soldier who was busily setting the timer on a high-tech bomb. "Ready, Vladimir?"

"Only a little more time..." said the Russian demolition expert. He set the timer, pushed a button then looked up and nodded. "T-minus 3 minutes."

Stan appraised the elevator doors, still closed. "Maybe we should have waited–" he started, but at that moment the elevator opened revealing a welcoming, empty interior. "Let's move!" he cried.

Ahmad shouted some orders in Arabic and the rest of the soldiers ran for the lift. Vlad squeezed in beside Stan, his cool blue eyes sparkling, a whisper of a smile on his lips.

By the time they reached the top, the old bus used to transport the facility's workers was rapidly jouncing down the pothole-riddled dirt road, away from the scene, gunned to the floor. Two Jeeps bounded over the surrounding dunes and skidded to a halt in front of the warehouse, picked up Stan and his men running to meet them, and roared away. Stan grabbed a transceiver and keyed it up as two armor-plated Commanche attack helicopters shot over the horizon. "All clear, Joshua!"

In the lead chopper, Matthew acknowledged the call. "Roger, Samson, see you back home! God speed." The ground location now secured, it was up to air support to finish the job. "Do it," he ordered the pilot.

A hard-looking man with a bullet-shaped, shaved head, grinned and swung the chopper around. A former arms dealer, Ivan Sergio had undergone an amazing conversion after seeing the abysmal destruction the earth had been subjected to in recent times, he had been instrumental in providing the military equipment for this raid. Gleefully, he broke into song. "Joshua fit the battle of Jericho, Jericho, Jericho, Joshua fit the battle of Jericho..." He thumbed up the safety cap and depressed the red trigger button, firing a Hellfire missile which laser-locked onto the target below. With a loud rush of heat and smoke the missile entered precisely into the hangar-like doorway to the secret desert facility. A tremendous concussion ripped through the warehouse, sending a boiling cloud of flame two hundred feet into the sky.

"And the walls come a-tumbling down!" sang Ivan, crowing at his accuracy.

Matthew looked down at the destruction, with awe. As he watched, the underground charge that Vlad had placed detonated. A circular section of earth some eighty feet in diameter lifted straight upwards, then the center erupted like a volcano, vomiting fire and smoke.

The aircraft, buffeted by the explosion, tilted wildly. With a cry, Ivan fought with the controls.

Matthew stared out the window, sickened by the fiery inferno burning deeply below and the plumes of black smoke, blocking the moonlight out of the sky. It was like looking down into the maw of hell and the glowing embers that swirled in the rotor wash were like millions of tiny, deadly demons winging forth into an unsuspecting world. Almost feverish with fear, he clutched his Bible tightly to his chest as its warnings and prophecies invaded his memory banks. The racket of the chopper's motor muffled his prayer, a cry that involuntarily fashioned itself into a long, horrified wail as he belatedly realized the implications of the destruction he and his followers had just perpetrated. "Dear God, forgive us. What have we done?"

Chapter 19

"Damn them to hell!" roared Masters.

Ahmad stood at attention in his official position just inside Jordan's palace office, undiluted apprehension tensing his every muscle. The world leader furiously faced a gathering of people: Lucretia Baylock and Derek Steele; Kumir, the chemical plant manager and Tanaka; Musa Hamadi, the Arabic President; and two others whose names Ahmad didn't know–a massively fat man who reminded Ahmad of Jabba the Hut from the early *Star Wars* films, and a pale, bespectacled German. Several more palace guards stood at attention with Ahmad at their usual stations.

"Whoever did this" growled Masters, "had to have inside information and the only people who knew about it are in this room!"

Ahmad swallowed thickly, trying desperately to control a nervous tic that had formed in his left eye. He understood that it was probably unnoticeable, but to him it felt like the entire left side of his face was contorting.

"What about the plant staff?" suggested Steele.

"They had no idea what they were working on," cried Kumir. "Except for a few key, highly-trusted scientists, all workers were told it was an agricultural insecticide. The leak did not come from inside."

"What about you?" said Steele, studying the man with cold eyes.

The man almost choked. "Me? How dare you! I was nearly killed! I had nothing to do with this calamity, you have my word on that!"

"Do we?" broke in Jordan, studying the sweating man. He speared him with his gaze like a bug pinned to a board, then abruptly broke away. "Well, I believe you."

The Manager began to breathe again.

Masters suddenly erupted into a shriek, "Because I know who our traitor is!" He tore open his shirt, displaying the disgusting amalgamation of melted skin and metal. "Do I have to remind you? I wear the medallion! I have the power! I know everything!"

Ahmad resolved that if he was going to die, he had to try to take the anti-Christ with him. He covertly slid his hand down and released the safety catch on his weapon. Jordan spun toward him, eyes blazing. "Take your finger from the trigger!"

Ahmad did as ordered, feeling as though his legs might collapse under him. The medallion began to pulse with light. Ahmad stared at it, frozen with terror.

"We will not need your weapon, my friend!" Abruptly, Masters pivoted, as the medallion's irised lens flew open. A blast of energy shot from it and burrowed into Derek Steele. His hair instantly burst into flame, the top of his head, eyebrows and chest flashing orange. He screamed in sheer agony as his skin melted, dripping off his face and body like wax. His eyeballs burst like boiled grapes and his quivering body crumpled to the floor. The whole thing was over in seconds.

"We will win this holy war!" screamed the man they'd made into a tyrant.

Ahmad could barely keep himself from fainting. The others all stared silently, appalled at the pulsating globule that only a moment ago had been a man. The smell of cooking fat filled the room, making him gag. He noticed, with a sickening feeling, that Baylock's eyes glowed only with excitement and approval.

Ahmad found himself filled with a deep, deep sorrow. Over the past seven years since he had been drafted into the Leader's personal elite guard the American had changed drastically. At first, Ahmad had been proud to serve. Everyone he knew thought that Masters was a truly inspired statesman, something like a savior, perhaps the greatest in all of history. But it hadn't taken him long to notice that Jordan was not actually making most of the decisions. The old man with the lumpy eyeballs and his entourage of international power figures were clearly manipulating Masters, sometimes subtly, sometimes with relentless insistence. Sex played a large role in the scheme of things as well, he was sure; the expert in that form of manipulation, of course, was that she-wolf of a woman who stuck to Masters like a tick on a dog. As time passed, Ahmad had with fear and dismay observed Masters metamorphosis from his earlier forceful, dynamic personality with great concern and compassion, to one of a power-mad, tunnel-visioned fanatic. The more Masters changed, the more deeply Ahmad's thoughts turned to his dear friend, Ibrahim Wazir.

The two of them had been traveling through the desert on assignment that day over six years ago when everything had changed. Best friends since they were young boys, Ibrahim always had a way of making Ahmad laugh, often at inappropriate moments. Ahmad's huge, boisterous guffaw had a tendency to turn heads, especially when he was around his friend who loved to tease him. He had been laughing that day. Ibrahim had just told him some outrageous joke and he had thrown back his head in uproarious joviality, wiping tears from his eyes. When he opened them, his friend was not there. He had vanished. Disappeared. In the middle of a flat stretch of desert, with nothing but sand for miles in all directions, his friend was suddenly gone?

How could that be?

Ahmad almost lost his sanity that day. He had searched like a madman, but had found nothing but Ibrahim's uniform, laying in a puddle in the sand. Then, just as he was about to go completely out of his mind, he saw something glint, half buried in the sand. He bent to pick it up, discovering a silver chain attached to a small silver cross. It flashed across his mind how Ibrahim had spoken often of a loving God and the prophet Jesus Christ and how his followers would be taken to heaven one day. Everyone else, said Ibrahim, would be left behind. He was so convinced of this that he had converted from Islam, and was now trying to get Ahmad to do the same. Ahmad had simply laughed off his friend's concern.

On that day, he had stopped laughing.

As he'd thought about Ibrahim, Ahmad had also thought about the men he worked for every day and wondered why–as powerful as they clearly were–they seemed to fear a seemingly inconsequential man, an American named Matthew Richards, and the message about Allah that he was spreading. Ahmad couldn't help but wonder if perhaps it was not the fear of revolution and unrest among the people that concerned them, but possibly something deeper and more significant.

So he'd begun to pay attention. During the many hours that he was responsible for Masters' safety, he not only guarded the man, but he studied him. He listened carefully to every word uttered, analyzed every decision made, trying to get into the leader's mind and understand his thought processes. On his own time, he secretly used the world-wide web to log onto the pirate Christian broadcasts. It hadn't taken long for him to draw his own conclusions. One truth led to another, and two years ago Ahmad had pulled his old, worn treasure box down from its hiding place in the top corner of his closet, taking from it the small, silver cross he'd found in the desert sand. He'd put the cross around his neck that night and changed his world view.

The horrifying act he had just witnessed was decisive. If any last, tiny grains of doubt had remained in Ahmad's mind, they were now banished forever. He shivered at the waves of coldness emanating from the murderous Masters. The leader of the world simply stepped over the bubbling corpse as if it were so much camel dung, leaving it there, perhaps as a frightening reminder to all present of the awesome power he held over them all.

Sitting at his desk, Masters folded his hands in front of him with eerie calmness. "So, Mister Tanaka, tell us. Where do we now stand?"

Tanaka, still staring ashen-faced at Steele's misshapen body, stepped forward, turned his back on it, and cleared his throat. "The fusion bomb used in the destruction of the plant had a most unpredictable effect," he said. "As you know the biological was designed to be harmless to humans, but we believe the radiation in the bomb caused it to mutate."

Ahmad knew this was a lie. He had seen first hand the results of exposure to the compound before any explosives had been set. Unfortunately, he could say nothing.

"Far from being destroyed, the resulting mutation spread with the ashes and fallout. The virus is extremely communicable. Within hours symptoms began showing up across a one-hundred kilometer radius. Within days, if it goes unchecked, it will spread globally."

Jordan looked stricken. "Can we stop it?"

Tanaka shook his head. "I fear not. And it gets worse."

He had everyone's undivided attention.

He spoke hesitantly, as if he, the messenger, would be killed for delivering the message. "The new disease seems to be affecting only people with a low-grade radiation level already in their systems."

Lucretia watched him like a cobra. "Just what are you saying?"

He pointed to his forehead. "I'm saying every person who is registered with The Masters System will be infected before the next full moon."

Lucretia grew agitated. "What exactly are these symptoms?"

"Blisters, boils, extreme sensitivity, thinning of blood vessels which will lead to frequent bruising and nosebleeds, excessive dryness of the skin. Not life threatening but ugly and painful."

Lucretia yanked back her sleeve, displaying a raw-looking ulcer on her wrist. She probed it, and it oozed a clear liquid. With a screech, she glared wildly at the men around her. "You stupid psychotics!" She turned and stormed from the room in obvious distress, side clipping Ahmad as she passed.

The tall German removed his thin wire-framed glasses, and spoke urgently in his thick accent. "We must keep this secret! If this is in any way connected with our System, people will hate us!"

Musa Hamadi, the Arab president, nodded his agreement. "They'll turn like an angry mob."

Jordan looked after Lucretia, coldly appraising the situation. "I concur. None of this information leaves the palace."

"There is a bright side," suggested Tanaka, quietly.

Everyone looked at him, questioningly.

"If nobody without the mark will be affected, it will soon be very easy to recognize our enemies."

Every man in the room slowly broke into shark-like smiles. Every man except Ahmad. It was good that his job required him to keep a straight face.

He knew, at that moment, that he was in deep, deep trouble.

The predictions were correct: it was a plague of biblical proportions. The highly communicable disease ran rampant, spreading across the globe in a matter of weeks. The symptoms were painful and ugly: boils, blisters, purple bruises on the face and body. Weakened blood vessels made nosebleeds as common as sneezing. Tissues swelled until people looked like over-stuffed sausages that often split the skin, now dry and brittle, under the stress. It wasn't unusual to see tears of blood running down a loved one's face. Those who had not practiced diligent dental care in the past found themselves spitting bloody teeth into their sinks or dinner dishes. Finger and toenails peeled up at the slightest force. Tongues often blackened and became swollen and dry, resembling a parrot's. Hair fell out in clumps so most people stopped shampooing altogether. Severely bloodshot eyes, looking more red than white, were the norm. Bodily discharges became highly acidic, so waste elimination became an agonizing experience every time. The all-around constant physical sensation was akin to a severe sunburn mixed with the sharp feeling of intense "pins and needles." In every person the symptoms varied somewhat, except in one detail: an early sign of the pestilence was always an eruption on the forehead. The invisible tattoos placed there during registration for The Masters Plan, became discernible in the most disgusting way: the skin blistered and broke into yellow, infected, distinctively swirled patterns. Even after healing, deep scars remained etched in the skin.

It was a living hell.

Ahmad abandoned the palace on the third night, when most of the staff had begun to show signs of the abomination. He had been standing at his usual post, when Lucretia, covered by festering sores, had become incensed at the sight of his unblemished skin. Flying into a rage she had attacked him, scratching at his face with claw-like fingernails, screaming, "What about you? Think you're special, little man? You'll get it too, then you'll see! You'll see!" Shouting obscenities, she'd stormed off, half mad, slamming her bedroom door with a banshee wail. That night, Ahmad had slipped out the barracks window and disappeared into the dark underworld of the suffering masses of New Babylon.

He was only one of many who had to hide or fight. Across the planet, those who did not wear the mark were unaffected by the plague, which only served to enrage those who suffered. For many it was flee or be killed by some pain-incensed lynch mob.

Many of the stricken tried to commit suicide. Miraculously, none succeeded, only bringing more suffering upon themselves.

"It is all part of God's plan," Matthew preached, to any and all who would listen. Most would not, cursing the name of the Lord.

Jordan Masters, seeking relief for the suffering, lifted all bans on narcotics and took steps to make them freely available all over the world. Marijuana and hashish were widely distributed. Cocaine was shipped in from South America by the ton. A huge variety of mind-altering pills could be purchased along with any Slushy at the local corner store. LSD and hallucinogenic mushrooms made a successful come-back, available in market places of any population center. Alcohol flowed by the millions of barrels. Even the more radical, expensive narcotics such as heroin and morphine could be bought over the counter at any pharmacy. Of course, none of these things were free. Billions in credits were used. The average person wiped out his or her savings.

After twenty weeks, the pestilence ultimately passed. Wet, cancerous-looking sores dried up and dead skin flaked away. Swollen glands returned to normal and bowels settled, allowing regular intake once again. Hair and fingernails began to grow back. Vision cleared. Bruises faded.

Millions, however, were now addicts–slaves to the drugs they had come to rely upon. Their dependence was abundantly clear in the hollow eyes, sunken cheeks and unhealing, crusty track marks along their veins.

On every sufferer of the plague, even those who made a complete and clean recovery, one sign remained: round swirls of thickened skin showing prominently on their foreheads, a scar in the familiar twisting pattern of the medallion given to Jordan Masters by the entity known as Gideon.

Chapter 20

"The disease lasted exactly five months," stressed Matthew Richards, "Five months!"

Cat Johnson turned to face him. They were meeting in her office at the network headquarters, an imposing suite on the fiftieth floor, with floor-to-ceiling windows that allowed an expansive view of New Chicago. The renegade preacher had been petitioning her for months for a meeting. She'd finally acquiesced, as much out of anger at Jordan Masters as for any other reason. "Can you get to the point, Reverend?"

"I quote." He opened a Bible.

Here it comes, thought Cat, with an inner sigh.

"A star fell from the sky and opened a bottomless pit." He looked up and described the attack on the chemical plant: the helicopter shooting a missile down at the ground, the destruction of the warehouse, and the subsequent underground explosion that opened what almost looked like the mouth to hell, as it billowed smoke.

"Reverend–" she started.

He quickly lifted the Bible and continued reading. *"And smoke rose as if from a big furnace... and locusts came down to the earth out of the smoke."* He looked up. "Helicopters. It's referring to helicopters."

"I don't know–"

Again, he interrupted, reading from the book. *"Their chests looked like iron breastplates and the sound of their wings was like many horses and chariots hurrying into battle."* He looked at her, pointedly. "Helicopters."

She blinked, a little surprised, mentally analyzing the analogy. It fit rather neatly.

Matthew continued to quote the scripture. *"To those not with God, they would cause the pain of a scorpion..."* he glanced up, "Meaning untold physical suffering," then finished the quote, *"for five months!"* He slammed the book shut and pounded it with his fist. "It's all there! Written two thousand years ago."

Cat studied him. "And the reason you're here, sir?"

"He must be stopped!" cried the preacher, "People will listen to you, Miss Johnson. You started this! You were there at the beginning."

The quotes from the Bible had an eerie, familiar quality to them, as if the author had, indeed, seen into the future. Cat, however, was unconvinced. "What about Gideon? What about The One?"

The long-haired man shook his head. "The Bible says–"

"The Bible was written by men, Reverend!" she snapped. "All the things described as 'acts of God' in those pages–everything that has happened in the past seven years–have perfectly scientific explanations! Nuclear detonations, chemical warfare, space ships, aliens, helicopters–you said so yourself! As I understand it, the Book of Revelation is based on the visions and dreams of prophets. Well, okay, if a primitive man saw those things he'd have no other explanation except God and angels and the devil! He'd have no other reference points. So even if I grant you that somebody, somewhere, once upon a time, did foresee these occurrences, their interpretation was clearly wrong!"

Matthew came at her and grabbed her shoulders in an iron grip. She almost cried out to security, but he merely spun her around to face a mirrored wall, pointing to the scar on her forehead. "What about that?"

"What about it?" she asked. "Due to the radiation used in The Master System tattoos, the skin didn't properly heal. Everyone has them."

He raised an eyebrow, skeptically.

"Almost everyone," she added, weakly. Matthew had no scar.

"It's the mark of the devil."

Cat shook her head. "The mark of the devil is 666. I saw *The Omen*."

Matthew held her eyes with his own a moment, then suddenly hurried across the room to where her purse sat on a small end table. He snatched it up and turned it upside down, holding the mouth wide open and spilling the contents out onto the glass surface.

"Hey!" she cried.

Ignoring her protest, he rooted through the pile of contents until he found an eyeliner pencil, picked it up, and returned. Again, more gently this time, he turned her to face the mirror. Using the pencil he pointedly traced the faint lines of her scar, ignoring the outside circle but starting at the end of each line that touched it. Starting with the first one, he traced the curved line inward, continuing around the inner circle until it touched itself. It was a perfect 6. He then did the exact same with the other two.

"Six. Six. Six," he said, firmly.

Cat stared, taken aback. There was no denying it, the pattern clearly formed three perfect sixes, each one sharing a common bottom loop. How had she never noticed that before? She swallowed, to moisten her suddenly dry throat. Her voice came out husky. "Yeah, well, like I said, the facts may be right but the interpretation is wrong."

The man of God didn't anger, but he looked at her imploringly. "Miss Johnson, don't you pay attention to your own news reports? There were no reported deaths from those who suffered the disease."

"So, it wasn't a fatal–"

"No reported deaths, Miss Johnson!" he said, with urgency.

"That's not true–"

"It is. Many died during this horrible time, true. In fact, nearly one hundred fifty thousand from Israel alone were killed, murdered for spreading the gospel."

"How do you–?"

"Believe me, I know. These are facts. But another fact is that none of them wore the mark. None of them were sick. In the past five months, Ms. Johnson, in spite of untold suffering, in spite of thousands upon thousands of suicide attempts, no one with this affliction died! Do you know the astronomical odds against that? It can only be a miracle!"

So it was true. Numerous times upon reading the day's news reports over the last five months, Cat had questioned just that phenomenon. She'd even suggested research on it and her Director backed her up, but the network brass had squelched it, claiming that it was ridiculous and that they didn't want to give people "ideas." Cat knew there was a logic to that, if you suggested to people that they couldn't die a number of lunatics would likely attempt to prove you wrong and she certainly didn't want that on her conscience, so she'd dropped the subject. Now, for the first time, she began to wonder if there hadn't been an ulterior motive for rejecting the story, and if, perhaps, the orders had come from a higher source, from someone with a different agenda.

"So, you're saying–" she started.

"The sinful were meant to suffer!"

"I see. Nice God," she said, derisively.

Richards clearly heard her sarcasm but ignored it. Instead he met her gaze and said, pointedly, "Yes, to give them a second chance! To provide them with a small taste of hell so they could choose a different path for eternity!" He moved away, shaking his head, woefully. "The Antichrist tried to shield them from it, you know."

"Excuse me?"

He picked up a magazine up off a table and tossed it to her. On the cover was a picture of Jordan Masters with the headline: *Drugs Legalized!* "He used drugs to numb them to the horror that will be their fate if they fail to repent. And now there are tens of millions hooked. Addicts! He who controls the drugs, Miss Johnson, controls the people."

"This has nothing to do with God."

"It has everything to do with God! And the devil."

"Give me a break, Reverend! You say one thing, the Jews say another, the Hindus another, the Buddhists something else! Christ, Krishna, Buddha, what's the difference? I don't think–"

"The problem, Miss Johnson," said Richards, cutting her off, "is not that you don't think, it's that you over think! You analyze and rationalize! You talk yourself out of the truth because you've seen hypocritical 'holy men' preach one thing and live another! I understand that. Oh yes, I do. I was one of them. Because of people like me, Miss Johnson, people like you disdain God!" He looked at her with imploring eyes, pleading. "Don't do it. Please. Don't blame God for the weakness of man or the warped interpretations of His word or for the atrocities committed in His name. Search instead, for the truth. There is only one. You won't find it out there," he said, waving toward the city beyond the picture window. He turned back to her, reached out, and gently touched her heart. "You'll find it in here."

His touch sent a inexplicable shiver through her.

Someone knocked on the door and immediately Roger Jackson entered her office without waiting for an answer, as was his habit. He, too, bore the scar on his forehead. "Excuse me, sorry to bother you..." He trailed off, staring at the darkened mark on her brow.

Cat roughly wiped the eyeliner away with her palm. "What's up?"

"Assignment. It seems there's been a guy in Jerusalem preaching nonstop for months."

Cat looked at him, puzzled. There were multitudes of preachers, worldwide. "So?"

"*Nonstop,* Cat," he emphasized. "No sleep, no food, no potty breaks?" He raised both eyebrows and looked at her quizzically as if to say, *weird enough for ya?*

Matthew hurried across the room to him, obviously excited, but also looking perplexed. "One man?"

"One who can do that ain't enough?" cracked Roger.

"No," said the preacher, thoughtfully, "There should be two." Cat looked at her guest, who seemed to have been expecting this.

"He's getting a lot of attention," continued Roger, "And the word is that Masters is planning a confrontation. Could be on his way anytime now."

Cat turned to Richards. "You know something about this, Reverend?"

The preacher smiled happily. "Oh yes."

"Would you like to share?"

Richards met her eyes for a moment, as if searching for something behind them. Then, apparently, he came to some conclusion and sprang into action. He strode across the room and hurriedly replaced the items he'd spilled back into her purse, then pointedly added his Bible to it as well, zipping it up decisively. Handing it to her, he announced, "I'm coming with you."

She considered the man before her. He was obviously determined. She glanced over at Roger, who simply rolled his eyes and shrugged, as usual, ready to flow with anything. She thought about the danger. If Jordan really was planning a confrontation, then he, the preacher, and Matthew Richards would all be in the same place at the same time. The results could be explosive. She had to admit, it would make a terrific story. Still, she hesitated. Something about the long-haired preacher had touched her. His sincerity clearly ran fathoms deep, and despite his misguided faith in a book of myths, she didn't want to see any harm come to him. She shook her head, negatively. "I don't think so. We don't know what's going to happen."

The preacher laid a gentle hand on her shoulder. "It's okay, Ms. Johnson, because..." he smiled enigmatically. "I do."

Chapter 21

It was raining in Jerusalem. The taxi moved slowly through the deluge, the wipers feebly swatting at the downpour, attempting to clear the windshield and meeting only defeat. The ride from the airport to the walled city took twice as long as it usually did. The driver dropped them near a huge archway that was filled in with bricks. "That is the legendary Eastern or "Golden" Gate which was walled up by the Turks in an attempt to stop the Messiah," explained Matthew, "According to certain beliefs He cannot arrive until those doors are open."

The short walk to the "wailing wall" left Cat and Roger drenched, in spite of their over-sized umbrellas. Roger kept his digital camera close to his body under his loose rain poncho, trying to keep it as dry as possible. Matthew walked beside him without an umbrella, his hair plastered down along the back of his neck and falling across his shoulders, his beard dripping like a waterfall. He didn't seem to mind the rain in the least. In fact, he appeared to be reveling in it.

As they approached the square, a huge African-American man loped toward them, looking like a pro football linebacker. "Matthew! Welcome to Jerusalem. I was so thrilled to get your call."

Matthew turned to Cat and Roger. "Catherine, Roger, this is Stan Washington. Stan, Cat Johnson and her partner Roger Jackson."

Roger beamed at the introduction. "Pleasure to meet you, my man." They shook hands.

"Miss Johnson. Of course I'm familiar with your work," said the big man, shaking her hand. "It's an honor to meet you."

"Thank you, Mister Washington," she said, surprised at the gentle grip. "My pleasure."

Stan Washington turned to Matthew and suddenly gathered him into an excited bear hug, grinning from ear to ear as if they shared some sort of wonderful secret.

"Is this what I think it is, Stan?" asked Matthew, looking up at the big man.

Stan's smile grew even wider. "Come on," he said, with a mysterious voice, "let's get out of the rain." He looked at the others and added, "You ain't gonna believe this."

Eagerly, he led the way.

A huge crowd was gathered watching a lone robed figure standing on a high, rickety-looking platform, preaching. As they reached the outside edge of the crowd, the rain abruptly quit. Puzzled, Cat looked back and felt reality spin. The rain still poured down on the city, on the walls surrounding the square, and right up to the edge of the crowd, but there it stopped. On the crowd and the preacher, the sun shone. Cat exchanged incredulous looks with Roger who, from the flabbergasted look on his face, had clearly also noted the bizarre phenomenon. Scrambling to pull his equipment from beneath his poncho, he quickly started filming.

It took Cat several minutes to tear her eyes away from the sky and focus her attention on the stage. The Semitic looking man on the distant platform had long dark hair and a beard, worn in a style similar to Matthew's–which was no style at all. Although he was outdoors and had no amplification equipment, his voice carried clearly to her. He spoke English with a thick middle-eastern accent, reading aloud from a tattered book that Cat assumed to be the Bible.

"*'On their heads they wore crowns of gold and their faces looked like human faces. Their hair was like a woman's and their teeth like a lion's.'*" He looked up from the pages and pointed to an object on the stage, covered with a large cloth. "Behold! This is what they packed the poison in!" Dramatically, he ripped the cover away. Under it was a metal barrel which she immediately recognized from Matthew's earlier description of the chemical laboratory raid. The crowd reacted with gasps of shock and astonishment. The picture on it matched the biblical description perfectly.

Slowly, aided by the giant man's gentle persuasion, they made their way through the mass of humanity toward the stage. Most of them, she noticed, were scarred on their forehead, but many were not. In fact, she had not seen this many people without the mark gathered in one place since before the plague. As their group approached the platform, Cat saw Matthew stiffen, apparently recognizing the man on stage. Stan Jackson broke into another wide grin, obviously delighted at his friend's reaction.

Matthew gazed prayerfully at the man on stage. "Ahmad," he whispered, with unmistakable reverence. Cat recognized the name from Matthew's earlier explanation.

Ahmad, soldier turned preacher, continued without interruption. "*The locusts had a king who was the angel of the bottomless pit. His name in the Hebrew language is Abaddon and in the Greek language is Apollyon.*" Again, he gestured at the barrel, clearly marked: APOLLYON.

Roger turned to film the crowd's intense reaction of fear and anger. Cat, herself, found the coincidence entirely unnerving.

Matthew turned to Stan with a look that seemed to say, I should have expected this. "Ahmad. Ahmad is The Witness!"

Stan nodded happily, then a dark cloud crossed over his face. "But there should be two, isn't that right?" he inquired, somberly.

"These chemicals were the devil's work!" proclaimed Ahmad, in a ringing voice. "Jordan Masters! Jordan Masters master-minded their creation!"

A fat man with a smarmy-looking pencil mustache stepped forward in the crowd. "This is true! I was there. I myself was the manager of this evil facility, may Allah forgive me! He speaks the truth!"

Before his listeners could absorb this statement, a man in a dark burnoose lurched forward through the crowd in the direction of the stout man. Cat saw the gun in his hand too late to shout a warning. The assassin pressed his weapon against the other man's stomach and pulled the trigger. The weapon roared, the fat man's eyes and mouth flew open in silent surprise, and he fell backwards. The crowd screamed and scrambled to get away. The assassin jumped up onto the platform, aiming the gun at Ahmad's face. "Lies!" he spat. "You preach poisonous treason!"

Ahmad faced him calmly, without fear. "Do not do this, child, you will only harm yourself."

"Die, traitor!" snarled the assassin, pulling the trigger, point blank.

The gun blew up in his own face. The hammer shot backwards, turning into a projectile as deadly as any bullet, passing through assassin's right eye and entering his brain with explosive force, killing him instantly. His lifeless body dropped to the wooden floor like a puppet with his strings cut.

Cat stared at the corpse at Ahmad's feet with numbed awe. What had just happened? Then, she and the rest of the crowd watched, paralyzed with shock, as the preacher stepped off the platform down into the crowd and moved to the slain gunshot victim. Next, to everyone's astonishment, he gently began helping the man back to his feet. The stout man gazed down at himself, apparently unharmed, then up at the preacher. Ahmad smiled reassuringly. It was difficult to tell if the fat man's legs buckled from the shock or if he was acting out of reverence, but he fell to his knees in front of the preacher, sobbing like a child saved from a nightmare. Others immediately followed his example, kneeling, keening and praying.

Cat stared at the resurrected man, utterly confused, her emotions in turmoil. His forehead was now smooth, no longer blemished by the ugly scar that had been there moments before. It took her a moment to break out of her paralysis. "Roger," she cried, urgently. "Did you get that? Tell me you got that!"

Roger, panning the camera over the genuflecting crowd, followed the preacher who was even now moving back toward the stage. "Oh, I got it." He added under his breath, "Don't freakin' believe it, but I got it!"

Matthew spoke quietly to Stan Washington. "You are right, my friend. There must be two."

He broke away from the small party to intercept the Arab. Catching up with him just below the stage, the preacher immediately recognized him and broke into a brilliant smile. They embraced warmly. "Matthew, my brother. I wondered when you would come."

"Sorry I'm late."

"You are not. You have been spreading the word even longer than I. But now..." He shrugged and sighed. "I fear it is time."

Matthew firmly took the smaller man's hands in his, and squeezed. "Fear not, my friend."

Together, the two men of God went up onto the platform.

Across the large square, in a small apartment above a souvenir shop, Lucretia Baylock lowered a pair of binoculars and threw them across the room. "I don't believe it!" she cried.

Sitting at a small table, Jordan Masters clutched the edge of the wood with white knuckles. "He failed." It wasn't a question. He felt cold tendrils of fear creeping through him.

"The gun blew up in his face!" She whirled on a guard that stood near the door. "You! Go down there and blow that smug little camel-jockey away!"

"It would do no good," injected Gideon, coming in from the tiny kitchen.

"You're telling me he can't be killed?" she asked, incredulously.

"Of course he can be. But in only one way." He looked at Jordan, pointedly.

"Me?"

"Yours is the power."

Masters touched his medallion with an almost sexual pleasure. It was true. He had the power. He was invincible. He could almost feel boiling acid pulsing through his veins and electricity jolting between his fingertips. "And the kingdom," he muttered, "and the glory."

"That's insane!" cried Lucretia, crossing the room to him, "You go down there now, they'll tear you apart!"

Jordan felt a rush of fear replacing the prior power surge. She was right, it would be suicide. He looked to Gideon, not wanting to appear frightened, but searching for an excuse not to pursue it. "They *have* lost their faith..." he began.

"It can be restored." said Gideon matter-of-factly, cutting him off.

Both he and Lucretia looked at their savior questioningly.

The silver-haired alien smiled, his deep blue eyes as blank and vast as the sea. "Perhaps the time has come to introduce the world to me."

Chapter 22

Matthew stood on the stage, holding the barrel marked Apollyon high above his head. "Witness!" he cried. "Understand! Believe! Everything depends on it!"

A mocking voice called loudly from the back of the crowd. "Everything depends on it?"

Cat turned with the rest of the people, stunned by Jordan Masters' sudden appearance. As the leader of the United World Coalition made his way through the mass of humanity, the crowd was clearly angered by his presence, yet still appeared to be mesmerized by him. They parted like the red sea to let him pass.

"Depends on what?" called history's most famous statesman. "A God that does not exist?"

"He exists!" cried Stan, standing in the crowd.

Jordan whirled on the man. "Then why are innocent children of good parents born crippled?" he asked, quietly.

The gentle giant reacted as if he'd been punched.

Jordan continued toward the front edge of the stage, raising his voice. "Why then, when there were young girls among us, were so many terrified because their fathers visited in the night? Why was our nightly news so filled with stories of violence that we became numb to it?" He leaped up onto the stage and faced the assembly. "If there was a God, would man hate man because of the color of his skin or even more incredibly because of the way he chooses to worship? Look around you, people! A hundred religions–all insisting that their laws are the true laws! If God exists, why does he not come forward and tell us who is right?"

"Because there is no God!" a female voice called.

Cat looked at the source and felt her skin crawl. Lucretia Baylock stood in the crowd, between two bodyguards.

Masters took center stage, righteous indignation exuding from every pore of him. "The Christian Crusades: slaughter in the name of God! The Spanish Inquisition: torture in the name of God! Millions living in abject poverty but worshipping in mosques plated with gold. Nations torn apart! Catholic hating Protestant, Jew hating Moslem, Moslem hating Hindu, neighbor hating neighbor! War after war after war. Illness and terrible accidents happening all the time to innocent people!"

Cat watched him, transfixed. The man had an incredible ability to make it appear as though he were addressing each and every listener individually.

"Sons and daughters ostracized because of sexual preference," he continued, building to a roar. "Women oppressed, innocent animals slaughtered! All in the name of God!"

"In the name of a God who does not exist!" shouted another voice.

Cat whirled, drawn by the familiar voice. *Gideon! Where had he come from?* She exchanged worried glances with Roger, who immediately focused the camera on this new presence. Recognizing him from the early tapes and pictures, many in the crowd dropped to their knees in reverence again, gasping his name. This was his first known public appearance.

The alien walked slowly through the crowd, apparently reveling in the adoration, and made his way up onto the stage. He turned and waited for silence, then addressed the crowd. "You know who I am. I am Gideon, of The One."

A woman fainted, but no one paid any attention. They were all riveted on the extraterrestrial visitor.

"The One has visited your planet on numerous occasions since we seeded it tens of thousands of years ago. From the very beginning we have been called Gods, angels, demons." He shook his head, like a tolerant parent. "You were primitive children seeking to explain what you could not comprehend. You misunderstood when we taught that there were not many Gods, only The One." He seemed genuinely sad. "It was merely a poor choice of words, errors of language and translation, that has led to a misunderstanding that has lasted millennia."

Matthew, who had been standing dumbly by, seemed suddenly energized. He strode across the stage until he was face to face with the alien. "You twist the truth! You mold the words to interpret whatever meaning you want."

Gideon smiled, sardonically. "Now there's something that man could never be accused of. Certainly not in the case of important teachings such as, oh say, the Bible."

Matthew reddened. "You're no alien. It's a lie. A trick."

Gideon's hair suddenly lengthened and turned a deep chestnut color. Two of the strands thickened, then twisted around the crown of his head, like vines, hardening and sprouting large, sharp thorns. A dark beard sprung out of rapidly thinning cheeks. His nose lengthened, his lips thinned, his skin darkened. His eye color remained unchanged, still bluer than blue, but the animosity in them melted away, replaced by deep sorrow, compassion and understanding. The morph happened within the blink of a firefly, and Matthew was suddenly standing before the living likeness of his Lord and savior.

In the audience, people crossed themselves. Many fell to their knees, mumbling prayers.

Cat, staggered by the moment, gasped, "Jesus Christ!" Roger shot her an odd look.

The embodiment of Jesus laid a bleeding palm gently against Matthew's cheek. "You are wrong, my son," he whispered, compassionately. "As wrong now, as you were earlier in life."

Matthew made a pained sound deep in the back of his throat.

Abruptly, just as rapidly as the first transformation, the figure morphed back to his Gideon likeness. He continued to watch Matthew, studying his reaction.

It took a moment for the man of God to find his voice. Finally, he croaked, "*Good* trick."

With a tolerant smile, Gideon turned to the stupefied crowd. "I ask you this, Earth people. What is a God? One who bestows a planet with life? One who watches over the universe? One who tries to guide you to a better way?"

"If that is so," said Masters, stepping up next to Gideon and placing an arm around him, "this alien, this friend of mankind, is the closest thing to God that exists!"

Gideon looked at him, warmly. "My powers work only through you, Jordan Masters." With those words, Jordan's medallion pulsed, bathing him in its glow. The crowd murmured.

"There!" cried Lucretia, pointing to Jordan. "You see? There is your God!"

Jordan thrust a finger out toward Ahmad and Matthew, acid dripping in his voice. "These men are false prophets! They sow dissent in a world which has finally–*finally*–harmonized!"

Gideon spun and kicked over the empty chemical barrel, violently. "They are also the men who brought the plague to you!"

Cat was taken aback by Matthew and Ahmad's reaction to the accusation. Both men looked as though they had been physically struck–guilty as the devil.

The crowd seemed to sense their culpability as well, and anger began to boil. Matthew faced the crowd and began to protest.

"Will you deny it was you who released the scorpion?" roared Gideon, cutting him off.

Matthew and Ahmad exchanged glances. "No," said the Arab, "but–" The angry explosion from the crowd drowned him out. Most of them had suffered grievously during the five-month hell, and many still felt the pain burn in their joints with every movement.

"They must be punished!" cried Jordan. His medallion began to glow steadily, growing in intensity. Ahmad started to back away in fear, eyes fixed on the phosphorescent glare. Matthew reached out and steadied him, gently. "His will be done," he said softly. Ahmad met his friend's eyes, and his tension dissipated. He nodded in acquiescence and the two men knelt in prayer.

Cat watched, frightened, as Jordan ripped open his shirt and the glowing medallion irised open. The crowd backed off, covering their eyes from the intense light that emanated from it. The stout chemical plant manager who had been shot earlier pushed his way forward, pointing at Ahmad. "He cannot be harmed! He has the power of God!"

Jordan's medallion exploded with an energy beam that shot across the stage, enveloping Matthew and Ahmad. Both men stiffened as, almost instantly, all moisture was sucked from their bodies. In one sickening moment that would be etched into Cat's memory for as long as she drew breath, the two figures were mummified. Muscles shrunk over bone, skin shriveled and dried, eyes receded into sockets, faces became leather-covered skulls.

She screamed in horror.

There was another scream, near her, but it was a scream of triumph. Lucretia Burton, eyes glowing with excitement, shouted like a woman in the throes of passion. "Yes! Yes! Yes!"

Gideon watched unblinkingly, a slight smile on his lips.

Cat shielded her eyes from the glare as Jordan's medallion beam suddenly fanned out around the crowd. The majority of the throng stared at each other in awe as the 666 marks on their foreheads glowed as if radioactive. Jordan gave a long jubilant cry of exhilaration, then the light retracted into him and the medallion irised shut.

The crowd fell into silence, traumatized with shock. Roger slowly, mechanically, lowered his camera, looking ill. Cat leaned against him, feeling weak-kneed.

Matthew and Ahmad were dead. They remained where they had knelt side by side, hands clasped, frozen in prayer, cobwebbish beards and hair fluttering in the breeze.

Jordan Masters turned to the crowd, flushed with power. "If you must worship a God, I stand before you!" he shouted, thrusting his fists into the sky.

To Cat's dismay, much of the crowd erupted with cheers, whistling, and cries of support.

"Witness!" screamed Masters, pounding his own chest and making a mockery of Matthew's words. "Believe! Understand! Everything depends on it!" The assembly roared its approval. Masters, with his almost hypnotic powers, had won them over once again. Lucretia climbed up on the stage, fawning over Jordan like a teenage girl meeting a rock and roll star.

Rain began to fall everywhere now, soaking the stage and the bodies, still motionless on their knees.

Lucretia shifted her gaze to them and curled her lip in disgust. "Get rid of this trash," she ordered one of her bodyguards.

"No," countered Jordan, firmly, "Leave them! As a lesson." He turned to the crowd, putting his arm around Lucretia with the smile of a proud parent, then looked directly into Roger's news camera. "Let this be a week of rejoicing!" he declared. "We, mankind, have been united through pain and suffering! Like a Phoenix rising from the ashes of a cleansing fire!" Again, he raised both hands high above his head triumphantly, and shouted at the top of his lungs. "We are reborn!"

The crowd became unhinged. Jordan grinned and kissed Lucretia long and hard. The crowd whooped their approval, many of them grabbing the first person they could and doing likewise.

Stan appeared between Cat and Roger, shaking his head, forlornly. "How quickly they turn." Cat could hardly tear her eyes away from the horrific frozen tableaux on the stage. She had never witnessed anything so dreadful. Stan spoke gently, soothingly. "It's okay, Miss Johnson, it's okay. It's all part of the plan." She shook her head, unable to comprehend his inexplicable calmness.

"Have you lost your mind?" rasped Roger, weakly, sounding as distraught as Cat felt.

The big man only smiled his compassion, putting his bear-like arms around them both. "Read your Bibles."

Chapter 23

Cat Johnson lay in the darkness of a London hotel room, staring at the ceiling, unable to sleep. The events of the past few days had disturbed her greatly. She could not erase from her consciousness the sight of the two preacher's bodies mummifying before her eyes. Every time she shut her eyes it played on the back of her eyelids like a Hollywood horror movie, except infinitely more terrible because it had actually happened. As she thought about the moments leading up to the living nightmare, it seemed to her that Ahmad Ahwadi and Matthew Richards had known beforehand what was about to occur but had made no attempt to avoid it. On the contrary, it almost seemed as if they had expected, even welcomed the event. The faith of those two men facing hideous death had not wavered, and the immense power of that faith moved and haunted her.

She snapped on a bedside lamp and opened the small drawer below it, searching for the Bible that could always be found in every hotel room. The drawer was empty. She checked the other drawer. Also empty. She got off the bed and checked each of the bureau drawers. No Bible. She had a sudden paranoid thought, wondering if the Bibles had been purposefully removed. But why and by whom? She pushed the thought aside and rose to get a light sedative out of her large handbag. In it was something she had forgotten was there. Matthew's Bible.

Turning the book over in her hand, she ran her thumb gently over the slash where the book had taken the knife blow, miraculously saving Matthew's life in an incident he had told her about. The sight of the gash quite unexpectedly brought more tears to her eyes. A small sob escaped as she held the book to her heart, thinking of the compassionate, gentle man who had given it to her. His words returned. *"Don't blame God for the weakness of man or the warped interpretations of His word or for the atrocities done in His name. Search instead, for the truth. There is only one. You won't find it out there. You'll find it in here."*

Cat climbed back onto bed and stared at the book in her lap for a long time. Eventually, she wiped her eyes, opened it, and began to read.

Unfamiliar with its layout, it took her a few minutes to find what she was looking for. Of course, it was the last place she looked, the final book of the Bible. Revelation.

As the words unlocked her comprehension, she could almost hear Matthew's voice speaking them. On the ninth page, she almost dropped the book, uttering a small moan. She reread the passage again. Revelation 11.

"And I will give power to two witnesses to prophesy. They will have the power to afflict the earth with plague and to stop the sky from raining and if anyone tries to hurt them in whatever way, in that same way that person will die." Two prophets. Matthew and Ahmad. Two men responsible for releasing the plague. The incomprehensible miracle of the selective rainfall. The way the assassin's gun had blown up in his own face.

She read the passage a third time, then continued marveling at how events had paralleled the allegory. *"When the two witnesses finish telling their message, the beast that comes from the bottomless pit will defeat and kill them."* Again, the agonizing image of Masters' medallion-beam ripping through Ahmad and Matthew projected itself on the back of her mind. *"The bodies of the great witnesses will lie on the street of the great city where the lord was crucified. And every race of people, tribe, language and nation will look upon them and refuse to bury them."* She thought of Masters' words. "No, leave them as a lesson. Let this be a week of rejoicing!"

The bodies, in fact, had not been removed. The dreadful sight was continuously featured on numerous World Web internet sites, as millions celebrated. It had turned into a party the world hadn't seen the likes of since New Year's Eve 1999. *"People will rejoice and be happy because these two are dead, these two prophets who brought much suffering."* She was blown away by each succeeding pronouncement was taking on yet another meaning for her, every line so undeniably paralleling the real events. Was there more to this book than ancient writers' imagination after all?

Cat's primary function as a newswoman taught her to deal with facts–cold, hard, facts, not wild theories. She had always strived to be a good person, living basically by the golden rule of Do unto others as you would have them do unto you. The Ten Commandments made sense, by and large, but were they actually rules handed down by God? Did a Creator even exist? Masters had made some awfully good points in his argument against that belief.

Still, the facts were clear, and she'd have to break her own rules of logic in order to ignore them. The predictions of two thousand years ago were coming true. There was no doubt that this part of the Bible, at least, was proving to be right on target. Was there was more to the rest of it than she had previously considered?

Her attention totally focused, Cat continued reading. The very next paragraph caused her to leap out of bed throwing on her clothes as quickly as she could.

Roger Jackson was roused from an uneasy, nightmarish sleep by the sound of increasing banging on his hotel room door. He rolled over and flipped on the bedside light, wincing as his eyes adjusted to the brightness. The clock read three AM. "Hold on. Hold on!"

A familiar female voice filtered through the door. "Roger!"

"Cat?"

"Yeah."

He hurriedly pulled the bedcover around him, his heart beginning to race. For years, ever since they first started to work together, Roger had been fascinated by Catherine Denise Johnson. He'd watched her development from an awkward newcomer to the business to one of the most respected television journalists in the world. During years of working by her side, and covering numerous stories together, he had supported her in every way he could with unfailing loyalty. They'd climbed out on many a shaky limb together but always managed to land on their feet. She might be the voice and ears of the world, but he and his camera were the eyes. In fact, he was so used to looking at the world through his camera that if he didn't see something through a lens it almost didn't seem real.

He and Cat were the ideal team, he figured. Inseparable, each one's work incomplete without the other's, dove-tailing in every respect. Except one. In all the years, in spite of numerous subtle overtures, he had never been able to reach her romantically. She loved him, he knew, but only like a brother, a close friend. Unwilling to risk jeopardizing the relationship, he had never let himself express his private feelings. And she, who seemed obsessed with the great Jordan Masters, had never indicated any interest in pursuing a more intimate relationship with him or any other guy. Until now. Here she was, coming to his hotel room in the middle of the night.

Nervously, he opened the door. He had thought about this moment many a lonely evening in many a lonely hotel room, and had rehearsed his witty repartee time and again. Now, as he saw her standing before him, hair tousled carelessly, his cleverness melted away. "Well, hello," he managed, in a husky voice.

"I need you."

He looked at her, deeply serious. "And I you."

"Huh?"

Reality hit him like a cold cement block. "You aren't here for social reasons, are you?" he mumbled.

She gave him an odd look, then brushed by, stepping into the room efficiently. “Get dressed.”

Feeling like a fool, Roger did what he always did when in an awkward situation, he reverted to humor. “Avert your eyes. I’m naked under this sheet and you ain’t ready to see that yet! It’d ruin all other men for you.”

She didn’t even smile, appearing too distracted. “We’re going back to Jerusalem.”

“Jerusalem? Why?”

“Because it’s been almost three days since they were killed.”

“Huh?” He was totally confused.

“Let’s just say,” she said, tossing him a worn book, “I got a hot tip.”

Chapter 24

The sun scorched Jerusalem. No clouds promised relief. The city was packed with revelers, celebrating as if it were Mardi Gras. Cat and Roger had pushed their way into the main square and stood only yards from the large roped-off platform now littered with garbage and glass tossed in drunken glee at the petrified bodies. The immobile figures knelt almost within a stone's throw of where the man Jesus had been crucified, over two thousand years earlier. The imposing figure of Stan Washington knelt on the stage near the bodies, watching over them in continuous prayer, a self-appointed guardian angel.

Roger sat in one of the portable chairs he had brought along and began to read the Bible he had accepted from Cat, who watched his eyes, looking for a reaction. He closed it and stared at the small gold cross embossed on the cover. "You buy this stuff, Cat?"

She had asked herself that same question, over and over again. "I don't know. I just..." Restless, she paced.

He checked his watch. "It's past noon."

"I know."

"Well past 90 hours."

"I know."

"The book says three and a half days, Cat. *'After three and one half days–'*"

"I know, I know!" she snapped, annoyed at her own lack of conviction. Her internal conflict was driving her mad. "How do you do it, Rog?"

"Huh?"

She sat next to him. "These past seven years, you and I, we've seen it all, the worst there is, but you..." She shook her head in amazement. "you're always there with a laugh." She smiled, remembering some of his antics, then grew serious again. "You know, you, Roger Jackson, are the one thing that's kept me going." The enormity of her own words hit her hard as she realized just how true they were. He was the only constant in her life, the one thing she never had to worry about, always there for her. Always. She studied him closely, realizing how very much his opinions mattered to her. "What do you believe in, Rog?"

He considered the question for a while before answering, his eyes never leaving her face. "Courage. Truth. Honor. Intelligence. Beauty."

It dawned on Cat that he was talking about her. The very idea set off a flood of confusing and unfamiliar emotions. Afraid to continue the discussion, she fell silent. Instead, she took the Bible from him and turned to Revelation again. "When will we know, do you think?"

"When?" He shrugged. "I don't know when."

She shut the Bible with a thunk, suddenly filled with an urgent need to get as far away as possible from this place of unparalleled historical horror. "Okay, this is insane," she snapped, "I don't know what I was thinking. Let's get out of here. Let's go home."

Roger looked like he was about to protest, then he just shrugged. "You're the boss." He began to pack up his camera equipment.

"No!" said Stan, calling from the stage, "You must not go yet!" He rose off his knees and started toward them, but abruptly stopped and stood gazing at fast-gathering clouds unpredictably filling the sky. Cat followed his gaze upward as a shadow fell over her. The sky was quickly growing inky, like an unexpected solar eclipse. They were not the only ones to notice; others roaming in the square were also reacting to the ominous weather change, stopping to watch the increasing darkness with apprehension. Many hurried toward shelter, anticipating an imminent storm. Cat and Roger exchanged glances with growing unease. Stan turned back to the tableau of Matthew and Ahmad's stone-quiet bodies and knelt again in agitated prayer. Cat noticed with curiosity that he moved further away from the two figures. Why?

Black clouds boiled from horizon to horizon, blotting out the sun. Her reporter's instincts urging her into action, she nudged Roger. He immediately grabbed his camera and started filming.

Everything grew still. Even the clouds ceased their restless movement.

The former revelers stood mute, gazing fearfully upwards at a sky that was now almost as dark as night. Waiting. The whole world seemed to be holding its breath.

If Cat hadn't herself witnessed the event that followed, she'd would never have believed it. Even as it unfolded before her own eyes, it was like watching a special-effects enhanced scene from a Hollywood spectacular.

One cloud melted away allowing beams of sunshine to break through. The brilliant rays radiated downward and specifically illuminated the mummified bodies on the raised platform like personal spotlights on a theater stage. The tableau began to glow; a sculpture surrounded by a soft, incandescent halo.

The uneasy onlookers shied from the sight, withdrawing in awe from the eerie brightness. One man, however, did not. A beatific look transformed the features of the big black man on the platform. Stan Washington remained on his knees, his hands clasped together.

As the light surrounded them, the desiccated corpses shimmered, their aura becoming brighter and brighter until, like the sun, the brilliance was too intense to look at directly. Cat had to shield her eyes, squinting and blinking. An awed murmur ran through the watchers, many turning away. After a surge of absolute blinding radiance, the light diminished somewhat so that Cat could again see without migraine-like pain. She dared a peek at the stage and what she saw left her speechless with disbelief.

Matthew and Ahmad were standing on the stage, alive, unblemished and fully restored to their original selves. Smiling. Then, awash in shimmering, incandescent light, they slowly began to levitate. As they rose into the air, the throng gasped, unsure what to make of it all. Was it some kind of a trick?

Cat fell to her knees, overcome. Almost to a person, the crowd followed suit as the two men hovered overhead, thirty feet above the ground. The one with the white streak through his hair smiled upon the throng, spread his arms toward them, and spoke. He did not raise his voice, but Cat had no trouble hearing the word.

"Witness," he said.

"Understand," added the Arab holy man, floating beside him.

Stan gazed up at them, tears of joy filling his eyes. "Believe," he added, in a choked whisper. Matthew and Ahmad smiled down at their friend and the light suddenly retracted back into the clouds, taking them with it.

As they disappeared, the heavy atmosphere rapidly dissolved and the desert sun burst forth again, in its full glory, washing over the supplicating crowd. Most were too overcome to move. Only Roger, still filming, remained on his feet.

Cat found her vision blurred with tears. When the sun's cleansing rays touched her she'd experienced a stunning epiphany. She now knew the truth and, in the enormity of it, she was overcome by regret that she had ever doubted. And shame, not just for herself but for the whole human race. The lessons taught in the Bible–

Even as she grappled with the undeniability of it all, the next chapter of the prophecy sprang unbidden into her mind. A deep, dread welled up within her. "Oh no," she whispered, "Roger, we have to go!"

Roger had lowered his camera to search the sky. His arms were trembling. "Cat! Did you see that, Cat? Did you?"

She leaped to her feet in near panic. "We have to get out of here!"

"Why?"

She grabbed him by the shoulders and pulled. "Now! We have to get away! We have to get away! Please!"

But it was too late. Without warning, the ground began to tremble. Cat stiffened. With a explosive rumble the earth heaved, tossing her to the ground.

When the earthquake hit, it hit hard.

Cat screamed. People all around her panicked and tried to flee, but were thrown off their feet like rag dolls. Every structure in sight began to collapse, raining lethal debris everywhere.

"Come on! Let's move!" Roger shouted, pulling her to her feet, but they realized in another heartbeat that there was no safe place to run to. No way to avoid the raging juggernaut.

Cat screamed again as an ancient building buried a shrieking couple, evoking vivid memories of her parents' death. Sheer abject terror possessed her. She folded her arms tight across her chest, almost fainting, drained of her habitual presence of mind by the emotional and physical impact. The shrieks seemed endless.

The piazza broke apart as a huge chasm tore across the square with a sound like a jet taking off. The ground lurched violently and Roger was catapulted into the air.

As Roger fell, the ground seemed to rise up to meet him, slamming into him with a bone-jarring crunch. He managed to take most of the impact on his shoulder, while instinctively protecting his camera. He rolled onto his back, pain shooting through his arm, amazed to see Cat, still on her feet. She stood motionless, surrounded by the ongoing destruction, repeating a strange sounding phrase over and over again. "El Diablo era el panico. El Diablo era el panico. El Diablo era el panico."

Around them the worst was yet to come. More of the piazza and streets beyond opened up like a gaping mouth, swallowing vehicles, animals, people, even entire buildings. Those structures not devoured were shaken into piles of dust and rubble. Explosions from gas pipes rocked the air and flames shot high into the sky.

Even the world famous "wailing wall," a traditional place for worship and prayer for centuries, succumbed to the relentless unleashed forces and fell, strewing tiny pieces of rolled up papers everywhere. The prayers that the devoted had stuffed in the cracks scattered with the wind, like so many denied dreams.

Still the reporter stood, frozen, chanting her mantra. Roger fought the rolling ground in a determined attempt to reach her when a tremendous cacophony of noise came from a distance behind Cat. The ancient bricks sealing the Golden Gate were shuddering and shrieking, literally exploding into dust. With a huge crash, the massive structure fell.

Instantly, the earthquake stopped.

His heart threatening to break through his rib cage, Roger took a shaky breath and looked around him.

It was a disaster the likes of which hadn't been experienced since the nuclear holocaust, seven years earlier. Everything surrounding them seemed utterly destroyed or pitifully damaged, but he and Cat remained on a small island of safety, unharmed. On his knees, he looked up at her, speechless. Slowly, she knelt down beside him and took his hand, the warmth of their grasp comforting him immeasurably. Feeling weak but thankful for their deliverance, he leaned against her.

"Remember you were asking when we would know?"

"Yeah," she said.

He attempted a smile. "When."

"You okay?"

"Yeah."

"Then you're still on the company clock, right?" She gave him a shaky smile and pointed at his hand. He looked down, amazed to see that he was still clutching the digital movie camera. She looked at him expectantly. Chuckling softly he touched her face with a featherlike caress and they got back to their feet. He raised the camera to his eye and waited

Cat stepped within his focus and took a long, fortifying breath, composing herself. Finally, she looked directly into the lens. Roger sensed a change in her before she even said the words.

"Ladies and Gentlemen, this is WBN. I'm Cat Johnson." With deep emotion, she began her report. *"Today our almighty Creator showed us that, without any doubt, He does exist."*

It took Roger a moment to realize what else was different about her.

The geometric scar on her forehead was gone.

Chapter 25

"Blast her!" shrieked Lucretia Baylock to Frederick Marco.

She was watching a huge television monitor rebroadcasting Cat Johnson's report from Jerusalem for the umpteenth time. Located deeply underground on the sub-basement level of the Imperial Palace at New Babylon, the room held an uncanny resemblance to the old White House Crisis Management Center where she had first introduced Masters to her husband, the President of the United States, years ago. The tension in the air was also uncomfortably similar to that melee. Barely suppressed panic. A high state of agitation. Many of the powerful, international junta, the men Jordan first met on that initial flight on the black Gulfstream jet, were present. She could tell by their expressions that they were experiencing an emotion that was completely foreign to their usual attitude: the icy fear of doubt.

Everything had changed. To see two men ascending in the air under no visible power and disappearing through the purple clouds had shaken the people of the earth to their very souls. Because WBN's cameraman, unaccountably close to the action, had captured every moment of the life-altering experience in full digital color, the most incredible piece of film of all time was now running over and over again on every news channel in the world. Matthew Richards and Ahmad Ahwadi's teachings were taking on a new validity for millions who had not previously listened to their message. Unprecedented, unforeseen events in Jerusalem capped by Cat Johnson's pronouncement, "Today our almighty Creator showed us that, without a doubt, He does exist." had shifted the balance of power.

Several dozen monitors were all tuned to different newscasters in different countries. Lucretia didn't understand most of the languages, but so what? She knew they were all saying the same thing. The old man was beginning to show signs of strain for the first time since she had been approached by him in a strip bar at age sixteen and taken on as his "special project." He had molded her, groomed her for political greatness, exposed her to an elite world of power and taught her the fine points of political manipulation. He had taught her pleasure, pain, sincerity and deception. He'd taught her to betray with a kiss. She had seen him give millions to charity and she had seen him order up death like it was a shrimp cocktail. She'd seen him laugh and, yes, she'd even seen him cry. But in all the years by his side the one thing she had never seen in him was doubt. Until now. "It's not just her," Marco was saying. "Newscasters everywhere are turning on us. People everywhere are turning!"

"Remain calm," said Gideon, the only serene figure in the room, "All is under control."

Tanaka looked up from a bank of computers. "Under control? We have reports that armies are mobilizing!"

Jordan paced the room like a wounded jackal, his hair uncombed, his eyes wild. "Forget their armies, I'll drop them where they stand!" He tore open his shirt, revealing the medallion. It gave out a steady, blue pulse, infusing his body with barely-repressed energy.

"We must return to Jerusalem," announced Gideon.

Jordan stared at him like he was out of his mind. "Jerusalem?"

"Yes," said the alien, without emotion. He turned to the decision makers. "Spread the word that we'll be there. They will come, which is exactly what they must do."

"I don't understand," said Jordan.

Neither did Lucretia. Nor, apparently, did anyone else in the room. They all waited for Gideon to explain.

The space visitor gazed placidly back at them, shaking his head, as if speaking to slow children. "Do you not realize what happened today? Who do you think caused the illusion of the traitors rising, knowing it would divide the people of Earth?"

Lucretia was the first to get it. Realization broke through her clouded mind. "The One," she whispered, with undisguised hatred.

Gideon nodded, solemnly. "They have returned."

The word went out and, true to Gideon's prediction, military contingents from all over the world traveled to Israel, determined to destroy Masters and the "alien," now believed to be the anti-Christ and the devil himself. Elite military forces from twenty-seven different countries converged on the city of Jerusalem. It was a cooperative military mobilization the likes of which had never before occurred in history–nation after nation joining together to destroy a common enemy.

And Gideon welcomed it.

Chapter 26

The world was in mourning.

The ancient city of Jerusalem lay in ruins, one tenth of it having been utterly destroyed in the devastating quake. Masters and his minions had now turned the square near the leveled west wall into an armed camp. Ahmad's platform had been reconstructed, and Masters now paced on it, back and forth like the pendulum of a clock counting down the minutes. The tension in the air crackled.

Gideon stood alone, apart from all. He remained unobtrusively at the top of the wide steps overlooking the square, staring across the distance at the now open Golden Gate, his face contorted with hatred.

A Humvie pulled into the square and soldiers tensed until they recognized it as one of their own. It stopped in front of the platform, almost directly under the spot where Matthew and Ahmad had levitated. Doors were thrown open and Cat Johnson emerged, seething with anger. In an efficient military maneuver, she and Roger Jackson had been abducted from their news studio in front of many witnesses, three of which were left wounded or dead. Seeing Masters on the stage she yanked herself out of a soldier's grip and stormed over to him, climbing directly up onto the stage.

"Why have we been brought here?" she demanded.

He was seemingly unaffected by her anger. "Because I need you, Cat."

His soft tone and the gentle, almost puzzled, look in his deep blue eyes took her off-guard. He reached out toward her and for a moment she softened, confused. In spite of everything, the man's presence affected her in an almost physical way. He touched her forehead gently, curiously. Then, puzzled, he looked at Roger, who had followed right behind her.

Cat knew exactly what the man was looking at. Their scars were gone. For a moment she fantasized about his seeing the light, coming back to his senses. He would take her in his arms, whispering abject apologies, and together she and he would use their considerable persuasive powers to guide the world on a true spiritual path of peace and harmony.

Instead, his face hardened. "The entire world must witness this," he said emotionlessly, sounding dead inside.

A wave of deep personal disappointment washed over her. She should have known he'd kidnapped her only for her professional service. In spite of her bitterness, she tried to reach him one more time. "Jordan, listen to me! Please. You're being used. We were both used. Lied to. I know you think you're doing what's right, but Gideon is not what you think. Gideon–" She cut herself off as the alien himself stepped onto the stage.

"Speak of the devil," mumbled Roger, dryly.

Gideon raised his eyebrows. "The devil?" With an amused grin, he leaned in close to Roger. All at once his head was twice its size, eyes flashing bright yellow, his nose an animal snout, curved horns erupted from his forehead and his mouth opened impossibly wide, revealing huge, jagged, shark-like teeth. His skin flashed-cooked into the bright red of a boiled lobster and he let out an ear-splitting roar, like a furious lion. The transformation was instantaneous, a mind-blowing, heart-stopping moment.

Cat screamed.

Then, just as abruptly, the monster vanished, resuming the image of the benevolent silver-haired gentleman.

Roger's eyes bulged from his face and his throat worked, but no sound came out.

Gideon burst out laughing.

Roger remained frozen in place, his face the gray color of ancient bones.

Cat tried to stop the terror-induced pounding of her heart. Masters leaned in close to her, whispering obscenely in her ear. "Oh, Cat, I'm deeply, deeply..." his voice turned to ice, "disappointed in you." He slapped a cellular phone into her hand and forced her fingers painfully around it. "Call the network. Tell them we're going live."

That was the moment Cat snapped into full realization. So much for her idiocy. Masters' hypnotic alien device embedded in his body suddenly lost its seductive power over her and she saw the man for what he really was. A dangerous, ego-filled puppet. A sad excuse for a decent human being. Her eyes flashed with fury. "I will not!"

Jordan Masters stared at her, clearly surprised, then broke into a superior smile. "Oh yes, you will, Madam Reporter."

Across the planet, regular television programming everywhere was interrupted by a large logo. The symbol was extremely familiar–hundreds of millions bore it etched on their foreheads. A driving tune kicked in: the latest theme song for the WBN Evening News. Images began to flash across the screen: Jordan Masters hugging an African man, Jordan Masters with his arm around a Chinese woman, Masters with a rabbi, Masters signing a treaty, sitting on a fire truck, chatting with some smiling policemen, waving to a crowd, and so on. Every image was a positive action, specifically designed to leave the viewer with a warm, fuzzy feeling. All featured Jordan Masters. A title spun forward, in bold, electric blue letters. WBN SPECIAL REPORT.

"We interrupt this broadcast for a World Broadcast Network special report," said a deep, clipped voice. "Here now, is "the voice of the world, Cat Johnson."

Roger signaled Cat. They were live.

She stared at the camera, silently, defiantly. Standing next to her, world leader Masters waited patiently, smiling warmly, leaning casually on a baseball bat. He was wearing stone-washed jeans, a faded blue shirt rolled up at the sleeves, and a baseball cap. Behind Roger, Gideon hovered, like a hungry predator. Cat was livid. She would have spit in Masters' face and walked away except that, just off camera, a soldier held a gun to Stan Washington's head. Moments after she had refused to do as they demanded they had brought him up onto the stage as a hostage. She wondered, too, about the purpose of the baseball bat. To the viewing public it would evoke images of an all-American guy, but to her it held the underlying threat of a weapon which he might use on her or Roger if they refused to do as he asked.

With few choices left, knowing their lives depended on it, she began to address the world, choosing her words carefully but not bothering to hide her anger. "This is Cat Johnson speaking... from a place I don't want to be. I'm standing in the ruins of the ancient city of Jerusalem tonight, surrounded by military expeditions from all over the world who are demanding the surrender of this... individual."

Interrupting, Jordan stepped in front of her and took the microphone away with a charming smile as if they were the best of friends. "Thank you, Cat." Dismissing her, he spoke directly into the camera. "It's true, I'm surrounded." He rested the bat across his shoulder. "Three strikes, I'm out. Game over." The man's smile faded and he grew quietly serious. "Okay, I give up. You want my blood?" He shrugged. "That's okay, too. If my death will bring the world together as one then believe me, my friends, I will gladly give up my life for you."

God help them, thought Cat, *they will believe him.*

In the Israeli desert, an elite squad of Mossad agents watched on a small portable television.

"Because I am not the enemy!" said Jordan Masters, "You will understand that soon although," he shook his head sadly, "I pray it will not be too late. You must understand..." he removed the baseball cap and tossed it aside, as if throwing in the towel, "or we all will die."

The soldiers exchanged glances. *What the hell did he mean by that?*

Inside a large, gray, canvas tent, three kilometers outside the old city, three Chinese Generals watched their enemy with wary attention. The man didn't look at all frightened or defeated despite the odds he faced. He only looked sincere and deeply troubled. Why?

"My friends," said the fallen leader, "we are about to be engaged in the most important battle in human history. The battle *for* human history! I'm not talking about you against me. Our minor conflict means nothing. I am inconsequential. No, my friends, our upcoming battle is much, much more important. The whole population of the earth is about to go to war. With... The One."

As those words were converted into Chinese by the translator, the military men froze. Shock and alarm replaced the resolve to exterminate the man on the screen.

In a seedy bar on the outskirts of Tijuana, a group of rough-looking caballeros stared drunkenly at the ancient television set behind the bar, mesmerized. One of them slammed his bottle of tequila down on the scarred counter top. "You hear that? The space spooks are back!"

"Make no mistake, this alien species wants to eradicate us from the face of the planet, like bothersome insects," continued Masters from the black and white picture. "They have manipulated us, using our primitive superstitions to divide us. But we will not be fooled!"

Cat watched as Jordan held up the baseball bat. "See this?" He slapped it solidly against his palm. "This is real! Look at the person next to you!" His smiling eyes met Cat's and he put an arm around her. She felt herself flush with anger and pulled away. "That is real!" He stepped away from her and began to meander across the stage. Roger backed away, tracking him with the camera, as Masters approached Gideon. "Now," he said, with a disarming smile, "look at this."

Totally unexpectedly, catching everyone completely off-guard, Jordan swung the bat with all his strength. It connected solidly with Gideon's head, splattering blood across the stage. Cat screamed, involuntarily. Jordan swung again. Bone crunched. And again and again. Grunting with the effort, sweat flying off his brow, Jordan violently beat the alien to death.

In the Tijuana bar, the men reacted with approving yells, cat calls and high fives, spilling mescal across the bar. "Whoa! Si! ET go home!"

Cat was aghast. In death, Gideon's bloody and battered body reverted to its alien form. Lying in a spreading pool of blood, it began to pulse and shift, skin bubbling and stretching. Muscles reformed and bones cracked. Fingers fused, extended to points, became more insectoid than human. A sharp, spiny ridge ripped through the back of his shirt, his back arching into a ridged hump. Skin hardened, forming an oily-looking exoskeleton. His nose and lips melted away, shifting into something reminiscent of a bizarre crustacean from the bottom of the deepest ocean crevasse. The bulging, black eyes were multi-faceted, like a fly's.

Cat backed away in revulsion.

Jordan, fire in his eyes, stood over the body, holding the gore encrusted bat. "Look!" he screamed, pointing at the beast. "Look! That is real. That alien insect is what wants to annihilate us! Lead us *not* unto extinction but deliver us from evil!" He threw the bat aside, breathing hard. "Now you know why I have gathered the world's military forces here in the holy land, in the shadow of Mount Armageddon. For this, Earth's final battle!"

On the communications deck of the United States aircraft carrier Oklahoma, deployed to the Mediterranean Sea, Admiral Justin Pendleton watched the broadcast with fascination. Jordan Masters stood over the body of some repellent alien thing and shouted, "Let's show them we human beings are not insects, but we can sting like a swarm of hornets!"

"Abso-bleeping-lutly right!" cried the Admiral, tossing his cigar aside.

Now it became clear. The real enemy had been unmasked.

"We will fight!" shouted Masters.

"Right, again, son!" shouted the Admiral.

Every Navy man in the room raised their voice in agreement.

"Fight for our planet!" hollered Jordan Masters.

The small crowd gathered in the square cheered.

"Fight for our lives!"

Stan suddenly broke away from the guard watching him, ran across the stage, shoved Jordan aside and faced the camera, pleading. "No! We must not fight! For the sake of our *souls*!"

Suddenly his leg was yanked out from under him and he dropped below the camera level. He landed hard and found himself face-to-face with a very much still alive, extremely aggressive alien beast who was clutching his ankle in one sharply-clawed hand. It became immediately clear that the entire attack had been faked, the blood and crunch of bone simply more of Gideon's appearance-changing illusions. The hideous creature snarled loudly, baring hundreds of needle-like teeth. Stan screamed and punched the beast in the face. It reeled back.

Roger swiveled to direct his camera toward the alien to show it was still alive but Lucretia lurched across the platform and grabbed the cord leading from his camera to the broadcast equipment, yanking it. The camera slid off his shoulder and crashed to the stage.

Stan frantically crab-walked backwards, bumping into Roger who was scrambling after his camera.

"Slick move, Blood!" yelled Roger, exasperated, "Punch the all powerful demon ruler-of-the-underworld in the nose?"

The beast leaped to its feet with a furious growl and rose to a full nine-foot height, towering over the two of them.

"Now he's ticked!" cried Roger. Across the stage Jordan stood alone, looking stunned to see the insect's resurrection. Roger pointed him out to the approaching beast. "Hey, he's the one with the bat! Remember him?"

Stan reached into his coat and pulled out a large crucifix, holding it out in front of himself as he backed away. With an angry snarl, the creeping horror snatched it.

Roger turned to Stan, exasperated. "That's vampires!"

The cross suddenly glowed red hot, searing the creature with a hiss and a smell like burnt sewage. With a howl of pain and rage, the alien dropped it.

The cross fell to the stage floor, inexplicably shattering it like a pile driver instead of a six-ounce crucifix. The floorboards splintered and split, creating a rift across the entire stage. The cross dropped through to the ground, which reacted in the same way. The surface trembled and split at the point of impact. A deep fissure opened up, filling with an ooze of dark liquid. Still glowing red hot, the cross dropped into the fissure. Simultaneously, the entire stage broke in half with a tremendous crack, center stage dropping. They all slid downward funneling toward what now looked like a hell pit just below them. The cross had ignited the ooze, black oil from a heretofore unknown deposit.

Stan rolled, grabbing at Roger on the way. They flew off the outer edge of the platform together, landing hard on the ground outside the fissure. The Creature sprang to safety on arachnid-like legs while Masters also dove for safety, landing successfully on a pile of rocky rubble.

Cat found herself dangling above the raging inferno, choking on black smoke, clinging to the outer edge of the disintegrating structure. Lucretia, screaming, fell past her. Reaching out desperately to stop herself, she grabbed Cat's ankles. The jolt of the sudden extra weight nearly dislodged Cat, magnified by Lucretia's effort to clutch and claw her way to safety. Cat gripped the splintered wood for her very life, but her strength was ebbing too fast to hold them both. Lucretia grabbed at Cat's clothing but the material tore away and she slid down again, with terrified screams. Once more she saved herself by grabbing one of Cat's boots.

"If I go," she spat at her lifeline, "You go!" Splinters dug deep into Cat's fingers. Slick blood made her grip even more tenuous and she began to slip. Sucking up her last ounce of strength, she hissed through teeth, "Go... to... hell!" Her boot came off.

Lucretia plummeted, crushing the empty leather in her grip, clutching at the air, shrieking. Cat clamped her eyes shut, trying to block out reality, but her ears were assaulted by the woman's screams as she disappeared into the liquid inferno. Then she, herself could no longer hold on and also began to slide, following Lucretia's path.

Out of nowhere, a hand shot out and caught her wrist. Half fainting, Cat looked up to see Roger, his face contorting with the effort to pull her to safety. With a cry of desperation he heaved her up and she collapsed in his arms, weeping, eyes closed.

"Hey, hey," he said softly, "It's okay. I got ya." He kissed the top of her head.

Weakly, she whispered. "Thank you."

He looked steadily into her eyes. "Anytime." He held her like a baby as she struggled to regain her equilibrium, her ability to breathe, to think. Gazing at him, Cat saw something that she had never noticed before. Something wonderful and rare. She suddenly understood that it was nothing new, that it had been there all the time but she had been too narrowly focused on Masters, her career, and the world's tumultuous events to see it. At that moment, Cat knew she had been focusing on all the wrong things. Tears ran down her cheeks and she offered a silent prayer of thanksgiving to a God she had never truly prayed to before and turned her head into Roger's chest in abject apology for her blindness in the past.

Suddenly they both realized that the heaving and din had stopped. All was still. Cat gently pulled away from his sheltering arms and looked around, dazed. The fiery pit had disappeared, the chasm closed as if a bulldozer had filled it in. A pale Jordan Masters was staring dumbly at the place it had manifested, moments before. He turned to the insectoid alien in obvious puzzlement.

The creature morphed back into Gideon.

Stan hissed, in a repulsed tone, "Lucifer."

For a time, nobody moved. Five sets of eyes, stared at each other, sizing each other up, struggling to understand what had just happened and how they might deal with it. Breaking the silence, a strange whistling sound increasing in volume came from the stratosphere. Everyone slowly looked up.

"Now what?" asked Roger.

With a sonic whoosh, a missile shot out of the clouds and landed on the city of Jerusalem with a tremendous explosion of dirt and rock. All five of them hit the ground. Another missile hit, only fifty yards away. Then another. And another.

Just outside the city, a platoon of soldiers was sent scattering in all directions as projectiles rained from the sky, sending bodies flying. A General stumbled out of his command tent. bellowing, "Return fire!"

"At what, Sir?" cried a frantic, young lieutenant.

There was another explosion, and a screaming private painfully pulled a wickedly sharp shard from his leg, staring at it incredulously. "It's ice! It's freakin' hailing!"

The General looked up in disbelief. Sure enough, the sky had opened up in a torrential downpour of massive hailstones, some of them weighing close to one hundred pounds. The ground began to shake. At first the General thought it was caused by the hail, but quickly realized it was more than that. The desert sand started to shift and swirl, forming a whirlpool. An armored troop carrier was sucked into the ever-enlarging funnel, quicksanding under a waterfall of earthly debris. Rippling like liquid, the ground began to swallow more military equipment and dozens upon dozens of screaming soldiers.

Throughout the entire world, similar events were occurring. In Rome, Italy, the ground swallowed buildings, cars, trees, statues and people alike. The great Roman Coliseum, after thousands of years, collapsed inward. Giant hailstones battered the city. The destruction was unspeakable.

In Dublin, Ireland, a pub full of patrons were buried alive as the walls around them abruptly imploded. The heavy slate roof came down with a crash, burying the revelers.

In Las Vegas, Nevada, congregants in the Central Christian Church held hands in tight community. One of the worshipers was Lisa Keeler, who had quit her airline hostess job after that terrifying flight seven years earlier. She listened as all hell broke loose around the building, and wondered at the contrast within. Although they could hear tornado-like winds, hail, and other terrifying weather outside, the church itself and those within it sheltered, didn't seem to be affected. She closed her eyes and prayed, thanking the Lord for their deliverance. "Our Father, who art in heaven, hallowed be Thy name..."

At the WBN studios in Culver City, California, the fifty-four story building swayed. Windows shattered, sending knife-like shards of glass raining down on the panicked people in the streets. Floors buckled, ceilings collapsed, walls crumbled, elevators plunged dozens of stories. Electricity sizzled from equipment and light fixtures, electrocuting anyone unlucky enough to be in the vicinity.

Roy Robbins, News Director, put his life into the hands of God and sat without panic in his chair in the producer's booth as the glass wall separating him and the set shattered. With a sigh, he reached up to his forehead and ran a fingertip lightly over the raised welt, tracing the circular pattern. With a disgusted grunt, he dug one fingernail into the flesh under the scar and ripped it away. The entire blemish pulled off his brow with a soft tearing sound. There was little pain and no blood. Roy stared at the small, ragged circle of latex rubber with contempt. He had hated wearing it. He felt it was a betrayal to God and a denial of his faith, but the small patch of theatrical make-up had made his life oh-so-much easier the past few months. The idea had come to him during the plague when he was accosted one night by an angry mob who resented his freedom from suffering any afflictions. Misery loves company.

As the Director at WBN News, Roy had first-hand, inside knowledge of the workings of Jordan Masters' new government, and although the man had accomplished some amazing things, Roy noticed a number of contradictions that disturbed him. Censorship, for one. In a series of moves similar to the

Nazi propaganda, Masters and his cronies had carefully manipulated what the public saw, heard, and–ultimately–thought. The very idea of this kind of control made Roy shudder with revulsion. Nothing made him want to listen to Matthew Richards more than being told that he could not. So he became a regular viewer of the preacher's underground broadcasts. What the preacher said, in many ways, made sense. His point that the new monetary system would make the government privy to every personal move had disturbed him greatly, so he had refused to register, thus avoiding the illness that the radio-active mark brought to its victims.

After his near fatal encounter with the incensed mob, Roy knew he had to do something to avoid further confrontations. Before his career as a director, he'd been a make-up man for television and films. Using those skills, he simulated with theatrical make-up many of the scabs, sores, scars, and other symptoms of the plague, thereby blending in with the afflicted. Teaching many of his fellow "outsiders" the same techniques, he had undoubtedly saved numerous lives. After the sickness had run its course, he had created the fake 666 scar. It allowed him to continue his employment as News Director, thereby keeping tabs on the movements of the man who Roy now believed was, indeed, the anti-Christ. He knew that his make-up trick was a necessary subterfuge–all non-marked employees had been fired–but every time he looked in the mirror he had been filled with self-loathing. Now, he took one last look at the piece of flesh-colored rubber and tossed it angrily aside. No matter what happened now, he would never hide behind false symbols again.

On the Mediterranean, great waves and gale force winds lashed the US aircraft carrier Oklahoma. Admiral Pendleton was unconcerned. His command was, after all, as large as a small city and built to withstand anything Mother Nature could dish out. Nothing could capsize her. Short of the sea simply opening up and swallowing her, there could be no significant danger.

So he was understandably astonished when the ocean did just that. The gigantic vessel dropped out from below him, hundreds of millions of gallons of salt water foaming in to greet the crew.

In China, entire army bases vanished without a trace as the ground they stood on transformed to sucking, bottomless mud.

The enormous faces of Mount Rushmore in South Dakota, got an unexpected nip and tuck as the famous features simply dissolved into sand and slid off the cliff as if it were melting.

Forty thousand feet above the Pacific Ocean, the black Gulfstream jet rocked with turbulence as hailstones and ear shattering thunderclaps battered its flight across the sky. An ear-splitting bolt of lightning ripped through the clouds and struck the craft, blasting the left wing completely off the fuselage. The aircraft dropped like a hammer but took almost a minute to crash. As they fell, screaming, Frederick Marco's cold heart stopped. Shigeo Tanaka and the other five men who had manipulated the lives of billions of people worldwide had a chance to realize that theirs was not the ultimate power in this world after all.

In New Babylon, the World Center Palace was hit by six hundred and sixty-six simultaneous lightning strikes. The entire structure, and anyone within sight of it, was instantly vaporized.

Chapter 24

"No!" screamed Gideon, drawing the word out with anguish and fury.

At that moment, as if his command held some ultimate power over the heaven and earth, the world grew still.

Cat Johnson slowly came to her senses and stumbled to her feet, looking around her in disbelief. The city was leveled, very little of its population evident. Less than a hundred dazed survivors remained in the square, clinging to each other, wandering like zombies. She deliriously wondered if she still was in the middle of some ghastly nightmare which had taken an implacable hold on her consciousness. The change was too much to be believed.

"Are you alright?" came a low, shaky voice. She turned to see Roger struggling to his feet, watching her with concern.

"I guess," she managed. "You?"

"Yes."

She threw herself into his arms, overwhelmed by the need to be held by him. They clung to each other for a long moment.

"Look," said Roger, looking over her shoulder.

She turned to survey the damage, then turned back into him to block out the sight.

"No," he urged, lifting her chin. "Look at the people. Their faces. Do you see?"

Realization washed across her like the heat of a rising sun . "No scar heads," she whispered.

He nodded. Not a single survivor had the mark of 666 on their forehead.

"Oh - my - God." he rasped, in a stunned voice.

She pulled away. "Roger, don't you dare blaspheme!" Under the circumstances, taking the Lord's name in vain was unforgivable.

"I wasn't, Cat," he whispered, gazing at the sky.

Stan, who had just lumbered onto his feet, dropped back to his knees.

Cat followed their eyes upward but the vision was too much to believe. The Mother Ship of all mother ships was descending through the clouds. Massively huge, larger than the city of Jerusalem itself, it looked like a futuristic metropolis whose spires were made of gold and crystal and pearl. As it turned and slowly approached, parts of it sparkled and shimmered blue, like water reflecting the heavens. The sunshine gleamed off its parapets. It was a breathtakingly beautiful sight.

Masters' legs buckled under him.

Stan clutched his cross.

Roger grabbed the television camera and began to film.

In the WBN World Studios, Roy Robbins, lone survivor, sat in his chair, shell-shocked, in deep prayer. Part of his building had come down around him, killing many of the people within it, but he had been spared.

Suddenly every dark monitor in the shattered news studio blinked with light, all screens carrying the same image. He watched the descending vision with awe for a moment, then stumbled to his feet, skirted around the dead body of Maggie Brinks, and with trembling hands, began to hit the switches that would send this live-feed broadcast out to the world.

In a nearly destroyed mall in Charleston, West Virginia, Laurel Venizio dug herself out from under a tangle of hangers, dresses and a circular metal rack. "Gene?" she called, frightened.

Her husband, a strikingly handsome man with a Brooklyn accent, answered from across the store. "Here! Are you okay?"

"Yes, I think so." Last thing she remembered was she was checking out the latest fashions while Gene watched a music video on the massive video wall behind the counters, when the trendy clothing store abruptly came apart around them. She trembled to her feet, chaos surrounding her. One wall had collapsed completely, opening it up to the shoe store beside them. All the acoustic ceiling tiles had come down, revealing a high cement ceiling beyond through which she could see patches of sky. The video wall was dark and silent, and the lights were out. Every rack in the store had crashed to the floor, now carpeted with the latest fashions. She stumbled across them in the darkness and threw herself into his arms. "What happened?"

He looked at her, his brown eyes deep with understanding. "I'm not sure, but maybe..."

He suddenly trailed off as the giant video wall crackled back to life. Not with the latest song and dance from some rock idol, but with a scene more spectacular than any Hollywood special effects artist could possibly produce. Laurel was immediately riveted to the sight of a spectacular space craft.

On the streets of Vegas, the single remaining giant video sign crackled to life, reflecting the same image. The few hollow-eyed survivors stumbling through the debris looked up, bewildered, then blinked with awe at the remarkable image.

Cat suddenly realized that Roger's camera wasn't plugged in. The cord connecting it to the monitor and remote broadcast equipment was lying on the ground beside him, apparently yanked loose in the earthquake. She was about to tell him when she caught sight of the small monitor in the bank of broadcast equipment. Her heart skipped because, impossibly, the image of the sailing city was appearing on the disconnected monitor.

Outside an electronics store in Tokyo, Japan, shaken survivors stopped to gaze with wonder as every television in a barely intact electronics store suddenly lit up with the image of the mother ship.

Most of them didn't notice that every computer monitor was also alive with the same scene.

At Central Christian Church in Las Vegas, Lisa and the worshippers stared in wonder at the awesome image of heaven descending to Earth. The large video screens on either side of the stage, which only moments before had been projecting sing-along hymn lyrics, now served as giant television screens. The crowd gasped and murmured, none more stunned than Lisa. As an active member of the Audio Visual Team, she knew that this wasn't part of the planned program and, furthermore, that the system was not equipped to receive television broadcasts at all.

Cat Johnson was filled with childlike enchantment. Thousands of small aerial crafts, each one glowing with blue-white light, were breaking off from the mother ship and shooting across the sky. The effect was stunningly beautiful, almost like fireworks, or clouds of fireflies... or angels.

With tears in her eyes, clutching Roger's hand, she erupted with delighted laughter.

In the rubbled remains of a small apartment in the almost leveled city of Los Angeles, California, John Andrew Hefron slowly removed his dark glasses, contemplating the television set in front of him with awe. Belonging to a roommate, the TV had fallen from the table and was lying on the floor tilted at a crazy angle, but the colors radiating from it were so beautiful he could barely breathe. Reds, yellows, greens, blues, violets– prisms of light! Shadows and shades of darkness! The scene he was watching, actually *watching*, filled him with such joy that he thought his heart might explode. He put his arm around the soft-faced golden retriever next to him and hugged the dog's neck. "Can you see that, Murphy?" he asked in a choked voice. "Because I can! I can!" Hefron, who had been born blind and lived all his fifty-eight years in total darkness, began to weep. The dog chuffed gently, and laid a paw up on his knee, in understanding. John's tears made the images sparkle and refract and, amazed and pleased, he then began to laugh and clap his hands. The dog barked happily, sharing the moment, then returned his attention to the screen, watching the amazing events as carefully as if he fully understood what was going on.

The titanic spacecraft touched down on a mountain. The earth and rocks were split and crushed, cliffs crumbled, the peaks leveled akin to a man stepping on an anthill. The smaller ships flew out in all directions, some hovering within sight, many disappearing into the distance with lightning streaks of speed.

In India, a small group of miserable survivors gathered around a small television watching a spacecraft as large as a city settle down, destroying an entire mountain. Raj was the most astonished of all. When he bought the TV years ago he had very little money so he had settled for an economic black and white set. But now, when there was no electricity anywhere, it was broadcasting in full, spectacular color.

Suddenly, in the sky directly above them, a streak of blue light shot by. And another. And several more. One of the radiant objects slowed and landed not far from where they sat, huddled together on the ground.

Cat clutched at Roger's arm and he pulled her close as, all around them, smaller crafts alighted gently on earth like magical circles of light.

Gideon glowered at the scene with a contorted face. Then, as if he had heard something they couldn't, he turned his attention upward. He snarled, baring his teeth, more animal-like than human.

Cat followed his line of sight. On top of a high gold and crystal spire extending from the largest of the crafts was a deeply-tanned humanoid figure dressed in a white robe, gazing steadily at Gideon. With no definable race or sex–the Being's features were basically human but without definition, blurred by a dazzling rainbow-like aura.

In a rage, Gideon roared at the Being, "No! You made these people the way they are. The blame is not theirs, it is yours! I find them perfect, exquisitely flawed creatures! They don't need your interference! Leave this world! It is mine!" He spun toward Masters, his eyes wild. "Jordan! They have come to destroy you all! Fight! Fight!" He grabbed Jordan's shoulders and twisted him to face the Being, maintaining his grip. Jordan immediately arched his back, as if electrocuted. He screamed in agony. His shirt front burned away in a flash of flame as the medallion glowed with intense energy.

Cat and Roger could only watch, horrified.

The energy rose in a palpable smoky-green intensity until it surrounded both Jordan and Gideon. In tandem, they screamed, Jordan in agony, Gideon with exhilaration. "Yes!" encouraged the alien, "Fight! You have the power! Unleash it!"

The alien's manner suddenly changed, from authoritative to fearful. Something clearly was wrong. The energy was not shooting out of the medallion but, to the contrary, was building up within it. Overloading. Masters clawed at the thing to open the lens, but it remained implacably locked.

Like a man holding onto another man being electrocuted, Gideon received an identical lethal charge. "No!" he screamed, vibrating with pulsing energy, eyes flashing an intense yellow. The cry built into a soulful scream of anguish as the charge ripped through him like a cosmic bolt of lightning, causing him to lose all self-control. Once again, muscles pulsed and shifted, skin tore, and he reverted to the visage of the hideous red beast.

A blinding orange flash of energy turned both figures into living torches.

Cat screamed in horror, burying her face in Roger's chest as the two fused, blackened and disintegrated into a heap of ash. Roger's strong arms enveloped her, holding her tight.

After a time, exhausted with so much unrelenting stress, Cat weeping, they looked up at the Being in white, standing high above. The face smiled down on them benevolently, radiating warmth and compassion. The whole area around the figure glowed softly in rippling and shimmering rainbow hues. The Being spoke in quiet tones, but everyone could hear. Everyone. Everywhere. On every television, video, or computer screen in the world, no matter what channel it was tuned to, no matter whether it was plugged in, turned on, booted up or not, the scene played. On every radio, CD player, headset, CB radio, walkie-talkie, personal pager, juke box, intercom system, speaker-phone, and talking toy on the planet, the message came through loud and clear.

"No more death," they heard. "No more destruction."

Roberta Rodriguez had been the doting mother of eight year-old twins, Edwardo and Paulo. Their disappearance had been devastating, more painful than she could have thought possible, leaving a black hole in her existence. In the past seven years she hadn't changed or even straightened up their bedroom, wanting to keep it exactly as they would remember, clinging desperately to the hope that they someday would return. She couldn't bear to think of living her entire life without holding her babies again and she had been drawn to Reverend Matthew Richard's teachings mainly because that was exactly what he had promised. When the earthquake started, she knew exactly what was happening: her precious ninos were finally coming home. She'd lurched through the rolling living room, down the shaking hall, and made her way to the twin's room where she collapsed on the bottom bunk bed, waiting patiently. Now that the quake had subsided she focused with wide eyes at a small dark screen in a red frame which was crackling to life in the corner of the toy-littered floor. Awestruck and apprehensive, she picked it up. On its screen, in full color, was a wondrous Being in white. "No more prejudice," said the entity. Roberta Rodriguez took a sharp breath and crossed herself quickly. This was clearly a miracle! Not the sentiment, although an end to prejudice would itself certainly be miraculous; not because she heard the words in Spanish, her native language; but because Roberta Roberts was holding an Etch-A-Sketch.

On the streets of Hong Kong, three dark-eyed survivors in a nearly destroyed movie theater stared up at the huge screen, stunned that the film had restarted. No, it was a different movie–some kind of a science fiction epic with breath-taking special effects. When the camera focused on a powerful-looking alien, somehow they all realized that this was no movie. "No more hatred," he said, in Japanese.

Michelle Larouche stood in the middle of the street in downtown, Montreal. From all around her came sounds. The gush of water from a sheared-off fire hydrant, a dog's frantic barking, the distant crash of a collapsing wall, a hiss from a broken gas line, the crackling of a fire, someone sobbing in relief at finding themselves still alive. Noises! Each and every one was welcome. She drank them all in, like a woman who had been lost in a desert would revel in a waterfall of cool water. Michelle had been in that desert ever since falling through some thin ice at age six had resulted in a severe ear infection, leaving her totally deaf. Now, inexplicably, she could hear again. Exquisite sensations of sound that she hadn't experienced in thirty-two years. From hundreds of radios and other speakers in the buildings around her, she soaked in the words, spoken in perfectly-accented French. "You, the faithful, the true, are reborn."

On the Hawaiian island of Maui, a young native couple stood alone on a high cliff overlooking the Pacific, awestruck, tightly holding hands. There were no radios or televisions for miles around, but words seemed to come from inside their heads, the pictures forming within their optic nerves, projecting on anything they looked at. They gazed, glassy-eyed, at the circular bay below, seeing only a strange-looking Being glowing with colors cast across the blue water. "It is a new beginning, for all," it concluded, in the language of their fathers and their father's fathers.

In Jerusalem, Stan stood apart from the others, taking in the vision before him through tearful eyes. "It's over," he choked, his heart nearly bursting with joy at the scene before him.

A familiar Arabic voice behind him answered softly. "Oh no, my friend."

Stan turned and squinted, shielding his eyes from the shining ball of shimmering substance that had landed nearby. Two figures stepped out, appearing only as silhouettes at first, then slowly coming into view. When he saw them, Stan's knees almost failed him again.

Matthew Richards and Ahmad Ahwadi, as healthy-looking as two men could be, stood smiling at him.

"It is just beginning," finished Matthew.

He and Ahmad moved aside. Behind them, Brenda and Katie stepped forward. Stan stared, unbelieving. Neither one had aged a day since he had seen them last. When she spied her father, Katie broke into a huge gap-toothed smile. "Daddy!"

The little girl ran to him. Stan was overwhelmed with emotion as he watched. Was it real? Was it possible? For the first time ever, his daughter was running. She wore no leg braces, and moved as surely as a young filly. Even in this time of miraculous visions, it was the most beautiful sight he'd ever laid eyes on. Whooping with joy, Katie practically bowled him over as she threw herself into his arms. Brenda wasn't far behind. As he held his wife's warm body to his own, tears of gratitude ran down his cheeks in small rivers.

"Where have you been, Daddy?" asked Katie.

He looked at her, his throat tightly constricted, struggling to speak. "I got lost, baby." He looked over at Brenda, meaningfully. "But now I'm found." Her eyes, too, spilled over as they kissed, melting into each other, together again at last. Forever.

Cat and Roger stood side by side, not far away, taking all this in. She looked up at him. "Roger..." She tried to speak, to tell him how she felt, how she had been lost, too...

"I gotta ask," he said, unexpectedly.

"What?"

He looked up and took a few steps toward the Being in white. "Tell us," he called. "Please. Are you...?"

The being looked down at him, smiling warmly. "Yes, Roger," he said, "I am The One."

Roger seemed to considered that. "By 'The One,' you mean–"

Cat stepped in front of him and placed a finger across his lips. He looked at her, questioningly. She smiled. "The answer's not up there, Rog. It's in here." She laid a hand gently against his heart. "And why are you even asking? You already know the answer."

Over his shoulder, she saw Matthew smile at her.

Roger broke into a grin himself, putting his arms around her. "Yeah, I guess I do."

She melted into his warmth, feeling, for the first time in her life, that everything was exactly as it should be.

Ahmad began to laugh, loudly and joyfully as his old friend Ibrahim stepped up beside him, joining in the laughter.

People started to stream out of the other small crafts–happy people. Jubilant people. People of every race, creed, shape and color... and children. Lots and lots of children.

The End